ONE PEOPLE

Guy Kennaway's first two novels, *I Can Feel It Moving* and *The Winner of the Hooker Prize*, were both published by Quartet and his short stories have appeared in many magazines. He is a past recipient of the Hawthornden Fellowship, was runner-up in the Shiva Naipaul Prize in 1989 and won the Collins Scottish Short Story competition in 1986. *One People* is the fruit of many years spent in Jamaica, mainly in Cousins Cove and Blackie's Bar where he was told many of the stories that appear in this book.

ONE
PEOPLE

Guy Kennaway

First published in 1997 by Payback Press, an imprint of Canongate
Books Ltd, 14 High Street, Edinburgh EH1 1TE

Reprinted 1998

Publisher's Note
This is a work of fiction. Names, characters, places and incidents either
are the product of the author's imagination or are used fictitiously, and
any resemblance to actual persons, living or dead, events, or places is
entirely coincidental.

British Library Cataloguing-in-Publication Data
A catalogue record for this book is available upon request from the
British Library

ISBN 0 86241 719 8

Typeset by Carnegie Publishing, Lancaster, Lancashire
Printed and bound in Finland by WSOY

OUT OF MANY, ONE PEOPLE
(Jamaican national motto)

CONTENTS

THE BIRTH OF JAMAICA

One moonless night a whole *'eap o' year ago*, the vast equatorial ocean stirred, and boiling black volcanic lava bubbled from its depths to explode onto the surface. Relatively quickly, within ten thousand years, the molten rock cooled and solidified. Over the next *couple 'ondred tousan' year* it was reshaped by earthquakes, and sculpted by wind and sea. The island was a terrible place: tempests blew for fifty years at a time, bolts of lightning cratered the earth, and peals of thunder sent massive boulders hurtling into the sea, crushing everything in their path. A drought lasted eighty years, and was only broken by downpours of sulphurous rain. Earthquakes shook the ground for weeks at a time, and rent great fissures in the hills that opened and then closed like abominable mouths. From one bottomless chasm, a scalding geyser shot steam hundreds of feet into the air with no warning, while another devoured with a gulp a river which flowed into its throat and was never seen again. Twice, the island dropped out of view entirely, once for over a century, before being catapulted up through the depths to break the surface again.

Millions of years later the storms *ease back*, the ocean *cool out*, aftershocks became infrequent, the land finally settled, and the sun, one bright day, rose on the newly born island of Jamaica. Compared to what was to come, it was an uneventful and easy birth.

One hundred and fifty miles from west to east, and fifty miles from north to south, its silhouette on the map was amorphous, though at either end of the island the shape of two heads was clearly discernible, each pointing purposefully in a different direction.

The north coast of the island was a necklace of windswept cliffs, sheltered bays, little inlets and white talcum sand beaches. Reflected in the clear turquoise water were the hills that rose a little inland; hills the shape of *good size wuman dem* lying asleep on their sides, or fronts, or even their backs, their mounds and curves thrusting into the sky.

From the rock, mysteriously, came plant life: lichens and strange mosses quite extinct today, that thrived in the tropical heat and humidity. Seasons carved themselves out of the year: a dry winter, a cool wet spring, a hot and rainy summer and a windy, stormy autumn, and not long behind them came leafed plants, flowers, trees, and animal life. A jungle grew up, covering the highest misty hill and the deepest shady valley, but conditions were so fertile that a second jungle soon grew on top of the first: whole gardens, including large bushes and trees, took seed and thrived on the upper branches of big trees, and plants which entwined themselves around others were themselves soon covered in a third growth. In places the forest collapsed under its own weight before picking itself off its knees and forcing its way once more through the suffocating blanket of broken branches, wist and creeper.

Off the coast, in the warm, sunny shallows, microscopic life patiently weaved pink and green reefs that kept the deep sea predators out of the sandy bays, making a sanctuary for the striped and spotted fish which dwelt there.

✳   ✳   ✳

The only scientific fact known about early human beings on Jamaica is that they were created fully formed by Jah and one day walked out of a cave to begin life on the island. Everything else was disputed. Some people said the first Jamaicans were descendents of monkeys and apes through an unlikely process known as evolution, and others that they were 'Mesticans' who arrived by canoe from Guatemala and Belize, but these two theories were considered far-fetched because they presupposed Jamaicans to be in some way the same as other people, which of course stretched credibility too far.

However humans got there, Jamaica proved to be so beautiful and bountiful that they thrived, and soon after the first people appeared, there were settlements dotted around the coast of the island, many of which are still in existence today. An interesting example of this is the ancient community of Lances Bay, in the parish of Hanover.

LANCES BAY

Lances Bay was the prettiest village on the north coast of Jamaica, with the exception of Negril, whose picture postcard beauty was to damn it. It had the benefit of a sheltered beach, a breezy promontory, a fresh-water river, fertile, easily turned soil, and productive fishing grounds. But it was the people of Lances Bay who were really remarkable. A tight-knit, determined community from the very beginning, they passed the desire for their village to prosper and grow from one generation to another. For this laudable ambition they suffered the derision of other less progressive villages on the coast, like their immediate neighbours, Cousins Cove, but were never deflected from their purpose by the criticism of the unenlightened.

In Lances Bay they learnt early the civilised art of enjoying themselves with moderation. They alone could meet in the wooden bar by the bend in the road, enjoy a few drinks, put the cork back in the rum, and go to bed sober. In other villages, like Cousins Cove, when a cork was removed from a bottle of alcohol, it was flung into the sea. But the next night, when the improvident drunks of Cousins Cove had *nottin fi* drink, the men of Lances Bay still had nearly three-quarters of their bottle of rum left. And not only were they clever in Lances Bay, but they were kind. If one of them began to lose more than he could afford to, playing dominoes, his friends refused to play any more with him, and more often than not escorted him to his yard to prevent him finding anyone else to whom to lose money. That was the behaviour of a community that really cared. In Cousins Cove, if a man hit a losing streak at poker, word quickly got round, and friends would get out of bed and hurry to the game so they could strip him of his last dollar.

Unfortunately, Lances Bay people got an undeserved reputation for being priggish and self-important. When a Royal Tour of the West Indies was made in 1984, the *foolish people dem* of Cousins Cove joked that Mrs Queen was only coming to the Caribbean to see Lances Bay. Lances Bay easily rose above the criticism; they knew Cousins Cove people to be lazy, irresponsible and incapable of taking the important things in life, like being a little mindful of what others thought of you, at all seriously. It is the lazy and irresponsible men, women and *picknee* of Cousins Cove whose stories are told here.

*   *   *

Cousins Cove stood around a sandy inlet twenty miles east of the western tip of Jamaica, under some forested hills the shape of a good *size wuman* lying curled up asleep on her side. The sun rose behind her knees, and set on the sea in front of her. The moon travelled the same felicitous arc, burning as it came up through the trees and throbbing directly overhead at midnight when it was full, so bright that one night half the village got up at two in the morning thinking the day had started. A river flowed from the woman's belly into the cove, duning the sand as it crossed the beach, and mixed in a filmy way with the warm water of the sea. The ocean, held in the cove by overhanging jungle, was invariably as flat as a pond, and always warm. It wasn't dangerous or frightening, like on the point at Lances Bay where it boomed onto rocks, but comforting and reassuring, as if, like the sun and moon, it had singled out Cousins Cove to be its friend. It made the village seem a blessed place, a little Eden made more interesting by the Fall.

The first people to dwell in Cousins Cove were the Arawaks over 5000 years ago, but little remains of their occupation because the corrosive effects of heat, humidity and tropical rain, not to mention the devastation of rare but regular hurricanes, left so little of the past on the ground. What few historical sites there are in Jamaica are suspect; Rose Hall, a slave plantation Great House, and one of the nation's premier tourist attractions, was built in 1975. The Arawaks were not the kind to build large monuments, mainly because cutting and hauling stone in that heat was punishing work, something the Arawak was careful to avoid. Their legacy can be found in the language and character of the modern Cousins Covite. Words they coined which are still in use evoke the Arawaks' easy life: tobacco, hammock and barbecue. From time to time they fished from canoes dug out from the abundance of towering cotton trees, but otherwise, at least in Cousins Cove, they did pretty well nothing but lie about. Up at dawn, have a smoke, put your feet up and wait for some barbecued snapper – that about summed their life up. They were way ahead of the field in refining the art of leisure, and it was still only the fifth century, when everyone else's life was nasty, brutish and short. The Arawak Heaven (they had no Hell) comprised intermittent feasting and sleeping, with sex thrown in whenever they wanted it. It was the sort of place Christians went to Hell for even thinking about.

Jamaica has always been the most fertile island on earth. If you snap a twig off a tree and ram it into the ground, a couple of weeks later leaves shoot from its top. Centuries after the Arawaks, when the first fence posts were hammered into the land, they regularly sprouted into crooked lines of trees. The forest was full of fruit; in Cove the Arawaks didn't have to plant a thing, they probably didn't even go to the trouble of picking it, but waited in their hammocks for it to drop fully ripe into their open palms. Most of all, the Arawaks loved harmony, and rarely fought amongst themselves. Disputes were settled by one side (the weaker) backing down just before they were beaten up. Nowadays, you can tell a Cove man by the way, when he has a ratchet knife pulled on him, he'll reach quickly into his own pocket, pull out a packet of Craven A cigarettes and offer the assailant one. The Arawaks were good carpenters, fishermen and cooks, but they were most highly skilled in *chat*, which unfortunately was a talent not in demand when the man-eating Caribs began to make attacks on the islands of the Caribbean.

✳   ✳   ✳

In all military history, there cannot have been an easier race to surprise than the Arawaks, and the Caribs made swift work of them. Big meat-eaters, the Caribs moved up from South America through the Leeward and Antilles. After a one hundred and fifty mile row from Cuba, they arrived, famished, at Lances Bay, three miles down the coast from Cousins Cove, and devoured the first eight people they saw, who happened to be the official reception committee. They were still laughing about this a few days later in Cousins Cove, when Carib canoes rounded the rocky promontory and headed into the calm inlet, where the village huts stood on the beach. The Caribs splashed ashore, raped and killed a number of women and children, and chased the men into the bush as far as they could be bothered to. They argued that people so cowardly couldn't possibly put up a decent fight, and anyway, after years of carnage, a feeling was growing amongst the middle-class Caribs that they should eat more vegetables, and hunt only for the pot, and the plump Cousins Cove *picknee* were quite sufficient for a good light meal.

The Caribs liked to fight, and they liked to party. They made noise all night, and torched vast tracts of forest for a laugh. Their songs were not noted for their melodies, harmonies or lyrics, but for their volume. Arawaks hiding miles into the jungle heard them and said, 'Mi kiant believe dem listen a dis fart.' Carib blood has given the modern Covite the ability to sleep soundly inches from immense speaker boxes. They were always beating each other up, and the men carried knives in their belts at all times, causing a number of accidental suicides when they tripped over rocks in the dark.

✳   ✳   ✳

The Caribs were just beginning to feel happily settled in Cove when the white man turned up. There was nothing superhuman about the white man, but when it came to fighting (which it always did with the Caribs), they had the edge because of things called muskets. The Arawaks came down the hill specially to watch the Spaniards slaughtering Caribs. Then the Spaniards turned their attention to the Arawaks, who gave themselves away by laughing too loudly.

The common enemy drove the Caribs and Arawaks into each other's arms. The Caribs swore they were really sorry for everything, and the Arawaks, in their usual way, forgave them, and introduced them to the delights of eating things that didn't walk around on two legs or talk. They lived deep *inna de bush*, coming occasionally to the top of the hill to gaze longingly down on the creek that cupped the calm sea at their beloved Cove. Their grandchildren saw the Spaniards replaced by the British, and, finally, their grand-children got to live back down in the village, though in somewhat less than desirable conditions, for by then *slavery days* had begun.

In the autumn of 1690 two hundred and ten black Africans, the property of an English adventurer called Edwin Fairfax, arrived at Cousins Cove after a one hundred and eighty mile march manacled at the neck, blinking with confusion, fear and loneliness. It had not been their year: captured in battle, taken from their lands, tribes and families, imprisoned under purgatorial conditions in boats which left a trail of corpses floating on the Atlantic, they were split into new groups, stripped of their language, religion and remaining friends, and sold to a man who genuinely believed he was doing them a favour feeding and sheltering them in return for a brief life of back-breaking toil.

Once in Cousins Cove they were quick to notice how fertile the red soil looked, how sweet the water in the river tasted, and how plump and plentiful were the fish in the transparent sea. In many ways it was a better land than the one they had left – but that only made them hate it more. On the first night one proud man escaped, and waded into the moonlit water to commit suicide.

They were set to work under a ginger-haired overseer called Swing, the offspring of a brief but sweet union between a Carib woman and a Scotsman, to build a sugar mill and slave accommodation. By the time the task was completed forty-eight had died from disease or accident.

Within twelve months the estate was milling sugar worth £25,000, though that of course was a gross figure from which annual running costs of £26. 11s. 6d. had to be deducted. Edwin's son, Thomas (Eton College and Oxford), visited his plantation for the first time aged twenty-one, and was shocked by the conditions his slaves endured. He immediately put some proposals for reforms to old Swing concerning diet, sanitation and hours of work, but when Swing explained how they would eat into profits (which were by then £128,000 per annum, £1.8 million in today's money), Thomas saw that the issue was more complex than he first realised. The problem was that his income was fully committed on a new ornamental lake, grotto and classical ruin on his Gloucestershire estate, so there was nothing for it but to put off the reforms until he could afford them.

There were many courageous attempts to throw off the yoke of slavery, but none emanated from Cousins Cove, where they directed their energy to skiving work and minor acts of sabotage like peeing in the sugar mill and adulterating Swing's flour with salt.

Priding themselves on their bravery, the men and women of Cousins Cove responded enthusiastically when a Coramantee slave called Tiger Taylor in Orange Bay, a village ten miles to the west, asked them to join a revolt he was going to start. For a few days they talked excitedly in whispers of butchering old Swing and Fairfax's agent, Knibb the attorney, simultaneously thinking that if the revolt looked shaky they could always not come out to support Taylor.

A rumour of the plot reached the authorities – from the goody-goodies in Lances Bay, everyone said – and on the day before the revolt a detachment of soldiers was posted to Orange Bay. When the platoon marched through Cove the sight of the muskets and bayonets made everyone's blood run cold. A ten year old boy ran the ten miles from Tiger Taylor to Cove with a message: because of the soldiers, the uprising would now have to be started by Cousins Cove.

There wasn't a coward in Cousins Cove, of course, but the idea of starting a revolt, rather than joining one that was already going well, did not have quite the same attraction, and everyone was subsequently subdued by the prospect. A deputation went to Maas Williams, the obeah man, to ask for magical powers of protection against musket balls. After throwing a handful of animal teeth and chanting some ancient African incantations he gave the assurance that not a single man from Cove would die. To ensure this *science* would work, he went secretly to Swing and said he feared a revolt. Within three hours a second platoon of soldiers arrived in Cove. The brave people of Cove agreed, reluctantly of course, that this ruled them out from starting any revolt. The baton was passed again, this time to Lances Bay, who declined to grasp it, declaring that reform, not revolution, was the way to ease the burden of slavery. With some satisfaction, Cousins Cove branded Lances Bay cowards, and the whole affair has been remembered ever since as one of the many heroic episodes in the history of the village.

Edwin Fairfax's great great grand-nephew, Sir Somerset Webb, sold the plantation in the late eighteenth century for a colossal sum. His daughter Jane inherited his money and diverted it into her pet hobbyhorse: the fight for the abolition of slavery. Her generous contributions to the cause helped bring *slavery days* to an end in Cousins Cove.

When news of emancipation reached Cousins Cove (some months after everywhere else), the new owner of the plantation, an uncouth Yorkshireman called Hogg, asked the slaves to continue to work for a wage. But by then they'd had enough of working for the white man, and argued that after two hundred years of slavery they were owed some time off, about forty years each man, not to mention back pay. So Hogg, like other owners, imported indentured labourers from India. In Lances Bay the Indians were resented because they took all the work, but in Cove they were loved for that, and one other reason: they brought with them the ganja plant, the leaves of which, when smoked, tasted sweet and minty, and took all your troubles and cares away. Possibly as a consequence of this development, the next one hundred and fifty years in Cousins Cove were somewhat uneventful. In an average life of sixty-five years, a Cousins Cove man spent twenty-one years dozing, a decade working on his appearance, eight years flirting, a month having sex, five years boasting about it, six years generally showing off, four years laughing and the balance in idle chat.

To Cousins Cove the twentieth century was very much like the nineteenth and eighteenth, and for that matter the seventeenth and sixteenth too. While the rest of the world strived to invent and use cars, planes, computers and the other paraphernalia of twentieth-century life, Cousins Cove got by fine with the wheel, the wood saw, the hammer, the machete, and a single slightly broken screwdriver which was always left lying in the dirt where the last person used it. The village did not prosper and expand like the towns and cities of the south coast, but stayed pretty much the size it was when Hogg, the owner of the plantation, went bust in 1878, blaming the uselessness of the local work force, and left to seek his fortune in America. The sugar mill and slave accommodation fell apart with neglect, and soon melted into the rising foliage.

For many years, the village stood on the beach and along the rocks just above the sea, but a tidal wave in the autumn of 1909 swept everyone back onto the flat pasture between the sea and the hills, where they felt out of reach of an angry ocean.

'It dangerous fi live too close to de sea,' they told one another.

'Ya man, we nuh gonna make dat mistake two time.'

The coast road, or track as it then was, followed the curve of the bay and then climbed a little hill and left Cousins Cove for Davis Cove, Green Island, Orange Bay and the Morass, where it petered out due to lack of interest in any place further west. An even rougher track led to the *symmetry*, where the village dead were buried. The track then bent right into the Back Street, where about ten wooden houses, raised at each corner on rocks to avoid flooding and deter ants, stood in yards worn to dust by children's bare feet, each about fifty yards apart in the dense foliage.

In 1939, the population of thirty-nine supported one shop, two bars, and eight churches. A year later, six men left to fight a distant war for the white man *inna foreign*, and the loss of business closed one of the bars down. Three of them returned in 1945, with paler skins and exciting tales of life outside Cove.

Even in the 1960s travel was rare. Montego Bay, thirty miles to the east, was considered a long way away, and some people only got that far once in their lives. At Christmas and Easter people walked the seven miles to Lucea, the nearest town, to get drunk and find someone new to have sex with. Otherwise they stayed in the village and had sex with the same old people. In 1971 a primary school was built, where subjects were taught in English, a language no-one spoke, so only a handful of exceptionally gifted pupils learnt to read and write.

In the 1970s, political rivalries made metropolitan Jamaica a genuinely terrifying place, with murder many men's preferred form of self-expression. Elections were blood baths in Kingston. In Cove they liked to believe they too could produce political violence, but somehow no-one ever got round to it. A gun did enter the village at one stage in 1971, but only for a couple of months, while its owner, a Kingston gunman, was in the lock-up waiting for someone to buy him out. Fortunately, it had no ammunition, so the men of Cove were free to make big boasts about who they'd use it on if only they had the bullets. When the gunman returned to pick up his piece, he brought with him six bullets, loaded the gun, and let the *yout* of Cove feel it in their hands. Roddy Perry, a facetious twenty year old farmer's boy, twirling the revolver on his forefinger, accidentally let off a shot which passed under his friend, Rushton's arm, making two neat holes in his shirt sleeve. Rushton, thirty, quick-tempered, touchy, and strongly built, was a man who wasn't afraid to get into a fight. Fortunately for Roddy, who was a weakling with stick-like legs and tiny fists, Rushton was stone deaf, and didn't notice the gun going off a few feet behind him, and although he asked what all the commotion in the room was about, no-one ever told him that he'd been shot by Roddy until years later, when Roddy had moved to Kingston.

It was during these years of ferocious political turmoil that the government decided tourism would play a leading role in the economy. It was a desperate plan, but there seemed nothing else left for the government to try. The country was bankrupt. Sugar cane was no longer a jackpot commodity in a world where a billion people were on low-sugar diets, and bauxite hadn't developed into the big winner the mineral companies assured the government it would be when they demanded the compulsory purchase of large tracts of fertile land in the '60s.

Everyone knew, even the government, that tourism in the capital was a non-starter. Kingston was, after all, the gun capital of the world, and proclaimed itself the *baddest* city on the globe, not without some pride. So in its time of need, the City of Kingston, once preeminent in the Caribbean, had to call upon the rural parishes for help. It was a national act of faith in the obscure towns and fishing villages of the sandy north coast, which were instructed to play host to the white man and his dollar.

Far to the west, tarmac was laid across the twenty-mile swamp called the Morass, to Negril, an isolated hamlet on a seven-mile white sand beach, whose entire population of twenty-six came out to watch when the first bulldozer crashed through the mangrove, all wondering why anyone wanted to connect them by road to Montego Bay. They soon found out.

The smugglers' airstrip at Mo-Bay was swallowed up by the Donald Sangster International Airport, and wide-bodied jets were soon releasing, on each touchdown, enough tourists to fill four big hotels. Within a few years Negril underwent a crazy, uncontrolled expansion. Wave upon wave of tourists broke on its delicate shore. It was a village cursed by a win on the lottery. They soon had to call it a town, but it actually had all the features of a Third World city: dereliction at its centre, grotesquely opulent and heavily guarded suburbs around its middle, and a shanty town multiplying on its boundaries. It developed chronic water, power and traffic problems, and a sewage crisis so serious that when *rain farl* Negril was virtually marooned on a lake of ordure.

While the *big people dem* built shoddy concrete hotels in Negril fast, *the little people dem* slowly erected bamboo sheds along the Main (as the coast road was called), and enthusiastically painted signs that read ONE STOP BEER JOINT FRY FISH, with a few even going as far as getting some beer and frying some fish, though these were invariably consumed by the owners of the sheds and their *bredren*, while they watched the tourists pass by, in air-conditioned coaches, speeding directly between the airport and the hotel lobbies. The white faces gazed back at them through the windows with varying degrees of boldness, the way they'd later gaze into the deep water under the hotel's glass-bottomed boat.

Cousins Cove was no longer out on a long limb, far from the rest of the world, but near the centre of the action, on the road between the airport and Negril, and the inhabitants began to think ambitiously about expansion and prosperity. If it could happen to Negril, whose transformation everyone envied, why not to Cousins Cove? Leroy, known as Joe, a bandy-legged, diminutive dreadlock, led the way. He was the head of the Williams family, considered, in Cousins

Cove, one of the most important dynasties in Jamaica, though outside Cove no-one had heard of it.

Joe worked as a mason at Coconut Grove Hotel in Negril, and had seen tourists close up. He was particularly impressed by their behaviour in bars. In Cousins Cove *the little people dem* went regularly to Zapo Bar on the Back Street, sometimes hanging out there all day long, but it didn't mean they actually had a drink. Mostly they just stared at the dusty Red Stripe and Dragon Stout bottles sitting on the shelf behind the bar.

'De whitey go inna bar and him buy one Red Stripe or one Appleton and him drink it fast, man, fast,' Joe reported to his friends, a damp and stained spliff resting impassively on his bottom lip. 'Ya kiant believe how fast dem drink it. And dem alway tip de barman. For sure, man. Dem just say keep de change, buddy, an' leave maybe twelve dallar or twenty or even one US.'

On the rare occasion a *bokkle o Red Stripe* was bought in Cove, it was far too prestigious an object to drink swiftly. On average a bottle lasted an hour, though Michael Blidgen, the village show-off, once eked out a Red Stripe for two days, carrying it with him wherever he went *fi brandish* it at his friends who couldn't afford a drink. 'And when dem want a smoke,' Joe continued, 'dem nuh buy one cigarette, dem buy twenty! Ya man. Mi gonna capture a piece o land and build one shed for de tourist dem bus fi stop at.'

So Joe picked a spot beside the Main on a slither of pretty land that ran down to the sea. Capturing land was a game of grandmother's footsteps. One sleepy afternoon when no-one seemed to be about, you surreptitiously framed up a little shed with ten pieces of wood and then laid low to see what the owner of the land did about it. If no-one complained you then gradually improved the structure until you had a proper house and a yard marked off around it, by which time it was too late for the landowner to get you off the land. The Police only threw people off during the first stage of squatting, before a yard was established, before the people could say, 'Afficer, dis a fi mi yard, man. Mi live ere, mi likkle son and darter born an' raise ere.'

When capturing land the trick was to do very little work on the shed each day – which suited Joe – in the hope that the landlord wouldn't notice the house going up. Usually it was pretty easy. Most of the land was owned by middle-class people who lived miles away, because no-one with money stayed in Cove any longer than they had to. Their land in Cove was pretty well worthless, and yielded nothing but problems; it certainly never produced any rent, and it was only the difficulty of getting rid of the land that made the owners keep it.

The bit of land Joe picked was owned by Varmer, a successful Asian businessman who lived in Vancouver. Varmer paid Maas Algy, a calm and dignified fisherman distantly related to the Willams', to keep squatters off his estate. Because the land lay between the seashore where the fishermen drew up their canoes, and Maas Algy's yard on the Back Street, Maas Algy walked past it every morning and evening. Joe therefore worked in the afternoons when he knew Algy was sleeping before his night's fishing, and sat with his friends in the shade of a baseda tree across the road to watch him pass by on his way to his boat. Each day the same thing happened: Maas Algy walked by, his trim figure as erect as a soldier's, his gaze fixed straight ahead of him, never even glancing at the logwood and bamboo shed which was slowly appearing beside the road.

'Yes, Joe,' he would say, without looking at Joe.

'Maas Algy,' Joe would reply.

No-one knew how much Varmer paid Maas Algy, but the bonds of community proved stronger than the bonds of commerce, and he turned a blind eye. And out of respect for Algy, Joe worked particularly slowly so as not to seem too brazen and put him in a difficult position.

Three weeks after Joe started, Roddy Perry began building on another piece of Varmer's land. Before his second timber was nailed onto his first, Maas Algy went and found him where he was skulking in Zapo's and told him to stop building or he'd call the Police.

While Joe built, the coaches swept by, back and forth between Negril and the airport. The drivers knew the road so well they drove *hard an fast, hard an fast*, only keeping themselves interested in the run by trying to trim minutes off the time it took, and duelling with other vehicles on the road. Ran, from Cousins Cove, achieved widespread fame and respect for piloting his thirty-four seater past the Mo-Bay Fire Engine, going flat out to a fire, on the tight, blind bend in Hopewell.

At the airport the coach drivers *group up* to exchange stories about driving other *unit* off the road and to laugh about how many goats and fowl they *bounce*. When the jets landed and passengers emerged blinking from customs looking anxiously for their tour reps, the drivers said goodbye to each other and prepared for the race to Negril in the customary fashion: with a large swig of rum, 'fi clear de eyes fi de road'.

THE FIRST STRANGER

The only tourists who stopped in Cousins Cove were those with a flat tyre, or those who *lick dem* car, which is why the bridge over the river was so useful. It had a vicious reverse camber and was built slightly out of line with the bend so that unless you knew the road well you had suddenly to correct the car's direction to prevent it ploughing into the river bed. Cove's first tourist entrepreneurs were the *yout dem* who sat under the almond tree on the seashore waiting to help whities out of the swamp in the hope of getting a few dollars' tip. American college boys on rental motorbikes were the most reliable crashers. Driving too fast on the wrong side of the road, high on a spliff, they didn't stand a chance on the Cove Bridge.

Three of the *yout dem* were from the Williams' family, and one, Granville, known as Oneil, was a Blidgen, one of the other noble houses of Cove. They were all present one windy autumn afternoon in 1978 when Billy, a black American man of about forty, stepped off a minibus. He was the first stranger any of them had ever seen voluntarily stop in the village. Up until then, strangers swept straight through without stopping on their way to Negril. Once or twice someone had engine trouble, or a flat tyre, but coming to Cousins Cove was an act of volition for Billy, and for this reason alone, everyone liked him.

Billy came to Cove on a search for 'native dancers' which
he said there was demand for on the cruise ships and in the
hotels.

'Most of the guys on the boats right now are dancers from
the States,' he informed a rapt audience who'd assembled
to watch Joe and his business partner Ione argue over a
hammer they were sharing while they banged a bamboo
extension onto Joe's shed.

It was thought an extension might make whities stop;
after all, Rick's Cafe in Negril, which was always full of
tourists, had a massive extension. They only had two-inch
screws for the job, but the single slightly broken screwdriver
that had served Cove for so many years had finally broken,
so they were banging the screws in with a hammer.

'The dancers on the ships pretend to be Caribbean, right?'
explained Billy. 'But they have to learn all the moves, and
are paid one hell of a lot for it, plus they're all joining a
union which the operators don't like one bit, I can tell you.
I figured you guys must know all the dances already, kinda
have them in your blood, and would be prepared to undercut
the market – though still make a packet by your standards,'
he added quickly. 'But I musta been in twenty villages so
far and nobody knows the traditional African stuff in any
of them. You know, old tribal dances like limbo and such
like. You don't seem to do them these days.'

It was true – although billed as a 'native' activity, the
only limbo in Jamaica took place in front of white people
at the hotels. To everyone in Cousins Cove it was a new
dance.

'It's one helluva pity, cos there's some money in this,
believe me,' sighed Billy.

'Mi can limbo,' Vinton piped up. Vinton was the gangly,
gummy-eyed thirteen year old nephew of Joe Williams. He

got his younger brother Maxwell, and Oneil, to hold up a stick of cane which he edged towards and collapsed under, getting up quickly to *tomp* Trevor and say, 'Fool. Nuh drop it, nuh drop it. Mi can do it. Watch.' The second time he succeeded.

'You don't know how to do the wheel dance, or fire dance?' asked Billy.

'Ya man. For sure. Dem mainly hotel style dance,' Vinton answered. 'Dem easy. Fi mi oncle know dem.' Uncle Tom had played banjo in a bright shirt provided by the hotel at Round Hill in the '60s, and told stories about the goings on there. 'He can tell we how dem run.'

Billy looked at Vinton sceptically.

'Fi sure man,' Vinton said, with a bright confident smile. 'No problem. Trost mi.'

The Jungle Rhythms, as Billy named the troupe, was made up of eleven guys – almost every available man in Cove – but dwindled by the third rehearsal to four: Vinton, Maxwell, Oneil, and Trouble. Billy produced a bit of paper which guaranteed each of them $2 US whenever they performed, which they painstakingly signed to prevent him backing out of the agreement. Even a single US dollar was an immense sum to the boys. The year before, Vinton changed a flat tyre for a tourist who mistakenly gave a greenback to Glenroy, his cousin, who was standing by, giving Vinton instructions, most of which had been wrong. It was the first dollar bill they had touched. It was such a curiosity it was worth more, in a way, than the eight Jamaican dollars it would fetch in the Bank of Nova Scotia in Lucea, so Glenroy kept it to show anyone who wanted a look.

Uncle Tom was no help with the choreography; he roared with laughter when they told him what they were up to, so the boys told Billy he'd taught them how the dances went in one intense session, and enthusiastically invented all the traditional dances themselves.

They should have been at school, but Vinton hadn't been for years. Originally, his reason for not attending was that he didn't have a school uniform or shoes, and was too proud to go in the rags he'd grown up in, but when, at nine years old he was thrown out of his mother's yard, an old lady of forty called Miss Liza, who needed the help of a *picknee* for things like moving the goat and *fi ketch water*, lured him to her yard with the promise of *a shoes and a khaki*. Life wasn't as easy as he'd anticipated at Miss Liza's but it was too late to move back in with Momma, so instead he spent hours dawdling on errands ignoring the faint shouts of *VINTAN* that wafted across the village from Miss Liza's yard. She did give him the shoes and uniform, but he didn't waste them on school. He was so proud of the outfit he *brandish* it all day long up and down the Main.

One day, Billy didn't turn up for rehearsals, and couldn't be found anywhere. Michael, Oneil's elder brother, was quick to laugh and say it was the last they'd seen of him. With his off-the-peg American clothes, Billy had displaced Michael as the village's *criss* dresser, and Michael didn't like him. But the boys were familiar enough with disappointment to have spent many hours boasting about their imminent fame and prosperity, so that if (or when, in the case of Cousins Cove) everything fell through they knew they had been admired, or more importantly, envied, by the rest of the village for a short time at least.

But Billy did return after a few days with a black eye, some revealing stage clothes and the news of an audition in Montego Bay. The fake leopard-skin loincloths were too small, but Billy said that that made them better, and with only Billy and a white man in the audience for the audition, the boys didn't get nervous, and put on their best performance.

But Billy, who would hear nothing said against the Jungle Rhythms, had to admit, to himself, that his group looked unlikely to pass the audition. In Cousins Cove the foursome seemed athletic and appealing, but with the critical eye of the white man beside him Billy suddenly saw how tall and spindly Oneil really was, how spherical Trouble looked, and how enormous Vinton's feet were. Maxwell, at least, was perfectly proportioned, and handsome by anyone's standards, but his problem was that he was minuscule.

They were quite unaware of their glaring shortcomings as professional dancers. Billy was so moved by their naïve belief in themselves, and by extension him, that after one particularly clumsy sequence (executed without an iota of embarrassment), he had to wipe a tear from his eye.

After the audition, Billy introduced them to the white man, whom he informed that all the dances were 'totally authennic', and were passed down to the Jungle Rhythms by a 'village elder'. In accordance with Billy's instructions they agreed with everything he said to the white man, and answered 'seventeen' when the white man asked their ages.

A week later, after spending an hour and a half at the public telephone in Lucea, five minutes of which was in conversation, Billy came away with the news that the Jungle Rhythms had passed the audition and were booked for a four-week cruise around Cuba on a Yugoslav shipping line. Carried by the conductor of a crammed minibus, the news got to Cove before Billy, where it swept through the population, though by the time it got to Fozzy, who lived in the last yard on the ball ground, the engagement was a residency in a Miami nightclub and lasted not four weeks but two years, and included a house, car and white girls.

When Billy turned up, the boys were *pon de street* exulting in their success. The first person he *buck up on* was Michael who, thinking Billy might not have heard the news, asked him if he could rejoin the Rhythms, for he'd dropped out at the second rehearsal. Billy shrugged him off, found the others, and got them all drunk on one Red Stripe each at Joe's shed. He was genuinely elated, and for the first time expressed surprise at their success.

'I never really believed this would happen, you know? I never really thought we'd get our shit together enough to make it to a professional gig. I mean when I first set eyes on you guys I thought Billy, forget it, this aint gonna work. But I was so goddam desperate ...'

Vinton was hurt by this. 'Nuh say dat, man,' he said. 'When you find we, ya buck up on a whole heap a talent.'

'Ya man,' insisted Maxwell.

'I know, I know,' said Billy, with tears of happiness welling up in his eyes. 'Well now I know. Hey Joe.'

'Ya Billy.'

'Another beer for everyone.'

'Irie.'

The boys were astonished. They'd never seen anyone buy someone two beers. Those who weren't in the Rhythms hung about in the darkness outside the shed, and had not shifted off when Billy, by then in a state of euphoria, left the bar with his arms around his boys. When they were past the fishermen pushing out their canoes he said, 'Isn't this the greatest feeling in the world? We're all here in this beautiful place about to begin a new chapter in our lives which we're all going to be in on together. Yeah? You know what I mean?'

'Ya man,' said Maxwell, who did.

'Ya man,' said Oneil hesitantly, because he didn't.

'And I gotta feeling we're going a good distance in each other's company,' said Billy, staring up at the stars.

'Just gimme mi passport and let we go,' Maxwell laughed.

'Passports. You guys got passports, right?'

'No man,' they told him.

'No problem. We'll get onto that tomorrow morning. But maybe tonight would be a good moment to get the haemorrhoids test over and done with.'

'What haemorrhoid?' Trouble asked.

'You know, piles.' There was a pause. 'They're a complaint every dancer has to keep a watch for. They've ruined many a career, I can tell you. Quite a few great dancers who coulda made a fortune had to throw the towel in on account of them. You ever heard of Baryshnikov?'

'No. Him fram Montego Bay?'

'No. He's American. A great dancer. Made a mint. Now he damn near lost his career to piles. But it's a simple enough test. Nothing to worry about. If you get on top of the problem early they're a cinch to eliminate. I just run my forefinger up your anus to check if you're likely to get any trouble. Trouble, you look a little tight in that region. I may be able to do a little work relaxing you down there at the same time.'

Trouble said nothing.

'Nobady put dem finger inna mi botty,' Vinton said.

'Nuh man,' added Maxwell.

'Cho,' said Oneil dismissively. 'Dat nuh sound right.'

'Who touch dat mi tomp im,' stated Vinton.

'Look, it's not that important, right? If anything crops up on board I guess the ship's doctor can handle it. Hey, check that out!'

Billy pointed to the distant glistening cruise ship inching across the black sea and sky. 'That's where we're headed, guys.'

'Ya man,' said Maxwell softly.

Trouble, Oneil and Vinton nodded, but said nothing. The ship looked a long, long way away to them. The prospect of leaving Cove suddenly seemed scary. They were to be away four weeks. The longest any of them had been out of the village was for the audition, nine hours. Each had their own gnawing worry: Trouble that he had no *criss* clothes, Oneil that he had no shoes, and Vinton that he wouldn't be able to use a flush toilet, for he, like everyone else, had always used the bush.

Oneil wisely waited for his father to be in a good mood before he asked for his birth certificate, so when he heard Mr Blidgen bragging that he'd sold the Green Island Police station a load of sea sand as salt-free river sand, to build the new cell block with, he put his request to him.

'What ya need age paper for, picknee?' Mr Blidgen snapped back. He looked so aggressive, like a boxer dog, and had once almost killed a bad boy with a tin of mackerel in a *lada* bag when he jumped out of the bush to rob Mr Blidgen.

'Mi gawn a foreign fi dance wid Billy, and mi need one passport, sah,' Oneil told his father.

'Ya tink Billy want mi fi go a foreign fi dance too?' Mr Blidgen asked.

'No, sir. Billy want ongle Vinton, Trouble, Maxwell an' mi,' replied Oneil apologetically.

'Well ya nuh de go, annerstan? Until mi go, nobady in this family reach up inna foreign. Ya tink picknee take first place to him farder? No sah. No sah. Tek up de rake and work, boy. You nuh go nowhere till ya pay ya farder the debt fi raise you. Gwaan! Tek it up.'

And Mr Blidgen in his turn took up a stick and set to work whipping his son's long thin legs as he raked the yard.

Later, Miss Linnet, Oneil's mother, gave him the birth certificate. 'Nuh tell ya farder. An' carry back com gimmi soon.'

'Ya Mamma. Tank ya.'

When Trouble, who was a year and a half junior to Oneil, asked the mountainous Miss Citarra, his granny, for his birth *surfaceticket*, she lumbered swiftly across the creaking wooden room, lifted her mattress and slid out the family heirlooms: a couple of disintegrating official letters relating to her brother Rushton's deafness, some blurred photographs, one or two of people she didn't know, yet treasured nevertheless simply because they were photographs, all the documents relating to her favourite son-in-law's conviction for assault and rape of two different women, and a couple of his painful letters from Spanish Town Gaol, a 1972 Jamaica Labour Party calendar, two prescriptions she couldn't afford to fill, and birth certificates of two of the six minors in her care.

'Ya send mi money each mont, y'annerstan?' she shouted at Trouble, even though he was just across the room. 'An' send down one bedcover and one cooker. Tek this.' She thrust the bit of paper in his hand.

When Maxwell and Vinton asked for their birth certificates, people heard Blackie's laugh on the other side of the ballground, actually only an average distance for Blackie, whose laugh was one of the Seven Wonders of Cousins Cove. She once laughed so loudly, a solitary fisherman working out of sight of land in his canoe heard her disembodied guffaws coming over the horizon.

Before she ceased laughing she went at her sons with the flat side of her machete, a surface which had more than once made high-speed contact with their flesh. But that Sunday *eveling*, when Blackie walked up and down *pon de street* in her finery, Trevor, as agile as he was naughty, slithered over the room partition through the nine-inch gap, and found Momma's papers. He climbed back with one birth certificate between his teeth – Dalton Wedderburn's – his own in the formal name no-one ever used.

Oneil, Maxwell and Trouble toiled over the first line of the passport application form until Billy took over and answered all the questions at an astonishing speed, which confirmed the idea they had that he was very clever, for he'd known the answer to the Kool-Aid radio quiz question that had foxed the whole of Jamaica for six weeks – Mr Moneyman asked, 'Eighteen King of France share de same name. What is dat name?'

When a caller said, 'Is de answer Dwight?' Billy laughed.

'What de right name, den?' Michael, who looked in through the window of Joe's shed, where a radio played on the bar, asked Billy.

'Louis,' Billy replied.

'Dat nat true,' Michael said, but a week later a caller said 'Louis' and won the accumulated jackpot of 600 J, which most people felt was at least partially owed to Billy.

Billy explained to Vinton that he had to go to the government office in Mo-Bay to get a duplicate certificate. 'Tell them your parents' names, place and date of birth, all that shit, and you'll get it easy.'

'But mi nuh know mi father name,' said Vinton shamefully.

'Ask your mother.'

'Mi ask fi mi mudder, but she nuh tell mi.'

'Why?'

'Mi sit down and tink about dat all day, Billy.'

Eight hours after Vinton was born in the Lucea hospital in 1966, Blackie, his mother, went back to her yard to wait for Aubrey, the *baby farder*, to come and acknowledge his son. She knew better than to walk to his yard with the infant. Her friend Babs had confronted her *baby farder* with his daughter when she was three days old and he had licked them down in front of his friends with a *hax hangle*. After waiting four days, Blackie's father, a drinker and a fighter called Harvest, shook Blackie in the night and demanded with overproof rum on his breath the name of the infant's father. She didn't tell him, or anyone else, and the next day tore up the birth certificate with Aubrey's name on it and gave her own surname – Williams – to the child. From that time on, she swore never to *business* with Aubrey again, however much *he sweet up her mout wid words.* This was why she never told Vinton who his father was, despite the fact that Aubrey lived on the Back Street and Vinton passed his yard practically every day.

'They'll give you the birth certificate with just your mother's name. Sure they will. And you know it might even have the name of your father on it.'

With *criss* clothes borrowed from around the village, Vinton waited for the minibus in the short, still, smoky dawn before the sun exploded over the top of the hill. He saw Michael, Con, Oneil and a group of little boys walking up the slope from the sea shore.

'Boggy,' called Michael, using one of Vinton's names.

'Ya man.'

'Con hear from Waller cousin in Mo-Bay dat Billy is one botty man.'

'Dem gonna dance pon one ship wid a botty man,' piped Con in his high-pitched voice, making everyone but Oneil and Vinton roar with laughter. They looked sick.

The thud of a bass line heralded a minibus called Dutchman, which came off the long straight and around the corner listing heavily with the G-force. Vinton didn't stop it. Nor did he stop Pomp Action, which careered by a minute later. He had to find out more about this.

He and Oneil found Maxwell bouncing barefoot down the back street slopping water from a bucket he was carrying, and singing at the top of his voice: 'Mi no more move cow dem, mi no more ketch water, mi no more rake de yard dem ...'

'Michael say Billy one botty man,' Vinton told his brother.

'Raas claat Michael is a idiot, fool. Him nuh like Billy. Everybady know dat,' stated Maxwell, adding, 'blaad claat.'

'Waller cousin hear in Mo-Bay, Billy try fi interfere wid one boy.'

There was a pause while Maxwell ruminated on this. Then he *suck teeth* and said, 'Cho.'

'Mi nah go pon no boat wid no botty man,' said Vinton.

'Nuh sah,' said Maxwell ambivalently, then added with more conviction, 'Ya kiant business wid no botty man.'

Oneil gravely agreed, relieved that this would mean he could return his *age paper* to Miss Linnet before Mr Blidgen found it was missing and beat her *bad*.

Shouts could be heard from Miss Citarra's yard, where Billy stayed, so the boys hurried towards them. Miss Citarra had moved the infant Craig, Dwight and Yvette into the octogenarian Miss Amy's bed in order to rent a room to Billy for a *couple dallar* a week.

The boundaries of the various yards in Cousins Cove were by and large invisible, but known and respected by all. They operated like a force field around either one, or a group of houses. Those whose yard it was could wander in and out from the street, but all outsiders had to stop on the border line – which often only someone from Cove could recognise – and *hail up* whoever they wanted to see in the house by calling out their name. It was on the boundary of Miss Citarra's yard that a growing crowd of curious people stood. Michael shouted abuse at Billy, who cowered inside. 'Botty man!' he called, 'move from here, botty boy ...'

An elderly woman, the usually kind and helpful Miss Joly, threw a stone, and a boy with an unbroken voice yelled, 'Pussy claat!'

Inside, Billy sat on the bed trembling with terror, occasionally peering through a gap in the louvred shutters, and jumping whenever a stone cracked against the thin wood clapboarding of the wall.

'Oh my God,' he uttered, crossing himself feverishly.

A minibus drew up, momentarily diverting attention. The door slid back, and after a moment Miss Citarra hobbled out, dressed in her best clothes. She looked almost uphol-stered, as though she were padded with springs and might even possess a pair of ball and claw feet. A visit to Dr Bury in Green Island, made on the expectation of the funds Trouble was going to mail her from the ports he'd visit on the cruise, necessitated wearing the finery.

'Faggot!' screamed Michael at the house. 'Ya one faggot, Billy.'

'Let 'im pass out. Let 'im pass out,' shouted Miss Citarra, parting the crowd before her. Inside, she said, 'Pack up ya tings in ya suitcase, Billy, an' jump trough dat back window, an' run off a back street.' Billy frenetically pulled his glad rags together. Another rock cracked against the side of the house. 'Gwaan,' she urged, 'ron now, ron now ...' But as he squeezed out of the back window she said, 'Hol' on now. De rent. Ya owe mi for mi rent.'

With one leg out the window, Billy dug into his pocket. 'How much is it? Three dollars?' He winced as another stone struck the house. The crowd was now a mob, and it was getting angry; Miss Citarra saw the strength of her negotiating position.

'Gimme ten dallar.'

'Ten?' cried Billy.

'Tree rent. Seven for cancellation.'

'Jesus,' Billy said under his breath, reaching for his wallet. While he clambered out the back of the shack, Miss Citarra went to the front to pacify the mob. 'Hol' on. Im just com. Let im pass out fram mi yard, annerstan?'

Afterwards, when the story of Billy and the Jungle Rhythms was told in the sheds and on the porches of Cousins Cove, no-one ever blamed Miss Citarra for this little deception, because everyone, with perhaps the exception of Michael, saw it for the simple act of kindness it was.

When the cry, 'Him roun' a back street!' finally went up, most people were glad that the three-minute start Billy got meant that he was pretty well out of the village before anyone could catch up with him. The Cousins Cove mob liked to make a lot of noise, but had little taste for blood, and had been known in the past to catch up with and run right past a culprit rather than attack him. At the ballground Billy's suitcase burst open, and a trail of bright clothes was laid across the bumpy cricket pitch curtailing in an empty case with a broken catch. The mob chased him around Bubbles' yard, parted into two around the primary school and met again on the other side to see Billy sprinting down the middle of the tarmacked Main in the direction of what the government had recently rather optimistically named Industry Cove. It was not a name that stuck. By then the Cousins Cove mob had run out of both venomous jibes and, more importantly, puff. Chasing Billy all the way down the hill would only mean walking back up in the increasing heat of the morning, so they slowed to a trot and then a standstill and laughingly congratulated each other on a good morning's work.

One night, over a year later, Trevor, Oneil and Vinton were scanning the shallows near the canoes with paraffin-soaked rag torches hoping to find *swimp*. Vinton and Oneil looked up to see a glistening, silent cruise liner hanging in the dark out to sea. Both were about to resume their search of the sandy shallows when Maxwell, a little way off, said, 'Remember Billy?'

'Ya man,' said Vinton.

'Billy cool,' Maxwell said.

'Ya man. Mi know,' answered Vinton.

'Remember when him buy we two Red Stripe?'

'Ya man. Billy kinda nice.'

'But him a wah botty man,' Maxwell stated, to stop himself recalling more good things about Billy.

'Ya man,' agreed Oneil.

'And ya kiant business wid dat,' Maxwell sighed. And all three bent back over the water to look for *swimp*, happy to think about something else.

NAMES AND ALIASES

Babies came into the world of Cousins Cove at the hospital on the windswept point at Lucea, where mothers nursed their newborn infants looking out at the white-capped ocean, while the Caribbean breeze billowed the curtains, and wafted the nurses' paperwork across the lino floors. The papers once got so muddled that Rushton, a Cove farmer, visiting hospital because he woke up stone deaf one morning, was given an enema and discharged, while a man who hadn't been to the *tilet* for twelve days had his ears syringed; both men were satisfied with their treatment and pronounced themselves cured.

No man from Cove ever went near the maternity ward. The subject of childbirth made men nervous in Cove. When a girl got off the minibus from the hospital with her newborn baby in her arms, every Cove man felt anxious until one of them acknowledged the child as his. An unclaimed baby put them all under suspicion, and it was years before a physical resemblance could unquestionably clear up the matter.

During her short stay in hospital a new mother named her child, and the doctor filled in the birth certificate. Baby *mudders* felt that as they'd given birth without assistance from the *baby farder*, they could probably manage to name it on their own, as well. In the feminine atmosphere of the maternity ward, far away from the dust and squalor of a

Cousins Cove yard, the women picked romantic and impractical names. While lying in the sweet luxury of a bed not only to herself, but with a mattress and pillows covered in crisp, clean linen, Yvette conjured up the name Nakissia for her first daughter and Najia for her second. Venezia and Tamara were named in the same fashion by their mother, Miss Rung, and other Cousins Cove products of the Lucea maternity ward were Doreenia, Hyacinth, Adolphus, Beresford, Viviena, Euphemia, Estella, Bevlie and Weeville.

They were not names that lasted long in the *roffness* of a back-street childhood, yet neither were they worn down into diminutives, but stored away in one piece, like something treasured, and replaced by a tougher name for everyday use. The name on the birth certificate was often never seen again except on an electoral roll, if they were lucky, a Police charge sheet, if they weren't, and a concrete headstone in the *symmetry* if they were rich.

New names, or aliases, sometimes grew out of the way you looked. Blackie was the blackest woman in Cove. Biggar, as a child, was *biggar dan de nex one*, though when he stopped growing, and his friends shot past him, his name changed to Likkle Biggar. Glenroy Williams, Vinton's big and talkative uncle, inherited the Williams voice which jumped from deep rounded bass to falsetto and back again sometimes twice in one sentence. Like most physical abnormalities, it was considered special, and often Glenroy would be stopped by someone who'd heard about his voice and asked to say a few words. He always obliged, being singularly proud of his vocal peculiarity. He first got called Piano by Biggar, during a game of dominoes, 'cas im voice sound sweet like one piana'. It was adopted by the other players, and became a kind of password for the Glenroy posse – the guys he hung out with *inna Back Street*. But it soon spread outwards from

Glenroy's closest ring of friends, first to everyone in his yard, girls included, and then to the Back Street, and finally the whole village *hail up* the man as Piano. It was around about then that the men he played dominoes with began to call him Voices, which they pronounced *Vices*. This caught on too, so a new nickname emerged to mark out the initiates from the rest. Some said Vinton thought it up, others Maxwell. They called him Bird, 'cas im sing so sweet'. This, months later, was developed into Blackbird. Everyone could tell, by the name someone used to address Glenroy, how long they had known him, and how close was the friendship.

More commonly, names were pinned on a person by events in their life, and in this way the contemporary history of Jamaica was recorded in the aliases of its people. Usually, only important events were commemorated, but in Cove nothing important happened, so they commemorated the insignificant instead.

Granville got the name Oneil on a strange fishing expedition in 1981. A man from *inna de hills* had come down to the seashore and asked Oneil if he could use his bamboo raft to fish from. Oneil took the stranger out into the cove and they dropped their lines into the coral reef. Their fishing tackle comprised a baited hook on a length of thick nylon wound round an empty bleach bottle. A float wasn't needed because the fish were so plentiful and tame, and the water so clear, they could be watched taking the bait from the raft.

Suddenly, the stranger pointed at something on the end of the raft.

'Go way fram mi! Go way ... Go way. Mi know you Oneil. Leave mi, leave mi!' he shouted feverishly.

Granville looked but saw nothing, yet the stranger grew more *vex* and confused, eventually hurling himself off the raft into the water, which was only a few inches deep because in places the coral grew from the sea floor right to the surface. He tried to stand up, but slipped over, gashing his hands and feet badly on the coral (when recounted later, that bit always made everyone laugh), all the time shouting, 'Go way Oneil, go way Oneil!'

Mental illness was considered so hilarious in Cove, that the story soon became popular, and lest anyone should forget it, the name Oneil was given to Granville. He was honoured by this, knowing the high status any association with the insane gave a young man, and was proud to have it conferred on him.

If you asked, 'Why dem call Maxwell Maxwell?', an inhabitant of Cove would answer, 'Cas him see one show pon television,' and leave it at that, as if it required no further explanation. Few pressed for more information for fear of appearing ignorant of the magical and powerful world of television.

What had happened was this: Trevor, on a trip to Sav to buy DDT with his father for their ganja plantation, saw a television in the hardware shop. Only Chicken George in Cousins Cove had a TV, a 36″ 1974 Grundig which he brought with him from *Shepherd Bush inna London*. It was one of the seven wonders of Cousins Cove. It was only black and white, but no-one except Chicken George knew. People came from all over the village to gaze at it from the settee in the lounge of his much-envied concrete house. Chicken George always explained how it would be even more exciting when the Jamaica Public Service company brought electricity to the village.

The television in the Savannah La Mar hardware store was different: it was switched on and showing a programme. The programme happened to be *Hart to Hart*, in which Robert Wagner and Stephanie Powers have a butler called

Maxwell. The one line of dialogue Trevor could remember, when a rapt audience outside Joe's shed quizzed him on his experience was 'Maxwell, take my coat', and it was from this gem of American TV that the name came which remained with Trevor for years.

WHY DEM CALL U-ROY, U-ROY

Jimmy *get a idea* to promote a music show when Roddy Perry told stories about the times he *party wid Bob Marley inna Kingston*, and all the Cove girls loved to listen and *did friend wid Roddy*. Roddy had returned from the capital to claim his late father's estate. The first thing he did was sell a plot of valuable seaside land and buy a Lada car, a transaction considered shrewd by the entire village and which made him even sexier to the *gal dem*.

Jimmy Fairfax was a slim, *high colour* man with darting eyes and lecherous hands which gave him a reputation amongst Cove men for being attractive to women. His old friendship with the singer U-Roy paled beside Roddy Perry's with Marley, a global star and prophet to black people everywhere. Questions had begun to be asked about just how well Jimmy knew U-Roy before Roddy turned up, and now they were asked again, louder. Why, for instance, did U-Roy never come to *check* Jimmy if they were such buddies? It was a question that Roddy need never fear, knowing that his friend Bob was lying safely in a St Ann *symmetry*. Jimmy therefore decided to stop the gossip and *big up his status* by getting U-Roy down to Hanover for a show.

Cousins Cove didn't have a venue for shows, but Lances Bay didn't either, so that was all right. The nearest place was Parkins Lawn in Orange Bay, a rubble strewn slope enclosed by concrete sheds and corrugated zinc. The lighting rig was a single 60 Watt bulb and the moon, but these could evoke magic. A big DJ, capable of drawing a crowd of 10,000 in New York, drew about 75 in Orange Bay, 'though there were always another 100 listening for free on the other side of the zinc. The dancehall stars played the little villages for pocket money, for girls, and to keep their acts sharp. If they could hold the audience in Orange Bay, New York was a breeze.

But Jimmy booked a new venue in Bulls Bay, owned by a tubby, effusive dreadlock who'd come back to live in Jamaica in 1987 with a *whitey* girlfriend from England who people believed was a cousin of *Mrs Queen*, the British monarch. When they got married, the Royal Dread, as he was soon dubbed, invited the press and TV as a surprise for his bride; but she had to tell reporters that there had been a misunderstanding about her relationship with *Mrs Queen*, and that people used the term 'cousin' in England rather more loosely than in Jamaica. The local guests felt that if there had been a misunderstanding, it was not one that they would have corrected. The ceremony nevertheless made the *RJR News*, the JBC television news (second item, ahead of the fall of the Berlin Wall), and the *Western Mirror* printed a photo of the white suited Royal Dread and his delightful bride under the headline NOT THE COUSIN OF THE QUEEN WEDS IN HANOVER.

Jimmy booked the Royal Dread's brand new venue, called Zion House, for a Saturday night, after negotiating a deal over *much bokkle o' Dragon Stout* with the dread. Both men were pleased with the agreement: the Royal Dread because he got Jimmy to pay an exorbitant rent for the venue, and Jimmy because he had no intention of actually handing over a single cent.

Jimmy commissioned four posters, and the week before

the gig persuaded the easily-bullied Devon to drive him up and down the Main and into the hills and valleys in Bessie, Devon's Hillman, with a megaphone strapped to the roof, announcing that U-Roy was going to play in Bulls Bay that Saturday. It was a euphoric few days. He sold, from a book of obsolete Seventh Day Adventist church raffle tickets, twenty-eight advance tickets, the money from which he immediately invested in Appleton Estate Special White rum. The car, the megaphone, and the importance of his position as promoter, attracted countless women, all of whom, after telling Devon to take a walk, he had sex with in the back of Bessie, once forgetting to *plug out* the megaphone and attracting a crowd of curious little *picknee*. But while he enjoyed himself on the back seat he was aware of a growing sense of unease, attributable only to the fact that it was four days before the show and he still hadn't got in touch with U-Roy. He had been meaning to check a girl in Blenheim who *did friend wid U-Roy* in the old days, and who knew a mechanic who fixed U-Roy's Benz on Hope Road, Kingston, and he finally went up on Wednesday, but Euphoria's yard was empty except for *tree picknee*.

'Momma reach up a Mo-Bay fi look fi work,' a little girl who was cooking a pan of dumplings over a fire told Jimmy.

'Tell her he must check fi her friend who know U-Roy mechanic, and tell her dat U-Roy must com a Bulls Bay Saturday night fi play one show for Jimmy Fairfax.'

Jimmy drove back down to the Level enjoying the feeling of relief that at last he'd done what he'd been putting off for so long. 'De job of de promoter easy!' he told Devon. 'Easy! Everyting gonna be all right.' This cheered Devon who was anxious about the money Jimmy owed for gas.

Jimmy celebrated with a couple of shots of Appleton Estate Special and a spliff, and told Devon to turn Bessie towards Salt Spring, a place sufficiently far from the Main that a man with a car was still an exciting, exotic rarity.

On the day of the show the Royal Dread preened his locks in his large mirror in preparation for his encounter with U-Roy. 'Mirror mirror 'pon de wall, who is the most beautifulest rasta of dem all?' he purred, flashing his locks with a laugh. It was an important meeting for the Royal Dread, who wanted to get his career off to a cracking start in Jamaica. Things in London had not gone well for him. He'd wound up forty years old with two ex-wives and eight kids on his tail for money, and a stalled career as a bass guitarist looking increasingly incapable of providing it. To get himself out of a rut he'd started to *friend* with a delicious looking white girl whom he met in Notting Hill Gate who wanted to scandalise her family. In England a man was made to feel guilty about going out with a rich girl, so he took her to Jamaica where he got the respect he deserved for pulling her. His wife took an interest in his career, and to ensure he could always get a gig she thoughtfully bought him a music venue: stage, auditorium, bar, the lot. He named it Zion House. His policy was to book the big names in reggae, Dennis Brown, Gregory Isaacs, Freddie Macgregor, then form a band and invite himself onto the bill as support act. When you had the kind of financial backing he had, it was easy to make it. That was the way the Royal Dread saw it.

He loved to perform in front of an audience, and loved an adoring crowd, and had already decided to get to the microphone to introduce U-Roy himself, using a lot of echo and superlatives. He might have to push the *likkle bald 'ead* Jimmy Fairfax out of the way, but he was a nobody from the middle of nowhere, fit only to be stepped on by the likes of the Royal Dread. His text of the day from the good book was *He who loves to exalt himself shall be obeyed* – a favourite with many rastas. Quite where it appeared in the Bible the Royal Dread was unclear, but no-one else knew either, so it was safe to make up a fictitious reference when he quoted it in conversation. He lit a spliff and meditated on Jah for a minute or two and then began to daydream about discussing future projects after the show with U-Roy over a *couple Dragon Stout.*

The night before the show Jimmy got a message down the line from Euphoria in Blenheim that U-Roy could do the engagement, but needed a *whole heap o dallar* brought to him in Kingston before he'd *reach up inna Bulls Bay.* Jimmy's good friend Driver, drawn down from the bush where he'd been thieving ganja by the pleasure of breaking bad news, brought the information. He stipulated the precise sum U-Roy demanded, but Jimmy didn't listen because although he had a lot of money, 125 crumpled and damp J in all, he knew U-Roy would want more.

Driver suggested during the long moonless night the two spent in each other's company that it was time to use obeah – black magic.

'Mi can set one curse 'pon U-Roy,' Driver told Jimmy.

'To make him com to Bulls Bay?'

'No man, fi kill him nex baby.'

This was Driver's speciality. He used obeah to kill Marva Blidgen's newborn child because of a dispute he'd had with her father, and his sister Bab's fourth baby died because she once *dis* Driver. Jimmy was tempted by it, but knew Driver would charge a lot of money, and knew also that it would not solve the central problem of what was going to happen when everybody went to Zion House to see U-Roy, and U-Roy didn't turn up.

'Dat no good, Driva. Mi need U-Roy a com, or mi dead man.'

'Ya man,' agreed Driver warmly. 'For sure you will dead. Mi tell ya what can save ya from dead: if ya can find one man who favour U-Roy ...' by which he meant someone who resembled U-Roy, '... but nobady know how U-Roy look so ya gonna dead.'

'Nobady know? Somebady moss know.'

'All dem know is de same as we. U-Roy always wear one felt 'at, a bellfoot pants and a big boots.'

'... And de felt always have one fedder in it.'

'Ya man, one fedder in him felt 'at. But dat all mi know. Dat all anybady know, dat's de problem.'

'If nobady don't know what him look like, den all mi need is one felt, one boots and one bellfoot pants, and mi can be U-Roy said way 'pon de stage, and nobady kiant know it nat U-Roy,' said Jimmy.

A smile, expressive of Driver's deep love of deception, spread upon his lupine features. 'And nobady kiant know cos dem never see U-Roy 'pon TV or in newspaper photo.'

'Ya man,' said Jimmy, 'cas dem illiterate.'

'And dem kiant read,' added Driver, laughing, 'cas dem ignorant.' Then he looked serious. 'What bout de lyrics, man? Ya kiant sing,' he pointed out.

'Cho!' chided Jimmy. 'Mi can sing so. Mi can sing fast, man, and hard. Ya man. Ya nuh hear mi pon de microphone in Bessie?'

'Ya man?' said Driver.

'Ya man,' insisted Jimmy. 'True one gal up a Dias say mi voice sweet.'

'Even if ya voice sweet, ya nah know any of U-Roy song dem.'

'Mi do so. What bout "Cheek a bow, cheek a bow, cheek a bow wow wow"?' he sang tunelessly.

'Everybady know dat one. Dat one ole song. Ya nah know U-Roy new song dem.'

'When U-Roy play him show him sing one ole hit, and den showcase new material.'

'But ya nah know him new material.'

'Nobady don't know it. U-Roy just mek it up inna de studio. It nat even out on record. Nobady don't hear it. So mi can mek it up miself. Driver, de entertainer like we fi tink it difficult fi write song. It nat difficult. It easy. Ya man. Mi could be one DJ if mi had de time. Serious. If mi nah had so much pressing ting fi do mi could be one top DJ.'

By the time Jimmy returned from Mo-Bay later that day with a felt hat, platform heel boots and flared trousers concealed in a lada bag (called lada because they, like the Czech car, suddenly flooded the island after the government made a bulk purchase), Jimmy felt things had turned out better without U-Roy. For a start he no longer had to pay the entertainer, or rather think of a way of avoiding paying him, and second he could forget that the last time he saw U-Roy he tried to *tief* his girl from him and made him *vex bad*.

At Zion House the road disappeared under a crowd which pressed at the turnstile. Lots of people held up church raffle tickets which Jimmy had instructed Driver, in the box office, not to accept. When Jimmy hurriedly got out of Bessie to avoid paying Devon his debt for gas, the crowd recognised him and surged in his direction.

'Security! Security!' he shouted, desperately, although when a bouncer elbowed his way through the crowd and held Jimmy protectively by the arm, he changed his tune to, 'Mek way for de promoter. Mek way! Move! Gwaan boy!'

He was propelled to a side door, but before going in turned to address the crowd: 'De management regret dem kiant accept no responsibility for illegal sale of forge ticket,' and with that he disappeared from view.

So few could afford a ticket, the inside of the venue was virtually empty. Jimmy headed for the gloomy box office where Driver was deep in the long and arduous process of deducting forty from one hundred to give an anxious white couple their change. The boy, a U-Roy enthusiast from Dortmund, said, 'I sink it is sixti,' so many times Driver was sure it was a trick. Eventually the girl, clinging to her boy-friend, said in German, 'For goodness sake, Helmut, forget it. It's only a few Marks, and he's going to get heavy if we don't go in. Come on.'

After they had left, without their change but with effusive thanks, Driver said to Jimmy: 'Ya kiant do dis, man. It kiant work.'

'Mi can do i', and mi will do i',' replied Jimmy. 'Go on troo ladies,' he added, freeing the turnstile to admit two pretty girls.

'But dem will kill ya if dem find out. You want fi dead wid bokkle an' machete?'

'Mi nuh gwine dead. Trust mi. Dem will never recognise mi. Never.'

'Ya can run now easy, man,' Driver whispered. 'Look. We 'ave four ondred dallar. Go on. Excape before it too late.'

'No Driver. Mi gonna do it.'

'Why, man?'

'Cas mi want fi do it.'

'Ya wan fi do i'?'

'Ya man.'

'Ya crazy, Jimmy. Ya crazy. Why ya want fi do i'?'

'Cas dis hat, pants and boots,' he said holding up the lada

bag, 'pull gal like magnet pull nail. Serious. When mi put dem on, dem mash op all de gal dem inna de place. Big entertainer like U-Roy have all de gal dem him can hangle. And tonight mi gonna be U-Roy, and tonight U-Roy gonna have trailer load of gal dem. Mi kiant wait fi start. Now. Listen. Mi gonna have couple Dragon. Come and find mi in a likker while and say, so dat people hear, U-Roy inna de place and want fi see mi backstage. All right? And bring all de money. Cool?'

'Ya man.'

'Then go a back of the building to the likkle window and wait.'

'Ya man.'

'Nuh worry, Driver. Everyting gonna be smooth and cool. Believe mi, smooth and cool.'

Jimmy spent the next two hours drinking *hot* Dragon stout and asking girls if they liked U-Roy. Those who replied in the affirmative he made a mental note to seduce later. He was interrupted by the designer who appeared with two of the four hand-painted posters advertising the show. They were delivered an hour after they announced U-Roy would be on stage, but Jimmy pronounced them *criss*.

'The other two I and I deliver nex week for definite,' the designer said. 'An' ya owe I tree ondred dallar for de four.'

'No prablem,' replied Jimmy. 'Check mi tomorrow or the day after and mi give it to you. Respect.' To the Royal Dread, who was sitting close by with his wife and friends Jimmy added, 'De same fi de rent fi de venue. Check mi nex week for it, man.'

'No Jimmy, mi mus haffi tonight,' the Royal Dread insisted. 'Dat's what us agree.'

'Easy man, easy. Mi head nah feel too good,' Jimmy said feigning illness. 'Mi will see what mi can do.'

The audience was growing restless. A Dandy shandy bottle, favoured projectile of Jamaican mobs, spun out of the crowd onto the stage.

'Oh my God darling, did you see that?' the Royal Dread's alarmed wife shrieked.

'Nuh worry wuman,' he reassured her (and himself), 'mi know dese people. It only fun. Dey mean no harm. It all for show. After all, dey nat gonna mash op de one place dat provide top class entertainment in de whole parish, are dem? Anyway, U-Roy soon come.'

'Him inna de place now, boss,' Driver announced to Jimmy. 'Him inna de dressing-room an' he aks fi see you, Jimmy. And here de money,' he gave Jimmy the wad.

'Give mi what ya owe mi now,' said the Royal Dread.

'After de show,' said Jimmy, 'like us agree.' He stood up. 'Likker while,' he said with a knowing smile, and walked backstage. But when he got to the dressing-room – a small concrete room full of crates of empties with one high, barred window, he found the Royal Dread lumbering along behind him.

'Jimmy. Mi want mi money, man. Serious. Nuh give mi nuh bullshit.'

'Hol' on. Let mi first hail op U-Roy.'

'Ya tink it possible for mi to meet the man?' asked the Royal Dread.

Jimmy's hand rested on the door handle. 'Can be,' he said, 'first him and mi have a likker business fi settle, and den mi will call ya. Wait a couple minute. Cool?'

'Ya man. Mi wait here.'

Jimmy opened the door a little and slipped in, crying out, 'U-Roy! Respect, mi friend!' to the empty room. After shoving some crates against the door he began his metamorphosis from insignificant fisherman to top entertainer. Holding his old clothes and the money, he climbed up to the window and softly called Driver's name.

'Ya man,' came a voice. 'U-Roy a com, Jimmy?'

'Fool, Driver. Course him nuh com.'

'Ya man. Mi hear ya talk wid him.'

'Idiot. Take dese. Go back a mi yard and wait fi mi. Okay?'

He pushed the bundle through the bars into Driver's outstretched hands. There was a knock at the door.

'Hol' an,' he called out. 'Mi deh com.'

He took a last look at himself in the broken mirror, pulled the felt trilby over his eyes, gave a pelvic thrust and flashed a wicked smile. Reaching for the door *hangle* he said loudly, 'All right, Jimmy mi friend, if ya nah feel so good, ya stay here and chill out. Mi check ya after de show, man,' then slipped out of the door, closing it behind him.

'Rastafari! King of Kings! Conquering Lion of de tribe of Judah. Jah! Welcome a Zion House, brudder,' boomed the Royal Dread, slapping palms and locking his fist around Jimmy's limp hand. The Royal Dread was thrilled. He was now on personal terms with the great U-Roy, who stood before him in his trademark felt, bell bottom trousers and platform heel boots.

'Yes mi friend,' said Jimmy warmly.

'Mi de proprietor,' explained the Royal Dread, 'everyting cool?'

'Kinda cool, but,' continued Jimmy, lowering his voice to a whisper and putting his arm around the rasta's bulky shoulders, 'mi nah trust de promoter. Mi know him since lang time, and him a friend, true, but mi nah trust him all de same, annerstan? Im say im have fever and want fi chill out, but mi tink im gonna run off without pay mi, and me afraid mi nuh get mi money.'

'He have de money in der. Ask him for it,' urged the Dread.

'No man, a performer get pay after im sing, nat before. Mi kiant disrespect de man like dat.'

'Brudder, can mi do anyting to help you, cas mi tink him try fi run off widout pay mi too.'

'Mi kiant believe dis! Dat man one bad boy for true, eh?' laughed Jimmy. 'But look, man, dis room have one lock. Ya have de key?'

'Ya man, right here,' the Royal Dread took a key ring from his pocket with a twinkle in his eye.

'Well let we lock im in till mi finish sing, den im kiant leave wid de money before im pay we. Jimmy try fi jinall ya, but ya cleverer dan him.'

'True,' laughed the Royal Dread. This was excellent. U-Roy must have felt an instinctive bond to trust him so. The Royal Dread turned the key in the lock. 'Now we know he is safe.'

'Ya man,' laughed Jimmy, 'now us know im safe and sound.'

The Jamaican entertainer never toured with a band. He couldn't afford the cost of transporting men and equipment whenever he performed, so, instead he sung to the rhythm tracks which local dee-jays played on their turntables. Because every performer had to use the same few backing tracks, each of which had a name, like Salt 'n' Pepper, and the evocative Corduroy, he was judged not so much on his music but his lyrics. It was out of this economy that the lucrative dancehall music, which spread so successfully in the States and Europe, was born.

Few preparations were therefore necessary before Jimmy took to the stage, though one was that the Royal Dread had to waddle to the microphone to make his introduction. His text for the day echoed in his mind: He that loves to exalt himself shall be obeyed. On stage he exalted himself: he raised his arms above his head as if everyone had come to see only him, and shouted, 'Yo!'

'Yo!' the audience thundered back, for by then the place had filled out with all the boys who had vaulted the wall and those from Cove whom Driver, drunk on power, let in for free.

'Ya man,' he purred indulgently, and then intoned the rastafarian incantation, 'Selassie I, Rastafari, Conquering Lion of Judah, King of Kings, Jah!' In response to this a *bokkle* spun through the air and splintered on something behind him. *Bald 'ead* people, by which was meant anyone without dreadlocks, did not hold rastamen in the high esteem they did themselves. Scared of what else might come out of the darkness the Royal Dread got on with it.

'People! Let mi introduce the greatest, the number one, the one and only, mi good friend U-Roy!'

The rhythm track started, the bass so loud it *tomp* you in the chest, and after a short pause, while Jimmy tried to extract a promise out of a girl he *buck up* on backstage a minute earlier, he strutted on. The Royal Dread retreated to the edge of the stage where he still felt sufficiently close to the centre of attention to satisfy his vanity. He was a happy man. His venue was buzzing. The rent he was due, which he had worried he would not see, was now safely locked up with Jimmy backstage. A star, albeit one a little on the wane, was only feet away from him. He could henceforth tell people he'd been onstage with U-Roy without lying. His large, well shod foot tapped out the beat. In the audience his gorgeous and beloved wife clapped her hands pretty well in time. The rest of the crowd moved more subtly, *skanking and wining* to the rhythm, their mood mollified by the appearance of the man holding the microphone. He held up his hand to stop the rhythm and make an announcement.

'Dis number,' Jimmy called out, 'is for mi good friend Jimmy Fairfax of Cousins Cove. Big up Jimmy! Big up Cove!'

The Cove contingent blushed with pride – with the exception of Roddy Perry, who *suck teeth* with jealousy.

The music kicked in again, and Jimmy began to sing.

'Put on your best dress, baby, we're going out tonight. I'm going to let you wear my crown, I'm going to make you the talk of the town ...' It was recognisably U-Roy's greatest hit, and with its rousing chorus, 'Cheek a bow, cheek a bow, cheek a bow wow wow', was a big crowd pleaser. All those with cigarette lighters (two in a crowd of 190) held them in the air.

To people's surprise, U-Roy's second song didn't seem to have any lyrics. Emboldened by the success of the first number, Jimmy decided to make the next one up, but unusually for Jimmy, words suddenly failed him. He had begun, 'All right mi friends mi could sing all night,' but couldn't think of a rhyme with night, so mumbled and hummed for a bit, and then, thinking of 'all right' struggled to get it onto the end of another phrase, but unable to do that, he began to panic as his mind emptied of any ideas except utterly irrelevant and useless ones. There was only one thing for it: a reprise of 'Put on your best dress, baby, we're going out tonight'. This got the crowd going again, so he scanned the faces at the front for any of the girls he'd checked out earlier.

When he sang the same lyrics for the third song, everyone knew there was something wrong. The Royal Dread said to the person beside him, 'Not a vintage performance, I grant you, but a good one all the same. Ya man.'

Driver, listening outside the venue, grimaced, turned, and began to walk briskly into the safety of darkness.

In the audience, the Cove posse, like everyone else, fell silent and stopped dancing. Jimmy leant down to shake a girl's hand, but she recoiled. Most of the crowd began to wonder if it wasn't U-Roy, but for those from Cove it was not a question of who it wasn't, but of who it was, for the moment U-Roy's hat slipped back on his head, throwing light on Jimmy Fairfax's desperate grin, Vinton said, quietly to those around him, 'Jeeeezus, dat Jimmy. Dat Jimmy. Mi kiant believe it.'

Jimmy froze when he heard his name being yelled from the audience during the fourth number (a song entitled 'Cheek a bow cheek a bow cheek a bow wow wow'). The game was up, but he had enough time to pull off his hat, flaunt his true identity to the masses and dance a triumphal jig centre stage before being driven off by a hail of bottles. He sped past the Royal Dread who called out, 'Hey U-Roy, maybe we can drink a couple Dragon and talk 'bout management.' But an instant later the Royal Dread was fully occupied on stage trying to save his expensive equipment from annihilation. Like the overwhelmed goalkeeper of Cove's football team he leapt one way, then the other, with his arms wide apart as bottles crashed and splintered against his amps and boxes. This horrible spectacle only ended when a bottle bounced off his woolly head and forced him, to loud cheers, to totter off the stage. The undefended equipment was *mash op* by the crowd which, when it ran out of ammunition, turned its attention to the bar and looted that. Vinton and the other Cove *yout dem* were at the fore of the mob, though Vinton was never so prominent he couldn't slip away quickly if the Police suddenly turned up. The crowd then fanned out onto the Main and gave chase to Jimmy, who had grabbed a girl by the hand and was sprinting as fast as his high-heeled boots and flapping bell-bottoms would allow.

Jimmy made it safely back to Cove where he lived a hero's

life, revered by the entire village as the man who *jinall* the whole of Bulls Bay, for at least a month, though the story was kept alive for much longer by the addition of U-Roy to the list of Jimmy's aliases. People noticed that for a while Roddy Perry stayed in his own yard, and when he did come out and walk up and down 'pon the street, he spoke much less about Bob Marley in case someone brought up U-Roy's great triumph.

By the time Jimmy caught up with Driver, Driver had *spend down* all the money, but to a man from Cove, glory was more important than material gain, and Jimmy had a whole *heap o' glory.* He carefully kept the hat, boots and pants, and from time to time, when he heard U-Roy was playing a show, he'd bring them out and wear them to bars near the venue, and they rarely failed to get him a girl.

FOR THE BRAVE MAY FALL
BUT NEVER YIELD

Chicken George *chat noff.* He started stories and only stopped when no-one was listening any more. As people liked Chicken George, and didn't want to *disrespect* him, they were often caught for hours by his tales of life at the wheel of the No. 22 bus which he drove for London Transport from Putney Green to Piccadilly Circus for twenty-three years. If you met him in the Back Street, it could take forty minutes to get past him, and if he came into your yard he could trap you for an entire afternoon. People, seeing him coming, plunged into the bush to hide, or vaulted corrugated zinc fences to avoid him, and eventually the only audience he could find was the village *picknee.*

When Candy, the captain of the cricket team, asked him to umpire the match against the Police, Chicken George was honoured, and after a fifteen minute speech, accepted. He had been looking for an opportunity to put something back into the village where *he born an' raise,* and which he left in 1954 for work in Britain.

Touring Cove each day, trilby on his head, furled umbrella on his bony wrist, he liked to feel he was reintegrating himself in the community. When he had thought about retirement in Jamaica, while in gloomy Shepherds Bush, he envisaged himself being in demand as a school governor, or magistrate, or in some other important role. He expected to be called upon for advice on weighty village matters. But that was not the way things turned out. People in Cousins Cove did not seem to realise that he had mixed in Britain with the very highest in the land. Twice he had shaken hands with Sir Marcus Bromley, chairman of London Transport. His next door neighbour in Shepherds Bush, with whom he was on excellent terms, was the daughter of a Cabinet minister, whom he'd said good evening to on more than one occasion. He had even seen the Queen on television.

Cousins Cove, it seemed to him, could little afford to ignore the talents of a man like him, who could boast (and frequently did) thirty-two years' experience in one of the world's greatest cities working for a massive organisation like London Transport.

But there was something appropriate, Chicken George felt, about being asked to umpire. It showed that he was respected, and could be relied upon to make good, even-handed judgements. It was a start to his career as community leader. He knew little about cricket, it was true, and had never played a full match, far less umpired one, but he had watched countless Test matches on TV in England, and it looked pretty easy to him.

The cricketers had actually only asked Chicken George because Jimmy U-Roy Fairfax, their regular umpire, had been beaten up by opposition supporters after the Dias game for a dubious run-out decision against the Dias skipper, and Chicken George had a white nylon coat – from his days working in the London Transport canteen when he was stopped from driving after his eyes started playing up – which Oneil mistook for an umpire's coat.

The year 1987 had not been a good season for the Cousins

Cove cricket team. So far they had played seven matches, drawn none, won none and lost seven. And 1986 had been worse: beaten nine times out of nine. Their best result in recent times was the draw against Blenheim in 1984, and that was only because rain stopped play just before Cove were all bowled out. The other clubs in the Westmorland and Hanover Senior Cricket League said that if Cove lost every match in the '87 season they'd be thrown out of the league. With only one match remaining, it was time for some soul-searching.

The weekly team meeting was held in Cove Primary School on Thursday evenings. They found that they had to wait for at least five days after each match to allow inflamed passions to die down. If they met too early, fights always broke out amongst the guys as they blamed each other for the latest disaster. Squeezed into the tiny classroom furniture, it was the only place the team ever looked like giants. The first item on the agenda each week was Candy's captaincy.

'Answer mi dis,' said Vices before the captain turned up. 'If a animal have no head it can't live, it kiant go up an' down, can it?'

'No, man,' answered some voices.

'... Cas de head control de body. We is de body and Candy is de head. If we go to lose cricket match it cas de head lead us der. If we drop de catch dem or let de ball fly pass we, it cas de head place we in de wrong part on de pitch. It Candy fault.'

The growl of Candy's motorbike was heard outside the primary school, where the meeting was held.

Vices continued: 'Bot, bot, we moss support our captain,' he said as Candy walked in looking apologetic. Everyone knew that any idea of deposing Candy was unworkable, since only Candy, who had a job at Hedonism, the biggest hotel in Negril, could afford to *fund ball and team food.* Hedonism had its own cricket team which was also in the league, but Candy wasn't good enough to be selected for it, so he had to make do with captaining Cousins Cove.

'Last Saturday we win a moral victory,' Candy declared. 'Dem only win cas dem change de ball.'

The opposition batsman had hit one of Kipling's long hops so far it was lost in the bush. The substitute ball, everyone realised afterwards, had some kind of spell cast over it.

'Nobady can catch dat ball,' said Vices, who'd dropped three catches that afternoon. 'Nobady.'

'Ya kiant ketch no ball dat Obeah man deal wid.'

'Dat ball one duppy ball. Mi swear. It hate Cousins Cove,' Candy stated. 'It nat we fault we nuh win.'

'Ya man,' agreed the guys. 'It nat we fault. It de ball fault.'

'Bot dis Saturday . . . ' started Candy, who was aware that the men, after twenty-eight matches and nearly four seasons without a victory, needed a morale boosting speech, '. . . tomorrer we gonna play like de champion team we really is. Ya know? And we gonna mash op de Police, and win every game nex season . . .'

'If we nah win gainst de Police der nat gonna be no nex season, cas dem gonna trow we outta de league,' pointed out Bell, so called because he was once sent a bell for a bicycle by an uncle in Wolverhampton. As he didn't have a bike, he mounted it on the broom he swept out his mother's yard with.

'David slew Goliat,' Vices said.

'And Samson slew de Philistine,' added Maxwell.

'But de Police alway slew Cousins Cove,' added Vinton.

'Byron must get healty and hearty,' said Biggar. 'We need Byron.'

Byron's maiden innings of 199 against Sandals Hotel in 1987 had looked like changing the course of Cousins Cove cricket, and was a frequently mentioned rare moment of sporting glory for the village. He had been run out on a stupid call by Michael, who'd tried to steal a run to get off the mark. Cove were 230 all out, and Sandals 231 for no wicket, but Byron's innings that day was another of the seven wonders of Cousins Cove. But it was sadly to be Byron's last innings, for the following week he fell seriously ill.

Vices examined his older, quieter brother, and declared Byron had *one worm in him stomach dat make im maaga*. His skin grew sallow and hung off his bones, his eyes were lack-lustre and bloodshot, and he hardly had the strength to lift a bat, though nothing could stop him, every Saturday during the season, dragging himself from his bed to watch Cousins Cove play cricket, not that that did his spirits any good.

For over a year Byron fought the illness. Miss Citarra and Vices, the top medical brains in the whole of Cove, worked unceasingly on the case. Byron was made to drink rum and sea water, lime and Epsom Salts, gallons of Bicarbonate of Soda, Breeze soap powder ('Fi wash out *de* worm,' Vices explained), and many many bush teas, picked and prepared by all the well-wishers in the village. He'd applied poultices of logwood ash, seaweed and *hog doo-doo*, but nothing worked. Byron, once a handsome, athletic and industrious fisherman, was a husk of a man, with pale, yellowish skin, assaulted by horrible stomach aches, and forced to live on his bed, vomitting blood and spume.

It was agreed that Byron had to play on Saturday against the Police, so cricket club funds were voted to pay for a visit to Dr Bury in Green Island. His friends helped him dress up in his best clothes, which were a necessity for even a dying man to wear on a visit to the doctor.

Dr Bury took two minutes to diagnose the problem.

'In my opinion, young man, you are afflicted with what is known as a Bellicium Piritis Stupendum.'

'Bellicium Piritis Stupendum?' repeated Byron slowly.

'You do nat know anything about medicine, do you, young man? You did nat study it, did you?' Dr Bury asked, looking keenly at his patient.

'Mi ongle know dis bout medicine: if you have one fi cure mi, please gi' it me soon, dactar, cas me belly hurt bud.'

'I'll do the very best I can,' said Dr Bury, looking relieved. 'Now,' he explained, 'you see Bellicium Piritis affects the gerundive fibulator ...'

'Dat some kind of worm?'

'In a manner of speaking.'

'Which ya can wash out?'

'I'm afraid not completely. You see the problem is, the gerundive fibulator is very tenacious, very tenacious, and very difficult to remove with only medicine.'

'It have claw like crab?'

'Quite like that ... Look, I will give you some pills that will prevent it from growing further and give you some relief, but an impacted gerund can really only be cured by a surgical procedure.'

'Inna de ospital?'

'Most certainly.'

'Dat espensive?'

'Nat really, not when set against your life. I can probably get it done for about five tousand dollars, or maybe four tousand eight hundred ...'

'Bot mi nuh have monny like dat.'

'How much do you have?'

'Mebbe five 'ondred J.'

'Five hundred dollars? Well, I'm afraid I can't do anything

about your stomach for that, but I'm sure we can find
something else. Do you have any warts that want removing?
Or ingrowing toenails? They're only three hundred J.'

Byron stepped off the minibus where the members of
the cricket team waited. He showed the men the bottle
of pills.

'Dr Bury say mi need one cut inna de ospital, but mi can
tek one pill every day and it will hold back the worm.'

'Bot ya moss play tomorrer,' said Candy, desperately.

Vices said, 'He will play, Candy, he will play. If one pill
stop de worm grow, all de pill moss kill de worm, so tek all
de pill at one time. Den ya can play wid ease, man.'

'If dat true, why Dr Bury say only a surgeon cut can cure
Byron?' asked Miss Citarra, who swore by Dr Bury and spent
every available cent she had on visits to his surgery.

'Ya man, why?' said Maxwell.

'Cas him want money, fool.'

'No man,' protested Miss Citarra. 'Surgeon Canute
Asquith at Lucea ospital tek dat money.'

'Bot him give som a Dr Bury. Cho!'

'No. No. De reason Dr Bury nat want fi cure Byron is
dis,' Vices said. 'Tell mi. Wishart de doctor in Green Island?'
By which he meant, where is the doctor's surgery?

'Before de Police Station,' Maxwell said, and everyone
suddenly fell silent. The plot was thus revealed.

'Right,' said Glenroy, his eyes glistening with the insight.
'And it true Dr Bury Police doctor?'

'Ya man, ya man ...'

'And it true we play de Police on Saturday? Dat why him
nuh cure Byron. Cas de Police feart dat Byron play in de
match. Byron.'

'Ya man,' came Byron's weak voice from where he'd gone
to sit in the shade.

'If one pill hold back de worm, all de pill gonna make it dead. Tross me ...'

This seemed to make sense, so Byron took all the pills in the bottle. He was bed-ridden within hours, and couldn't stand for a week after that, so everyone said Dr Bury deliberately poisoned Byron to keep him out of the match. It was a comfort to go into a game armed with a good excuse for losing it.

Despite the certainty of defeat, there was the usual fierce competition to get on the team, not out of hunger for sport, but because the Police always attracted plenty of female supporters.

On the morning of the game the team emerged from their yards with their usual self-confidence, and set off to the sloping and pitted ball ground, with the glad hearts of the doomed but brave.

The Police umpire was a lawyer called Charles Brown, referred to by everyone as *Liar Brown*, who did the job as a favour to the Police, in return for which bail was always forthcoming for his criminal clients. Chicken George and Liar Brown took the captains out to the wicket where Candy typically lost the toss, and Cove were put into bat. There was a shortage of *gears* because one or two items of Cousins Cove equipment had been *borrow* from Kendal after a match up *inna de hills* and it was felt wise not to parade it in front of the Police unnecessarily. But although Vices and Candy went out in old, broken pads and poor cricket bats, and the well-fed Police were all equipped with *criss gears*, their heads were held high.

Chicken George loved umpiring, and found he was good at it, better, certainly, than Liar Brown, who raised his index finger with a wry smile after an appeal for LBW on a ball that clearly struck Candy's bat before his pad, and could not possibly have got him out.

'De Ompire is one tief!' the Cove supporters shouted. But Chicken George was impressed that the Cove players accepted Liar Brown's decisions so compliantly. It showed sportsmanship and character which he thought they didn't possess. In fact, they didn't complain because they were so accustomed to the bias of the opposition umpire, who more or less counted as a twelfth member of the team, and fully expected Chicken George to do the same thing for Cove when he got the chance, which he did, the very next over, when Vices sprinted down the pitch for a quick run and one of the Police fielders flattened the stumps with a tremendous throw.

'Owdat!' cried the Policemen.

Vices smiled to himself. He knew he was out, but knew also that it was Chicken George who had to make the decision. With little hesitation, Chicken George raised his first finger.

'Out! Out! Out!' yelled the Policemen triumphantly.

An outburst of abuse erupted from the Cove players. 'Ya fool Chicken George. Ya nuh remember where ya live? Ya idiot man ...' all of which Chicken George rose above.

Candy was out for 7. Vices for 9. Biggar held out for two hours and notched up 8. Maxwell got 12, Oneil 10 in a record fifth wicket partnership, and Joe was caught and bowled for 8. By this point the Police looked happy and relaxed. Their laughter wafted across the pitch on the breeze to where the Cove team huddled together under a tree, their silence broken only by occasional outbursts of abuse from Blackie.

'Ya useless!' she laughed. 'Ya no good. Ya kiant bat and ya kiant bowl.'

The score was 61 for 6, and the fielders on the boundary held long, laughing conversations with people in the crowd,

as though what was going on in the middle was fairly un-
important. The Police batsmen folded their arms across their
full tummies and gave each other fat confident smiles.

'Look like we'll be home for Dynasty,' they joked, rubbing
in the fact that they had homes, not yards, and televisions.

Cousins Cove were all out for 87 at a tea, paid for by
Candy, of *tin mackerel, and some breads* which the Police
pointedly didn't eat. 'Maybe I'll get a burger at Burger King
in Mo-Bay later,' one said to another in earshot of the Cove
men. The newly opened Burger King on Gloucester Avenue
in Mo-Bay was an Eldorado for the *little people dem*, somewhere to be dreamt of but never attained in this lifetime,
and the Police knew it.

Candy, Vices and Bell sought out Chicken George, who
was mingling with the Police players.

'What ya do, ya fool? Ya want we fi lose?'

Chicken George lowered his voice. 'Are you asking me to
help you win the match?'

'Course we blaad claat are, ya raas claat Chicken George,'
shouted Vices.

'In that case you leave me no option but to make an
official complaint in writing about Cousins Cove Cricket
Club to the Standing Committee of the Marylebone Cricket
Club, the ruling body of world cricket, who meet in the
Long Room at Lords Cricket Ground, Wellington Road,
London NW8.' As the relief driver on the 119 bus, Chicken
George had stopped many times and stared at the impene-
trable brick wall of Lords Cricket Ground, envying the
conductor who could dash up the stairs to see the players
on the pitch. 'If this country was run by men half as dedicated
to fair play as the Standing Committee of the Marylebone
Cricket Club, then we would not be in the boat we are
currently in vis à vis corruption and immorality. Have you

never heard the saying,' he hissed furiously, '"It is not whether you win or lose but how you play the game"? In England we were proud of that saying.'

'Bot Chicken George, ya not in England no more. Ya back a yard. And we moss win dis match or dem trow we outta de league, an' if we trow outta de league den nobady gonna play de game gainst we, and cricket gonna stop in Cove,' explained Biggar.

'From what I have seen of this club, I think that would be a very good idea.'

'Ya blaad claat,' Vices cursed as Chicken George walked away.

It was just as the Police opening batsmen were happily padding up that the news came through. A police car tore off the Main, bumping onto the ball ground and drew up in a cloud of dust. Sergeant Dickinson from Green Island was at the wheel.

'Natty Morgan hold up de drinks truck wid one gun at Orange Bay,' he shouted, 'and tief farty-one tousand dallar. Every afficer is needed fi de man hunt.'

The drinks truck was a noisy open-sided lorry piled high with crates of Red Stripe, Dragon Stout and *saff drink*, on top of which three men perched. It hammered up and down the Main ignoring the shouted requests from the *little people dem* for it to stop and trade with the bamboo sheds and bars, on its way to the big hotels in Negril.

'Nobady kiant com now, man. We gonna bat,' shouted one of the openers.

'Dat gotta wait. Every man gotta come.'

'Who say so?'

'Sergeant Pinnock.'

'Dis match gonna finish anudder day,' announced *Afficer* Barnett, the captain, who'd once trialled for the Jamaican national cricket team. He'd achieved considerable fame by being bowled for a duck by Carl Hooper.

'No sah,' roared back the redoubtable Blackie, striding towards the Police. 'Dis match a go finish today. Dat what de rule is. Mi wait tree year for one win and no Police a go tief it now.'

'But we haffi hunt fi Natty Morgan.'

'So ya lose de match den,' shouted Blackie, crossing her mighty arms as she stood in front of the policeman ...

'We not going on no man hunt,' said two of the Police-men, *afficers* Nini Hibbert and Cop Holt, who were suspended on full pay pending an inquiry into their robbing the bank at Sav. 'We can bat.'

'No problem,' said the Police skipper. 'Hibbert, Holt, you two hold on till we catch Natty Morgan and kill him, den we can come back and finish de innings. Nuh get out, annerstan?'

'Ya sah.'

'Likker while. Soon be back,' Barrett called.

There was screeching of tyres and revving of engines as the Police jumped into cars and headed up the Main to Orange Bay. Hibbert and Holt padded up and walked out to the wicket.

Candy said, 'Alright team, gadder roun everybady, gadder roun.' Five men responded to his order, and to them he said, 'We must tek one wicket. Just one wicket, and we win dis game.'

'Unless Pinnock ketch Natty quick,' said Bell, 'and dem all come back fi bat.'

'Dat kiant happen,' laughed Vinton. 'Natty nuh gonna ketch easy. Tross me.'

'Dat right,' said Candy. 'Now come now, let we do it.'

'And God bless Natty Morgan,' added Vinton.

Everyone in the Cove team hated fielding. Considered by some cricketers to be a crucial part of the game, Cove players viewed it as something only little people did. Cricket was not a team game in Cove. It was a gladiatoral encounter between two men, the bowler and batsman. Nothing else really counted. Cove fielders wanted only to bowl, or perhaps field at slip where there was a chance of a glorious catch. Standing for hours in the sun, running after balls and flinging them back to the keeper was not for them, and it was their habit in practice sessions in the village to let the *picknee* field while they *chop ten* in the shade or patrolled the boundary looking for *gal dem*.

Kipling opened the bowling, thundering in on his stuttering twenty-five pace run-up. The ball left his hand, and was next seen skimming towards the boundary after travelling at considerable speed between Joe, the wicket keeper's legs. The fielders let loose a stream of abuse in Joe's direction, for any player who made a mistake was rounded on by his team mates *fi teach him*. The next ball was very short, and flew dangerously close to the batsman's head, though yards above the wicket behind him.

'Good ball, Kipling,' shouted Driver from the gully where he was smoking a spliff. Everyone agreed, believing it better to terrify a batsman than dismiss him.

After failing to take a wicket in his first over, Kipling put another two paces on his run-up. He then came in at an astonishing speed, but his accuracy, never his strong point, worsened, and the deliveries came down wider and wider from the wicket. Despite this, no-one suggested bowling slower. Indeed, as his fury mounted, Kipling added three more paces to his run-up. His team mates loved it. Better to bowl fast, and lose, than bowl slowly, and win.

Every man in the Cove team knew that total concentration

on the job in hand was what was required, but that didn't
stop them gazing at the spectators and finding girls to chat
to, or talking amongst themselves and letting their attention
wander from the business of fielding to idle speculation
about their imminent win.

'We gonna win, man,' Oneil was saying to Vices when a
ball nicked Nini Hibbert's bat and whizzed through his hands
where he stood at slip.

'Come on. Constentrate,' urged Joe, behind the wicket.

'Dat nat mi fault,' shouted Oneil.

'Ya man dat ya fault. Ya drop de ketch,' shouted Vinton.
'Who fault ya believe it is?'

'Shut up,' yelled Candy.

The batsmen dug in and took few chances, waiting for
Natty Morgan to be caught, and their team mates to return.
In the first hour they scored only 18 runs, but at the end of
the second hour, when the fielding grew really sloppy, and
another couple of chances had been missed at slip, they were
43. After three hours they were 68, though a report came
through to Blackie that Natty Morgan had slipped through
the Police net and was heading up to Grange Hill, where he
could hide deep *inna de bush*.

'Dem nuh gonna find Natty,' she told the players on the
pitch. 'So com now. Tek one wicket and win.'

So unaccustomed were the players from Cousins Cove to
victory, that even when it was placed neatly in their palms,
they let it, like numerous catches that afternoon, slip through
their hands. At about four in the afternoon, when the policemen got to 70, and needed only 18 to win, Cove's old friend
Defeat came clearly into view, and mesmerised Candy and
the boys with its hateful familiarity. Beaten by a team of
only two players. It was something that could only happen
to a Cousins Cove outfit, and everyone seemed to know it.

They began to laugh at their own mistakes, and make light of their bungled attempts to bowl straight, or stop the ball, as if preparing themselves for defeat. The Cove supporters fell silent, as the Police supporters became voluble. Word of the state of play seeped back into Lances Bay, bringing out astounded onlookers who would normally have no interest in the match to see for themselves the spectacle of a whole cricket team being beaten by two men.

The dreadful moment duly arrived when Cop Holt drove a ball through Gary's legs for two runs out to cover. If Vices' throw had been accurate, Joe might have run out Nini Hibbert, but it flew wildly over Joe's outstretched hands and the Policeman ran a third run while Vices shouted, 'Ya kiant catch ya blaad claat keeper,' at Joe. This put the Police on 86, one less than Cove.

Joe, behind the wicket, said to Oneil clearly, so Cop Holt could hear, 'Oneil, mi never see two batsmen bat for so long time and never hit no boundary.'

'Cas dem kiant,' Oneil laughed. 'De police don't have no strength fi hit a four or a six. Cas dem saft. Ya ever see a Policeman lick off a six?'

'Never,' said Joe, and then settled down on his haunches as Biggar, his bosoms bouncing up and down under his shirt, pounded in to bowl from the other end. As Joe hoped, the batsman took a mighty swipe at the ball, hoping to end the innings with a boundary, connecting with tremendous force. He hit it so hard, in fact, that he split the ball into two, one half of which flicked off the top edge and flew up into the air towards Vinton at third slip. Vinton saw it coming straight towards him and his first impulse was to try to catch it with one hand because it would look so good. Then the thought of dropping it flashed across his mind. It was a small risk to take, compared to the glory of a one-handed catch, so he ostentatiously put his left hand behind his back, and plucked the ball from the air with his right.

'OWSAT!' he shouted.

The fate of the other half of the ball was somewhat different. It took the full force from the face of Nini Hibbert's bat and skidded at high velocity along the ground and over the boundary, spreading a large group of Police supporters who were jumping up and down shouting, 'Four rons! Far rons! We win, we win!'

A second later, all the players and all the supporters converged on Chicken George, arguing furiously about the rules that covered this eventuality.

Chicken George was certain that a new ball should be found, and the ball played again, but something made him hesitate. It was perhaps the sight of his large and comfortable house on the far side of the ball ground, surrounded by the many other lesser houses of his neighbours' yards. A moment later, without raising his voice, he asked for the two halves of the ball, and after glancing at them he made an announcement.

'Under Rule number one hundred and sixty two, section three of the Marylebone County Cricket Club rule book, it says which half of a split ball is bigger shall count,' he told the crowd.

He then held the two pieces up to show that one was larger than the other. 'Batsman,' he said.

'Ya man,' said Nini Hibbert in the crowd.

And up went Chicken George's finger. 'You are out, sir. And in the absence of any other batsmen on your side I declare Cousins Cove the winners.'

There was tumult. The Cove team ran in a pack around the boundary, shouting and whooping in celebration of the first victory in living memory. The Police supporters moved

in on Chicken George, and began to push him and punch
him. It was only the appearance of two off-duty policemen
from Mo-Bay, who'd joined the crowd late in the afternoon,
and who escorted Chicken George off the pitch, which
prevented violence. Though as soon as they had him out of
sight behind the primary school, they pulled their service
revolvers on him and threatened to kill him if he ever 'tief
de Police again'.

Up until that afternoon, Chicken George had growing
doubts about whether he was right to have left Shepherds
Bush for Jamaica for his retirement. But from then on, when
he walked out, although he had the same old suspicion that
he was being avoided, he felt that when he did talk to his
neighbours, they had more respect for him – and he liked
it. Sometimes, Vices, or one of the *yout dem* of the village,
would say, 'Chicken George. Ri-spec! What dat Marley bone
cricket clob rule nomber dat you mek up for de Police game?'
and laugh.

Chicken George replied the same each time: 'I did not
make that up. That rule is in the book. I would never make
up a rule. Never.' And thus he settled into a long and happy
retirement.

THE PEOPLE'S GANGSTA

When Tyrone 'Natty' Morgan held up the drinks truck on a stretch of the Main beyond Orange Bay, the job went better than he could have hoped: not only did he get away with 41,000 J, but the robbery was reported by Radio Waves, the new Mo-Bay station, and made *Crime of the Month* on RJR, which meant that his name, with the prefix 'notorious gang leader' was broadcast twice a day, every day. It was the kind of publicity that gangsters dreamt of. He became such a celebrity a minibus owner in Sandy Bay renamed his unit 'Natty Morgan'.

Before this break, Natty was an unknown member of a Kingston gang run by Heart Disease, so called because according to a government broadcast on JBC radio, that was 'the nation's number one killer'. Natty decided to get famous by killing his old friend Heart Disease, but the job went wrong, he only wounded him, and had to leave the metropolitan area in a hurry, so headed for West Jamaica, where twenty years before he was *born an' raise*.

Sergeant Delroy Pinnock of Green Island, Hanover's hardest cop, was put on the *drinks chock* robbery. Everyone knew and feared Pinnock, who had shot dead six people including his wife.

Natty hid up *inna de hills while tings cool dung*, but 41,000J in cash began to *mad* him in a backwater where the people still bartered for goods, and money was virtually useless, unless you wanted kerosene – not the commodity the gangster had planned to celebrate his heist with. His single thrill was hearing his name on the radio, and so, long before it was safe, he took the minibus down the pot-holed road to Montego Bay to drink rum and *sport wid de gal dem.*

The moment he alighted on Sam Sharpe Square he could tell people recognised him from wanted posters Pinnock had distributed. It was his first direct brush with fame and he loved it so much he swaggered brazenly down Barrett Street trailing a gaggle of awe-struck *picknee* chanting, 'Natty, Natty, Natty ...' only shooing them away half-heartedly before climbing the stairs to an iniquitous go-go bar where he was confident of being recognised by the criminal clientele.

Natty had a *couple ounce of rum in him belly* and his arm around a *bit of browning* in a bra and G-string when feet pounded up the narrow staircase and two uniformed cops burst into the bar. Even though they had guns in their hands, and Natty had something altogether different in his, he managed to shoot first, killing one and leaving the other writhing on the floor. With the sound of reinforcements charging up the stairs Natty gave his go-go dancer an un-hurried kiss, vaulted the bar, ran through to the back and smashed a window with a chair. Shoving his Beretta into his belt he climbed onto the sill, leapt across the alley and grabbed a loose drainpipe on the other side. He would have got away if he hadn't stopped to *hail up som yout dem* who'd heard the shots and shattered glass and run into the alley to see what was going on. He was still striking poses and spinning his pistol on his trigger finger when Sergeant Pinnock, six foot four with a wide jaw and thick moustache, rounded the corner with his .44 in his hand and squeezed off a shot. Natty still didn't run; he waved his fist and shouted, 'Ya miss, raas claat!' making the *yout dem* roar with laughter.

Pinnock didn't miss the second time, and Natty half fell, half slid, down the pipe and collapsed bleeding on the filthy alley floor. Pinnock picked up Natty's Beretta and spilled three live rounds into the palm of his hand.

Cocking his own pistol with a click at Natty's brown temple he said, 'Nyam dem.' It was classic Pinnock: make suspects eat live bullets to soften them up for interrogation. Holding Natty by his short dreadlocks he stuffed the ammunition into his slack mouth. Natty's eyes opened and he spat them out along with a stream of abuse, so Pinnock forced him face-down in the gutter, and with a boot between his shoulder blades slapped handcuffs on his wrists. He then dragged Natty past the *yout dem* to the Police car. Seeing the boys made Natty defiant. Not wanting to disappoint his public he began to *cuss and use bad word.*

'*Nuh touch mi, pussy claat,*' he shouted, but Pinnock just *lick im* across the head and tipped his body into the boot of the car which he slammed and locked.

On the way to Green Island Pinnock deliberately drove slowly, and stopped for an hour *fi check one gal in Sandy Bay,* carefully parking so the bonnet and cab were in the thick shade of an almond tree and the boot in the searing sunlight.

Word that the gangster was in Green Island lock-up flashed up and down the Main. People held up their heads with pride that such an important individual as a gang member and Police killer was for once on the north coast and not in Kingston. The story of his capture quickly penetrated deep into the hills and valleys, and well-wishers gathered at the gate of the Police station so that when Natty awoke from unconsciousness on the floor of his cell, the first thing he heard was his name being called from beyond the bars.

After Natty *nyam* a dinner of chicken-foot and rice, spurred by a hatred of Pinnock and a desire to do something for the crowd at the gate, he formed a plan of escape, and in the darkness before dawn, he struggled through a hole in his ceiling, crept across the roof of the lock-up, leapt off into a thicket and ran away into the bush.

Mr Blidgen of Cousins Cove was responsible for Natty's escape, though he didn't know it, for he was the contractor who had supplied the load of contaminated sea sand that had produced the substandard concrete roof which Natty had burrowed a hole through with nothing more than a spoon.

Natty spent the day sleeping in the upper branches of a guango tree with Police and Army vehicles speeding along the road beneath him. When night fell he slipped through the bush to a silent coastal village where a long time before he *did friend* with a shy, pretty girl whom he knew he could count on. He hadn't seen her for four years but figured she'd be where he left her, as she was tied to her yard by a huge dragon of a mother to do the chores.

It was late, and the people who had grouped up to discuss Natty's escape and speculate on his next move had dispersed to their yards, little thinking that he was passing silently through their midst. He crept to the girl's house and whispered her name through the rotting siding boards, trying not to wake her mother, who had, he remembered, often predicted he'd end up in trouble with the Police.

'Who dat?' came a voice.

'Yvette?' whispered Natty again.

'Who dat?'

'Yvette, it Natty Morgan. Mi beg ya som help.'

Yvette got up quickly and quietly and tiptoed to the door. 'Natty?' she asked anxiously.

He took her hand and squeezed it.

'Ya in trouble.'

'Dem nuh gonna capture mi. But mi beg ya someting fi eat and som place fi hide till tings cool dung.'

'Mi can tek ya to de cave dem. Wait while mi get fi mi dress.' She pushed the door to, and turned to see Miss Citarra in the moonlight sitting up in bed on one massive elbow, *tree likker picknee* nuzzled up to her bulk.

'Who dat?' she shrieked.

Outside, Natty winced.

'Nobady Mumma.'

'Dat Natty Morgan.'

'Ssh Mumma.' There were seven children and two other adults in the three-roomed house and Yvette wanted none of them to wake up.

'What he want?'

'Someting fi eat.'

'Give him dat fry fish inna de pot.'

'Ya Mumma.'

'And mek him pay.'

'Mumma!' said Yvette.

'Mi don't have no money,' Natty growled through the boards.

'Him never change,' sighed Miss Citarra, then she asked 'What bout de farty-one tousand dallar from de drink chock robbery?'

'Mi nuh have dat now.'

'Ya nuh spend down all dat money, ya liard,' Miss Citarra said.

'Mi hide dat far away. Now let de gal com,' he whispered impatiently.

'Who dat?' a small voice asked. Everyone fell silent. A five year old boy sat up in Yvette's bed rubbing his big eyes.

'Go back a sleep, Craig,' Yvette whispered.

'Dat Natty Morgan?' he asked excitedly.

'Hush up, *picknee*,' Miss Citarra growled.

'But Mumma, mi hear one man say him Natty Morgan,' Craig said. 'Mi did.'

'Top ya noise *picknee* or mi lick ya,' shouted Miss Citarra, and he lay down, but was too excited to sleep.

Yvette grabbed *half a bread, tree fry fish an one jack dompling*, shoved the plate out of the door and hurried to the mirror to work on her hair. Dawn broke as they left the yard and headed across the pasture to the dark hills. Yvette planned to hide Natty in Ran's rocktop Cave which, although Cove's premier tourist attraction, was reliably deserted at all times. Occasionally Ran, who had painstakingly erected a sign on the Main, and built a bar and turnstile at the cave entrance, wandered up there to moon about on his own, to daydream about tourists and money, but he rarely went into the limestone caves, which Yvette, like everyone else *raise in Cove*, knew so well. Well, perhaps not so well; Vinton once went in with Oneil for a quick game of hide and seek and emerged shaken ten hours later.

Yvette and Natty walked fast through the salady grass with their heads down, and only looked behind them once they reached the mouth of the cave. They then saw hurrying along in their footsteps a barefoot boy in a *torn shorts and ganzi*. It was her nephew, Craig.

'Go in,' Yvette whispered to Natty, who darted into the cave. 'Craig!' she shouted. 'What ya do here, *picknee*?'

A large, round face with big blinking eyes and long lashes

looked up innocently. 'Mi want fi hail up Natty Morgan,' he said, 'so mi can tell mi bredren.'

'Ya nuh tell nobady nuttin, annerstan?' Yvette said.

'Bot mi moss tell Leroy mi see Natty.' Leroy was two years Craig's senior and an object of adulation.

'Natty Morgan nat here, annerstan? Ya never hear him, ya never saw him. Now gwaan back a yard.'

'Ya, man, but first mi hail up im.'

'Hail up who?'

'Natty.' Craig stood square to his aunt with his hands plunged into his pockets.

'Mi tell ya. Natty nuh here. Now gwaan.' She raised her hand to lick him.

'Him is here. Him in de cave mout,' Craig stated implacably. 'Mi see him go in.'

She tried to strike him but years of practice enabled him to evade the blow.

'Him in der,' he shouted, 'mi will show ya.'

'Bredren,' Natty uttered quietly, emerging into the light with his hand held out to Craig, 'hush now. Com ya,' he beckoned to Craig, whose eyes tripled in size and whose chin dropped onto his chest. He shot a satisfied smirk at Yvette and approached the gangster. 'Let we go inna de cave mout,' Natty said, taking Craig's hand. But Craig shook his hand out, puffed out his chest, and walked beside Natty like a man. Yvette followed them in, and in the cool of the cave dabbed aloe on a wound on Natty's *foot bottom* while Craig stared at his swollen and cut face.

'Pinnock beat ya?' Craig asked.

''Top your noise, Craig,' snapped Yvette.

'It nottin,' replied Natty. 'Bot mi gonna kill him for it.'

'Look at dis.' Craig pulled down his shorts to reveal a welt across the top of his buttock.

'Ya Momma lick ya?' Natty asked.

'It nottin,' Craig said, pulling up his shorts, 'but mi maybe gonna kill her for it.'

Yvette slapped him across the back of his head.

'Ya one bad boy, *picknee!*' laughed Natty.

'Ya man,' exclaimed Craig proudly. 'Mi bad like you.'

'Ya one bad raas claat, mi can see,' said Natty, before turning serious. He took hold of Craig's hand, and this time wouldn't be shaken off. 'Will ya do someting for mi?'

'Ya man.'

'Listen careful. When ya go back a yard ya nah tell nobady ya see and talk wid Natty Morgan. Nobady, annerstan?'

Craig looked into Natty's bloodshot eyes and felt scared. 'Ya sah.'

'Nobady. Not one friend or nobady. Cas Natty ron from de Police and nobady moss know where him de hide. Annerstan?'

'Ya man,' he gulped.

'If ya tell somebady, *picknee*, ya know what a-happen? Natty com an find ya in de night. Ya man. And ya know what him do den?'

Craig felt his hand being squeezed hard – harder than he liked. But he did not complain. He just stared into Natty's dark and dangerous eyes.

'Mi will slit ya wid one ratchet knife from ya belly to ya troat. Annerstan?'

The boy's face crumpled and tears poured down his cheeks. 'Ya sah,' he sobbed.

'But dat nuh gonna happen,' said Natty, releasing his hand and patting him on the back.

'Nuh bawl,' snapped Yvette.

'Gwaan now,' Natty waved them away. 'Tek a long way back a yard. And wuman, com tomorrow. Bring mi food, ya?'

Yvette *cuss and use bad word* to Craig all the way home. 'Ya nuh tell nobady. Nobady, or Natty will kill ya. For sure. Him will.'

'Uh-hu,' murmured Craig miserably, by now resigned to a horrible death in the middle of the night at Natty's hands because, sneaking out of Miss Citarra's yard at dawn after Yvette and Natty, he *buck up* on Yvonne, a neighbour, who was returning from a night's work in Negril, and had boasted to her that he was off to see Natty Morgan. When she called him a *liard* he pointed out Yvette and Natty hurrying across the pasture.

Yvonne Grant was a newcomer to the village, who worked in the tourist industry as a prostitute on the beach in Negril, and therefore for professional reasons *did friend wid whole 'eap o' police*. She was very pretty, *nice and fat*, with brazen, seductive eyes. She considered herself Cove's leading authority on Natty, because her boyfriend of the moment, *Afficer* Donovan, was stationed at Green Island, and leaked the latest Police intelligence on the case to her.

There was a battery-operated portable TV in Larmonds novelty store, in Lucea, which Yvonne had coveted for months. Its moulded pink plastic attracted pilgrims from miles away, but Yvonne was determined to make it hers. She was too superior to use the benches Chicken George had kindly arranged in his yard for people to sit on to peer through his windows at his 36″ Grundig. It *vex* Yvonne to watch Chicken George on his settee eating fried chicken by electric light while she sat salivating out in his yard. Others felt differently: for them, the luxurious composition framed by the open window, of the settee, the picture of the square rigger, the floral carpet, the lava lamp and Chicken George eating chicken, were as much of a draw as the rather incomprehensible foreign television programmes.

After watching Craig run after Yvette and Natty, Yvonne went into her house and shook *Afficer* Donovan out of his sleep.

'What ya want?' he groaned. 'Gwaan an' mek mi breakfast.'

'Mi know where Natty Morgan de,' she blurted.

His eyes opened. 'What, wuman?'

'Mi know where Natty Morgan de,' she repeated urgently.

He sat up in bed. 'Where?'

'What ya give mi fi know?' Yvonne said, her rich red lips widening into a corrupt smile.

Donovan lay back down and closed his eyes. 'Ya know nottin, ya liard.'

'Mi nah liard. Mi see him dis marning.'

'Wishart ya see him?'

'What will ya give mi fi tell ya?'

'Pussy claat, Yvonne ...' he sighed. 'Mi give you one shoes last week wuman. Ya never have enough new ting?'

'Him wear one green ganzi,' she said, 'and him foot limp.'

Donovan leapt from the bed and pinned Yvonne to the wall by the throat. 'Where ya see him? Tell mi.'

'What ya give mi?' she croaked.

Donovan squeezed her larynx. Her bright red fingernails clawed impotently at him. 'Talk, blood claat ...'

'Alright. Alright,' she gurgled. 'Mi tell ya.' He loosened his grip. 'Mi tell ya if you buy mi dat pink teevee in Larmonds.' He tightened his grip and began to beat her head against the partition wall. Next door, Kadim, her three year old daughter, woke up and began crying. 'Mi nuh tell ya,' Yvonne screeched. 'Mi never tell ya.' He threw her back on the grey sheet, grabbed his Police issue pistol from under the pillow, and pointed it at her head.

'In the name of the law, pussy claat, tell mi or mi kill ya.'

Killing Yvonne often crossed Donovan's mind. An *afficer* called Buckingham shot his girlfriend and Pinnock promoted him a week later.

'Ya kill mi Donovan, ya never find Natty, ya idiot.'

Paying for the TV meant hanging around for hours at illegal roadblocks near the big hotels to get bribes from terrified tourists with ganja. But leading Sergeant Pinnock to Natty Morgan would please Pinnock even more than shooting a girl.

'Ow much dallar is dis teevee?'

It was 2820 J, but Yvonne also desired a pair of spangled plastic high heels for her daughter, Kadim, so added the cost of them to the figure. 'Tree tousan J.'

Donovan thought for a moment. 'Alright. Wishart Natty?'

'Ya swear ya gonna give mi tree tousan J?'

'Dat what mi say wuman.'

'Ya swear?'

'Mi swear.'

''Pon de Bible?'

'Ya man, now where Natty Morgan de?'

'Hol' an.' Yvonne picked up her Bible – the only book in the house. Raising her voice over the sound of Kadim's bawling she said, 'Put ya hand 'pon it and swear ya will pay mi.'

Donovan, his gun in his left hand, did so, and with his right hand still on the Bible said, 'Tell mi where de blaad claat is, now.'

'Mi nah know.'

'Bumber claat!' he shouted and grabbed her again in fury.

'. . . Bot mi know who know . . .' she screamed. 'Mi know who hide him and who tek him food.'

'Who?'

✳   ✳   ✳

Yvette did not panic when she saw the Police car in the road by Miss Citarra's yard. It had been up and down so much she thought it must have *burn out* of gas, but when Sergeant Delroy Pinnock *hail up her* from the driving seat she felt her heart miss *whole heap o beat.*

'You Christella Knibb?'

'Ya,' said Yvette, letting her bag with the length of aloe and blood-soaked cloth drop softly by her feet.

'Gimme dat lada bag, gal.'

Pinnock glanced in the bag. 'Get in de car, gal.'

Miss Citarra, who'd watched from the house, staving off a heart attack with Old Testament prayers, pushed herself up onto her feet and hobbled down from the house and across the yard. To Yvette she whispered, 'If ya haffi tell him, mek him pay.'

Like all Jamaican cars, the *door hangle brok*, so Pinnock leant across to let Yvette in, lingering in the position to pat her on her knee. 'Ya gonna tell mi where he is now, or we gonna ride back a Police Station an' talk der?'

'Mi nuh understan ya question sah.'

'Good, cas mi like fi interrogate a pretty gal.'

He started the engine, and without looking behind, executed a swift U-turn, forcing Rushton, who was trotting by on his donkey, off the road and into a tree.

Craig crept into the house and hid under Miss Citarra's bed, remaining there all day, watching her swollen ankles and waiting for Natty Morgan to kill him. At dusk, when he heard the *picknee* in the yard play a game called *Natty a com fi we*, he could bear it no longer and decided to commit suicide. Once, when hungry, he'd eaten fistfuls of foam rubber torn from Yvette's mattress, and Miss Citarra, while beating his *botty*, screeched, 'Nah nyam sponge, ya craven *picknee*. Ya eat sponge ya will dead.' So he solemnly consumed two square feet of six-inch foam rubber and waited to die.

All night he felt as though he were about to expire, but in the morning found he was still alive. He decided that God must have saved him, and in return for this made a promise never to speak again, which was a big undertaking for the most talkative boy in a talkative village.

Pinnock posted nine men in Cousins Cove to search for Natty, and set to work on Yvette. Police Commissioner Cuthbert Macmillan telephoned from Mo-Bay and told Pinnock to go easy on the girl. Three politicians had made specific complaints about the treatment of suspects at Green Island, and the Commissioner asked Pinnock what plans he had to prevent similar complaints arising in the future.

'Mi gonna kill dem tree raas claat PNP politician,' he laughed. 'No Commissioner, seriously, the witness will not be harmed.'

The truth was that Pinnock never planned to use violence during interrogation. He invariably ended up using it, but that was out of irritation rather than by design, because suspects never talked. The brutality of *slavery days*, and the difficult years that followed, hardened the *little people* far beyond the point at which a beating could break them. Nothing could break a people who'd survived slavery. The Police knew it, and they knew it, which was why Bob Marley's taunt at the Police: 'Cas dem saft! Yeh dem saft! We know dem saft!' was so loved by Jamaicans. The silent strength of the slim, barefoot and badly clothed suspects *did mad* the well fed, well clothed and well shod Police. And out of sheer frustration, Pinnock, like the other cops, always gave them a kicking before letting them go. But after speaking to the Commissioner, Pinnock was determined in the case of Yvette not to lay so much as a finger on her.

Green Island Police station was a new, and run down, flat roofed concrete bungalow protected from the people by a tall fence and heavy gates. On one side a cell block housed suspects whose hands could be seen clasping the bars of the high windows, and whose shouts could be heard by their friends and enemies who waited for them, sometimes for days, at the gate. Inside the station it looked as though the place had been ransacked, as though a civil war had swept through the place: the large rooms were empty but for broken furniture, bloodstains and papers strewn across the cement floor. The Police lounged apathetically on the front step or in the charge room, concerned only with the visitors who brought vegetables, meat and sometimes even cash as gifts. Anyone who came with a grievance was carefully parried by an interminable wait before being half listened to, and run back to their yard in a Police car. No constable had any interest in the crimes of the *likker people dem*, so *the likker people dem* devised their own system of justice, handed out by the village mob.

For two days Yvette was walked back and forth from the cell block to a room with two chairs for interrogation.

'Wishart Natty hide?' Pinnock asked.

'Mi nuh say nuttin.'

'Christella,' Pinnock said gently, 'I am trying to help you. Keep you from big trouble. I'm your friend. Tell me, if dat towel in de lada bag not for Natty, who it for?'

'Mi nuh say nuttin.'

'Ya nuh say nuttin.' Pinnock sighed. 'If ya nuh say nuttin, I will charge you wid obstruction of de law.'

'Mi nuh say nuttin.'

'And aiding and abetting a convicted criminal, and being an accessory to murder.'

'Nuttin ...'

'Gal, ya can get ten year inna Spanish Town Jail for dat.'

'Mi nuh say nuttin.'

But Pinnock didn't want to charge Yvette. It was the last thing he wanted. Pushing a case through the Lucea Court was an exceedingly painful business, and he didn't want to waste days of hard work on this girl. He wanted Natty Morgan.

'Mi know ya know wishart Natty. Ya nuh leave dis room till ya tell we.'

'Mi nuh say nuttin to you, Pinnock. Mi nuh say nuttin to no Police.'

Back in Cove Natty tried to slip out of the cave, but was thwarted by one of Pinnock's constables who concentrated his search on Rocky's yard, near to Ran's Rocktop Cave, because he fancied Rocky's sister Marcia, a fawn-like fifteen year old who caused a lot of men to waste a good many hours hanging around her yard in a backwater of Cove called Egypt. Natty was also nearly discovered where he lurked inside the cave by Ran, the proprietor of the dud tourist attraction, who, searching for a spot to make some ancient Arawak paintings, walked within feet of the fugitive who withdrew into the deep shadows clutching Yvette's kitchen knife.

Pinnock couldn't make Yvette talk. For the first time in her life she had something a *big person* wanted, and she wasn't giving it away. She even made Pinnock doubt his instinct: when Donovan woke him for the midnight session on Yvette, Pinnock waved him away. 'Leave de gal. She nah know nuttin. Ya gal friend one liard, Donovan. She waste we time bad. Now go way fra here.'

When Donovan got back to Yvonne's yard he beat her *bad*. 'Ya jinall mi fi get one blaad claat teevee!' he shouted as he smacked her with the flat side of a machete.

'Mi nuh one liard Donovan,' Yvonne shouted back. 'Believe mi, believe mi. Mek dat gal talk and she will tell ya. She know where Natty de. Mi swear. Mi see dem pon de pasture. Mi can mek dat bitch talk. Give her to mi.'

Then something occurred to Yvonne. 'It nat only Yvette dat know where Natty de,' she said.

'Who else know?'

'De licker *picknee* Craig. Him know. Him follow dem dat morning. Mi see him too. Tell Pinnock fi talk wid de *picknee*.'

Miss Citarra lay on her bed studying the bible when Pinnock drew up with Yvette. Her reading wasn't so good, but she could feel the benefit of simply staring at God's words. Yvette got out of the car slowly. Her hair was matted with blood, her face twice the right size, and her limp tortuous to watch. Miss Citarra heaved herself onto her feet and hobbled across her yard.

'Sergeant Pinnock, 'ow can ya abuse de young gal like dat? She never done nottin wrong and ya beat her bad, man. Serious ...'

'De Police cannat be eld responsible for haccident dat occur to suspect durin custody. De gal buck up on one table and juke her foot. She clumsy, aunty. Dat nat Police fault. Annerstan? Now. True ya have one *picknee* in de yard name Craig Barrett?'

'Ya man.'

'Mi want fi talk wid him.'

'Wid de *picknee*?'

'Ya man. Call him.'

Up went the shout so familiar to all those who lived within a mile of Miss Citarra's yard: 'CREEEEEEAAAAAAAAIG!'

A few minutes later, Craig ran smiling round the sound of the house, making the guttural growl of the *ice chock* toiling up the slope from the *seaside*, and mimed changing down from second to first with his hand. He halted with a hiss of air brakes at the Police car.

'Get inna de car boy.'

'Ya man!' Craig exclaimed excitedly. He loved riding in cars. He could hail up all his friends on the Cove Primary playground, the school he was kept from so he could *ketch water for him Momma.*

'Mi want fi talk wid you.'

'Mi?' he said, pointing at his chest. He was pleased to be thought important enough for anyone, not least a *Police*, to have a conversation with. 'No problem,' he smiled. 'Let we go.'

'. . . Tell I 'bout Natty Morgan,' said Pinnock starting the engine.

Craig stopped smiling. Yvette shouted, 'Nuh say nuttin, Creeaig. Nuttin!' at the departing car, adding, 'Oh lard, oh lard,' to herself.

Tyres screamed as Pinnock pulled out into the path of a tourist bus full of *whities*, whose brakes were so badly adjusted it swerved sickeningly and looked for a moment as if it were going to roll. Vinton, watching, said to Oneil: 'Tour bos nearly stop in Cousins Cove at last.'

Craig made a second promise to himself (for the first he'd broken thirty minutes after making it), to say nothing at all. *Mi get Natty inna dis trouble*, he told himself, *and it mi moss get him out.*

Within two hours of Pinnock sweeping Craig through the gate of Green Island Police Station, news that Natty's fate was in the hands of a five year old boy reached as far as Ocho Rios, a hundred miles to the east. Another five hours later it got to the ghettos of West Kingston. Despite not being mentioned on the radio or TV, it was the lead news item for the whole of Jamaica.

Wherever people *group up*, harrowing and pitiful accounts of Craig's screams and whimpers were passed from one indignant person to another, in a long chain of tiny links that stretched across Jamaica. Craig's mother in Savannah La Mar, forty miles south of Green Island told everyone she met she was going to Pinnock to complain, but she had too much washing, and never made it.

As the hours passed, the crowd at the gate swelled and grew silent with outrage. By nightfall on the second day, when he had been held for thirty-seven hours, Police constables coming and going told Pinnock that the *people dem* wouldn't stand for it if Craig was held much longer. By the following afternoon a riot was said to be imminent. Inside the lock-up, Craig sat on a chair, both hands gripping the seat, his exhausted face stained with tears, his mouth firmly shut, and for the thousandth time Pinnock said, 'Tell we, Craig. Where Natty?' And the *tousand and oneth* time Craig shook his head from side to side as his eyes filled with tears.

Nearly all of the twenty-three members of Cousins Cove's population walked the five miles to Green Island to join the crowd at the gates of the Police Station. Only Yvette, who was too weak, Mr Blidgen, who, when he heard how Natty escaped from jail, decided to give Green Island Police Station a wide berth for a few months, and Chicken George, who secretly sympathised with the Police, were not present. When *Afficer* Buckingham emerged from the back door for a quick pee, he was jeered, and someone (six people claimed it was they) *fling one rock stone* at him that missed and shattered the window of the office where Pinnock was taking a nap.

Pinnock awoke so shaken that half an hour later Miss
Citarra proudly led Craig by the hand out of the station.
The moment he was through the gates, the crowd closed
around them to slap the boy on the back and *hail up* a hero.

Everyone in the minibus back to Cove felt honoured to
travel with Craig – Miss Citarra made sure of that – and the
conductor waived both their fares – at Miss Citarra's sug-
gestion. At Cousins Cove, Craig staggered out of the
minibus, crossed the yard and climbed up into the house
where Yvette was lying on the bed next to the cooker, looking
distraught.

He looked at his aunt with a serious expression. 'Mi nuh
say nuttin, Yvette,' he said, and collapsed beside her.

He lay on that bed for two days, and every one of Cove's
twenty-three residents came *fi check him*, though Chicken
George pretended he had only called round to borrow a
machete. It was a glorious time for Craig and for Cousins
Cove. Complete strangers, some of them *big people dem*,
speeding importantly between Montego Bay and Negril in
criss car, drew up in the village and asked after the *picknee*
who hadn't grassed on Natty.

Pinnock finally withdrew his men, and Natty took the
opportunity to *excape inna de hills*, coolly strolling into a
barber in Grange Hill for a shave and trim in full view of
the general public. The barber told the story of Craig, and
Natty said, 'Mi remember dat *picknee*. Im cool. Mi respect
im,' words which were in due course relayed to Craig, and
made the whole of Cousins Cove walk with their heads held
up proudly, even in Lucea.

As the barber dusted Natty's neck with powder, to help
remove the cut hair, he listened to Natty outline his plans.
By this time the shop was full, and at every window faces
looked in and listened to Natty: 'Mi gonna get one gun,

bredren, and mi gonna find Sergeant Pinnock wherever he de, and mi gonna kill him for what him don.'

The news, carried on packed minibuses and crammed old taxis, spread from Grange Hill deep into the most silent, overgrown hills and valleys, and down onto the noisy Main, where it sped by word of mouth east and west so that within days everyone in North Jamaica knew that Natty was going to kill Pinnock. With one notable exception: Pinnock himself, whom no-one dared tell.

It was only when a four year old boy in Salt Spring asked, 'When Natty gonna kill ya dead, sah?' that Pinnock began to suspect why everyone was acting so nervously around him. It also explained why his two best girlfriends said he couldn't stay in their yards till Natty was *inna de lock up or dead.* In a quiet corner of the Police Station he asked Buckingham if it were true. Buckingham said it was.

Pinnock grew windy, and was unable to sleep soundly at home, so decided to move into the Police station until Natty was back in custody. When he passed through the crowd at the gate with a *sponge* mattress on the roof of his car, they laughed and jeered at him. 'Ya can hide, bot Natty a com an' find ya Pinnock,' they taunted.

Even in the station with his bed right under a cast-iron desk his dreams were bad and sleep patchy, and once, when Commissioner Macmillan burst in without knocking, he jumped so badly he nearly fractured his skull on the bottom of the desk. There was a heatwave and sweat dripped off him even as he sat motionless in the station's three-legged armchair, daydreaming of Natty coming steathily down the corridor with a knife in his hand, but he couldn't go out to clear his head with a breath of fresh air because of the people at the gate whom he knew were only there because they wanted to be around when Natty killed him. Worse still, he could not prevent Hyacinth, the wife, visiting whenever she felt like it. He couldn't shoot her, because two dead wives was hard to explain, so he had to tolerate the visits. It was an attack on the very being of a Green Island *Police* to be accessible at all times to the wife. At the end of the day when the men went off in happy groups to find women to have fun with, they laughed to think that all Pinnock could look forward to was Hyacinth and a big plate of *jack domplin*.

Pinnock's public humiliation ended a week later, when Natty was caught in a shoot-out in Negril and died in a hail of Police bullets. He was interred at the Dovecote Memorial Park, which was besieged by people wanting to file past his corpse in its silk-lined coffin. The funeral was reported on JBC TV, and Yvonne promised Craig he could watch it on her new pink portable, if he cut her yard, but he ended up standing on the roof of her house holding the aerial while she lounged on the bed to watch TV and *nyam* fried chicken.

THE SPOILS OF THE WAR
AGAINST DRUGS

In the 1980s the Reagan administration declared war on drugs and made Jamaica a front line. Two United States Air Force helicopters were dispatched to recce for ganja plantations. They did not represent a threat to the Jamaican industry which was formed by numerous small growers with crops too insignificant to be spotted from the air. Ten dozen goats would have harmed the trade more, and saved the Pentagon a few bucks to boot.

In Cousins Cove the arrival, each week, of the helicopter, was a keenly anticipated event. It made them feel important to be the object of American interest. On top of this, items sometimes dropped from the pockets of the airmen as they leant out to survey the bush. Maxwell sported a pair of Ray-Ban shades that fell from the aircraft, and for a week, Joe built spliffs with a packet of American cigarette papers that wafted down beside his bar after the chopper had clattered away over the hills.

The Americans rewarded those parishes where the Police made drug seizures: the Ambassador came to the north coast in a *criss* Cadillac to give the hospitals of St James 25,000 US of, confusingly, drugs, and present Lucea, Hanover's principal town, with a big red American fire engine.

The fire engine was designed for a crew of four, 'though it never left Lucea with less than eleven men on board, and often with many more. Eight fire-proof uniforms, including coats, pants, boots, gloves and helmets were also supplied. These were shared by the twenty-three men of the Lucea Fire Brigade, who were all prepared to enter burning buildings only partially clad in protective gear. It soon became clear, however, that they weren't likely to come to any harm. In a place where no-one had a telephone, and the wooden houses took ten minutes to *bung down*, it was a safe bet the firemen were never going to confront anything more dangerous than a heap of smouldering ashes.

The Brigade's telephone rang incessantly, but always for one of the Grant girls, whose yard lay in the shadow of the fire station. Olga gave out the number as her own, and both her husbands, European men who'd fallen for her startling good looks and sexy body while on holiday, kept in touch with her regularly. This stopped only when the phone was disconnected for non-payment of the bill, which grew huge because the crew used it to *chat to dem relative inna foreign*. Appeals were made to the Jamaica Telephone Company to write off the debt in an act of civic responsibility, but the executives, who lived far from Lucea and would never need the fire brigade, refused to. The local member of parliament, Andy Chin, who'd recently been promoted to Foreign Minister, intervened, but was told to 'mind him own PNP business' by the JLP phone executives. He did as he was told for fear that the phones in his ministry, like those in the Ministry of Agriculture the month before, would be disconnected in an act of malice. It took the intervention of the only man more powerful than a telephone executive on the island, the US Ambassador, to get the fire station reconnected, and that was only to take incoming calls.

When Driver burned down D. Brown's shed in Cove because tourists kept passing Driver's bamboo bar, and stopping at D. Brown's – not, as Driver thought, because of an Obeah curse, but because D. Brown alone amongst Cove bar owners had cleared a spot beside the road for tourists to pull over and park on – people *group up* to watch the shed blaze away. It was customary to ask the first vehicle that passed on the road in the direction of Lucea to alert the fire brigade. The sound of a gear box changing down to negotiate the Cove bridge heralded a Lada station wagon driven by Ran, the fastest man in Hanover and St James, towing his minibus, the nose of which was buckled by yet another accident. It was a bad time for Ran; first, he'd *bounce* and killed a *crazy man* in Little London, which was easy enough to laugh about and forget, but then a week later he *bounce one picknee* in Sandy Bay, who was struggling for his life in Mo-Bay hospital. Leroy Mckenzie, Ran's boss, had *vex bad* at the cost of the bodywork to the minibus, and that was before Ran tore a hole in the front of the *unit* when he scraped a tourist car which wasn't driving close enough to the kerb.

Ran could not work out why he was having such bad luck. But he was determined to regain his reputation as the Main's fastest tourist bus driver, and had found something which steadied his nerves, helped his concentration, and made him drive harder and faster, though not necessarily more accurately, than ever before. It was called cocaine.

When D. Brown frantically waved down the two vehicles, Ran pulled over to check out what was going on.

'Mi shed bung down, man,' wailed D. Brown.

'Nuh worry, D. Brown, mi go a Lucea fi fetch de fire chock – fast. Mi will getti here before ya shed destroy. Tross mi.' With that, Ran nipped around the back of the two

massive almond trees on the beach, had a swift pipe of
cocaine, then ran back to the Lada. 'Nobady can drive
fasterer dan I,' he announced before piling into the car
through the passenger door.

'Ya man!' shouted a supporter in the crowd. 'Nabady can
beat Ran.'

'Unhitch de minibus, man,' Joe helpfully suggested.

'Ya man,' shouted the driver of the minibus, a friend of
Ran's.

'Nuh man,' said Ran, fired up by the drug coursing
through his body.

'Ya kiant drive fass and tow one minibus, man,' pointed
out Joe.

'We nuh have time fi unhitch de minibus, man,' replied
Ran, who needed the minibus in Lucea for repairs. 'Like mi
say: us in one horry.'

The Lada shot off with wheels spinning, the tow rope
cracked taut, and the minibus lurched forward, its driver
thrown back against his seat.

Getting to the fire station *fast* was a way to salvage his
reputation, and Ran screeched and howled his way through
the twists and turns of the coast road at a suicidal speed,
his minibus barrelling crazily along behind him. At Green
Island he overtook a nervous tourist in a rental car which
was clinging to the tight bend, nearly driving him off the
edge into the sea.

It was not the habit of minibus drivers to use their rear
view mirrors when in motion, their main purpose being to
enable drivers to admire their hairstyles during stops, so it
was only when Ran drew to a halt at the fire station that he
looked in his mirror for the first time.

'Where is mi minibus!' he cried, when he saw that there
was nothing behind the Lada but a length of frayed rope.

His minibus was in fact at that moment sinking gently into the swamp by the new pork sausage factory outside Lucea, which it had glided into when the tow rope finally snapped as Ran gassed the Lada as he came off the corner and onto the straight.

Everyone at the fire station knew it was too late to save a bamboo shed as far away as Cousins Cove, but the crew still sped into action, threw on their odd bits of uniform, climbed aboard and switched on the bell and siren. Olga Grant, the most beautiful of the sexy Grant sisters, on the phone to her Austrian husband, shouted out, 'Wishart de fire?'

'Cousins Cove,' someone answered.

'Hol' on, mi go dat way too,' she shouted back.

It was hard to believe that nothing rested on the speed of the brigade's response, when you saw how fast and dangerously the fire engine was piloted through Lucea and down the Main. A tourist, recently recovered from a near heart-attack when a car chased by a truly insane minibus driver practically drove him off a cliff into the sea, received a second life-endangering shock when a fire engine loaded down with men and women in fancy dress appeared suddenly around a tight bend and missed him by a gap no wider than the air ticket he had just decided to buy to get off the island as fast as he could.

Things were made worse by the siren, which in the US may have scattered people in front of the vehicle, but which in Hanover attracted them to its path. The vehicle was gunned at sickening speed down a twisting, narrow path, in places no more than ten feet wide, lined with adults, children and unleashed animals. As usual, the act of summoning the Lucea fire brigade put more lives at risk than any fire.

The truck drew up at the cooling pile of ashes which had

been D. Brown's shed, but few considered its journey wasted, for the sight of the gleaming American machine and the wail of the siren thrilled the assembled crowd. It seemed to them to more than make up for the disaster to D. Brown's shed. D. Brown didn't share this view and did not join the chorus of thanks and congratulations. While a fireman wearing shorts, T-shirt, and one fire-proof gauntlet hoisted a *picknee* onto the engine, and Cove men took turns sitting behind the steering wheel, D. Brown picked among the burnt-out ruins for any possessions that might have survived.

People felt sorry for D. Brown, a young, charming man who'd worked hard to clear a bit of bush, erect a shed and get a little business going, but no-one condemned Driver for the arson attack, although all knew he was responsible. It was D. Brown's own fault, they argued, for trying to capture land so near to the sea-side where Joe, Ione and Driver all had bars. D. Brown was cool, but D. Brown was an outsider. You could tell he wasn't from Cove – he ran a successful business. He came from the hills, not the Level. No amount of good vibes could efface that. But when he rebuilt on a piece of land nearer the edge of the village, everyone was pleased, and Driver knew that this time D. Brown did it with the blessing of the village, and even though, once again, because D. Brown bothered to clear a spot for cars to park on, tourists started to pull over and patronise his bar, Driver could not *bung down fi D. Brown shed* a second time without public condemnation. But that didn't stop him thinking about doing it night and day, night and day.

TREE BAD GAL

BABS

Babs was the village *bad gal*, until Olga Grant turned up on the *fire-chock* the day D. Brown's shed *bung down*. Babs was bad. But Olga was *badder*, and a year or two after Olga, came her sister Yvonne, who was the *badderest*.

Babs worked as a prostitute in Negril, or indeed anywhere, and *spend down all him money on coke*. She had a yard on the hill above Cove where her five *picknee* fended for themselves during her frequent stays in Pegasus – the new Police station in Negril that was named by the *little people dem* after the international hotel in Kingston that they thought looked just like it. In Cove, Babs was called Gregory, after Gregory Isaacs the reggae singer who was always being busted for cocaine. He, like Babs, was in such a bad way he disgraced himself on stage during a show at Zion House. The audience *bokkle him* and once again looted the bar and box office which the Royal Dread had only just refitted after the last riot.

Babs was strikingly tall, with a slender, aristocratic neck, Egyptian eyes, flattened nose and wide mouth out of which obscenities emerged thick and fast as she strode through the hail of friendly abuse the villagers shouted whenever she got out of the minibus and walked the curving path across the pasture and up through the thickening bush to her yard.

People knew that when Babs' kids were hungry she'd still spend her last cent on cocaine, so they turned a blind eye when they saw them *tief* fruit from another man's tree. Babs did *friend wid anybady* when she needed money, but only one man meant anything to her: Humble Dread, a silent, dreadlocked Rastafarian from deep *back a bush*, with a deeply lined face, matted grey locks and a mouth empty of teeth. *Omble* Dread was a Bongo Dread – that is, a real Rastaman who kept strictly to the salt free, pork free, ital diet, sang incantations to Jah, smoked ganja religiously, and led a peaceful, harmless, meditative life. There were two other kinds of Dread. The Commercial Dread, like Joe or Ione in Cove, who had the dreadlocks and knew all the Rasta rules but liked Dragon Stout and jerk pork too much to observe them all the time. The other kind of Rasta was the Rental Dread, to whom the whole thing was little more than a hairstyle which *white wuman dem* found sexy. They ate anything, smoked coke and *tief* money without hesitation. The centre of the Rental Dread community was the Cotton Tree Cafe in Negril, where scores of them grouped up every afternoon before setting out into the hot sweet night to seduce overweight whitey spinsters and divorcees. All they wanted to do was have sex and *sport* on the women's money, and, marvelously, that was all the women wanted as well.

When *Omble* Dread came down from the hills *fi turn wid Gregory for a couple night* she didn't take the minibus to the beach at Negril, *but rake de yard, sweep de house, shine de floor*, got a fire going, put a pot on it and cooked up some dumpling and yam for *Omble* Dread and the *picknee*. She put on weight and smiled when *Omble* Dread was staying, but when he picked up his rod and his bag and left wordlessly at dawn for the blue hills she went straight to Negril, took coke, and *draw weight* till she *look so grey and maigre* not even Jimmy Fairfax, who was not that choosy when it came to women, would pay 15 J to *friend* with her.

OLGA

Olga was *badder* than Babs, but in a different way. Like Babs, Olga wanted many things she did not possess; she wanted clothes and shoes, she wanted meals in restaurants and rides in fast cars – but most of all she wanted to get off the island of Jamaica. She wanted to board an orange and green Air Jamaica 727, leave far below her the squalor of her crowded, dirty yard behind the fire station in Lucea, disembark *inna foreign* and walk through immigration to a job, a decent home, and the easy life.

At fifteen, Olga was told by the careers' master at Rusea Comprehensive in Lucea that with her brain she could win a scholarship to Arthur Mannings Technological College to train to be a teacher or accountant. But neither of these professions would get her off the island. Even if she earned money at them, she could never change it for US dollars, and even if she found an illegal way of getting hold of US dollars, most countries, particularly the ones Olga wanted to go to, banned Jamaican visitors. An American, or European, went to the airport and boarded any flight they could afford to. To the Jamaicans, no matter how rich they were, half the destinations on the departure board were barred. It was impossible to get a visa for America, Canada, Britain, Germany or Austria unless you had family there, which Olga didn't. If a Jamaican wanted to see the world it was Central and South America, or a geography text book. But Olga didn't want to live in Belize or The Caymans. She wanted to go up in the world, not sideways.

Instead of going to Arthur Mannings Technological

College in Montego Bay, Olga went to the beach in Negril, a place far more likely to yield a US or German visa to someone with Olga's fresh, sexy looks and gravity-defying body, than any Embassy in Kingston. And on the beach she joined a much more highly regarded profession than accountancy or teaching, on the beach she became a prostitute.

Negril beach attracted a different kind of tourist to the ones who congregated in the cement bars and restaurants on Gloucester Avenue in Mo-Bay to eat American food and watch American satellite television, or sat in linen suits, red-faced and thinking vaguely racialist thoughts, being served rum punches by gloved waiters at the Jamaica Inn or Tryall Villas Hotel. The tourist who went to Negril was more of a traveller than holiday-maker, and tended to be interested in discovering something about Jamaica and Jamaicans, and this set him apart from the rest of the island's guests.

The people of Negril welcomed these travellers with open arms, literally. They were rich, and generous and friendly, and never got into conflict with the locals over lovers because the white men liked thin Jamaican girls, whereas Jamaican men liked only *good size wuman*, and the *whitey wuman dem* loved Dreadlocks men, who were held in contempt by most self-respecting Jamaican girls, so everyone got along fine.

On the beach at Negril, the traveller found things arranged particularly congenially. For a start, the place was fabulously beautiful. Fabulous, because it seemed as though, when you first kicked off your shoes and felt the talcum-fine sand press your instep, under the grove of coconuts that fringed the beach, that you were walking into some kind of perfect, fictional location. The seven-mile white sand beach had not a single stone to step uncomfortably upon. It shelved at the gentlest of inclines into turquoise, transparent, bath-warm water under a deep blue sky. Immersion in this sea, which lapped onto the beach in soothing, stroking curls, no more than a few inches high, was akin to drifting off into a dreamy sleep, and certainly no more strenuous.

Against this background, fine-looking barefooted Jamaicans ambled up and down wearing only the flimsiest of garments, many of which were easily slipped out of, like the sexual inhibitions and moral constraints the tourists left strewn behind them as they began to enjoy themselves. They learnt from their new Jamaican friends not to judge strangers, nor feel guilty about something done in the name of *sport*. Negril beach was magical: it made the fat feel slender, the pale feel cool, the self-conscious feel sexy, the provincial feel pioneering, the mean feel rich, the poor feel generous, and the timid feel brave. Everyone fell in love on the beach, and made quixotic declarations of lifelong devotion, which were cooled only by the drive back along the Main, the air-conditioned airport, and the gathering thoughts of forgotten responsibilities and commitments back home. In the early days, before the big hoteliers and coke dealers moved in, the tourists and the Negrilites were the same kind of people: easy-going, fun-seeking and peace-loving. Most of the tourists wanted to stay forever with the Jamaicans, but couldn't, and most of the Jamaicans wanted to leave with them, but couldn't. This made the last goodbye, on the porch of the cottage in the coconut grove, or by the mouth of the tent at the hippy campsite, all the more sweetly poignant.

Olga was so alluring in her silver bikini it did not take long before she was betrothed. Her fiancé was a large fifty-five year old Belgian called Hubert. In the company of Olga, who was then sixteen and a half, he smiled a lot and sweated gently. They married and honeymooned in Zoo, which was what the staff called Hedonism Hotel, because of its high chain-link boundary fence and the unrestrained behaviour of the guests kept behind it. Hubert returned to Brussels with the marriage certificate, and promised to get Olga's emigration papers organised so she could follow him to Europe. But nothing ever happened. He telephoned Olga at the fire station when he was drunk or lonely, but when Hubert twice put down the phone when a woman called his name, Olga could tell that he wasn't going to get her off the island. So without bothering with divorce, she married Rudy, from Vienna, the nineteen year old son of a prosperous industrialist. He also returned to Vienna to fix her papers and passport, but when he telephoned he had bad news: he had showed his parents a picture of Olga and they had demanded he divorce her. Of course he said he wouldn't, and that he loved Olga and had made a solemn promise to stand by her, but they threatened to take away his flat, car and all his money. 'Olga,' Rudy said to her on the fire station phone, 'please don't vurry, I haff a plan. I vill come back to Jamaica and find verk as a vaiter, und ve can live together in a liddle hut in the hils.'

'No, Rudy, nuh com dung a Jamaica wid nuh money. Tell ya farda, him kiant mek judgment pon mi, till dem meet mi. Dem moss fly mi inna foreign and moss meet mi, annerstan?'

'But Olga, ve love each uzzer, ve don't need my farder's money ...'

'No, Rudy, nuh com dung a Jamaica widout monny.'

Rudy rang the fire station three or four times a week, and Olga found it increasingly difficult to keep him in Austria. Meanwhile, her attention was caught by someone else. Passing through Cousins Cove on her way to and from work, she noticed a white man constructing a *board house* on a piece of land that sloped down from the Main to a little lagoon that opened onto the creek. Every time she flashed through Cove on the minibus, she caught glimpses of him first clearing a space in the jungle and then erecting a three-room clapboard house with a pitched zinc roof, in the old style.

She only found out who this was when one day she found herself in Cove on a search for *sick picknee*. Olga liked the high status prostitution gave her, with its enviable contacts amongst the tourists and Police, fine new clothes and easy cash but, for some reason no-one knew, the Police started coming down hard on prostitutes, so she developed lucrative side-lines, like drug dealing, massage, hair braiding, and her sick children scam. She hit on the *sick picknee* idea when Yatta, her eleven year old brother who lurked under the coconut trees on the beach learning the art of the *hossler*, was suffering from an oozing eye infection. An American who wrangled for half an hour over paying 15 US for sex with Olga, when he saw Yatta's eye, took a 10 US bill from the wallet in his swimming trunks and gave it to the boy.

'You seen the doc about that, son?'

'Ya man. Him give me one pill paper,' Yatta said, showing the *whitey* the prescription, 'but mi kiant afford fi buy i'.'

'Go and get that prescription right away,' he told Yatta. 'I'm serious, or you could lose that eye.'

Yatta ran off across the sand with the 10 US in his fist, and Olga only caught up with him after a very hurried sex session, at a tourist stall buying himself a T-shirt. She ripped the note out of his hand.

'Tief,' she shouted, cuffing him over the head.

'Mi nuh tief, de white man give I dat.'

'Raas claat,' Olga shouted.

'Dat fi mi money,' Yatta said impotently. 'Dat fi mi money,' and stamped off across the sand, rubbing his inflamed eye.

'Com, ya, *picknee*,' Olga called, and pulling out a filthy, soft Jamaican bank note from her bikini briefs, said, 'Tek dis. Nex time mi give ya more.'

'Nex time?' Yatta asked.

'Ya man.'

Thus was their business partnership born, which led to the *sick picknee* scheme. With the prescription, the steadily worsening eye infection, and Yatta's pathetic assertion that he had no money, Olga took hundreds of dollars off men and women on the beach. It only came to a stop when one day Yatta took some money and bought the antibiotic cream at the pharmacy because his eye was hurting so much. Olga tried to get the tube of ointment off him, but he hid it in a hiding place in the coconut grove, and try as she might, she couldn't prevent him applying it. She was philosophical about the set-back; one thing the back streets of Negril were not short of was sick and suffering children, and she went out to get hold of a new one. For a week she had a boy with a foot wound that, as it turned green and began to smell rank, raised money faster than the beach's best hookers, and for a few days she worked with the victim of a minibus crash with a terrible head wound. He was going very well but died suddenly one night after work. After this, Negril *baby mudder dem* grew wary of leasing their sick children to Olga, so her search took her beyond the town boundaries, which were themselves moving outwards by the day, to places further down the line like Cousins Cove, where one afternoon, on her way to work, she stopped the minibus because she saw a promisingly malnourished little girl hurrying down the road.

The girl was Joy, Babs' eldest, and she was on a mission to Miss Netta's shop to beg for *half a bread* on credit for her mother and for her siblings, Sanjay, 10, Simone, 9,

Marshalyn, 8, Kaysia, 8 (but not a twin), Andy, 6, and Tulia, 5. Babs had *spend down* all her money on coke and the youngest *picknee* had moaned through the night with hunger. Actually, Babs had done more than *spend down the money*, she'd stripped siding boards off the house and sold them to Mr Blidgen for money for coke, so the breeze now blew straight through the house across the bed the children all slept on. But at six o'clock that morning, when Babs *cuss and use bad word* at Mr Blidgen because he refused to give her any more money unless she stripped the corrugated zinc off the roof, because he didn't want any more siding boards, Joy set off down the hill to *beg one bread*, so as to save the zinc and keep the family dry when *rain farl*.

'*Picknee*,' Olga called to Joy, 'com ya.'

Joy approached Olga shyly. Olga looked appreciatively at her open sores, and the bones that prodded at her skin. She would raise a *couple dollar pon de beach*.

'Ya want fi earn a few dollar, gal?'

Joy could tell Olga was a prostitute from her expensive denim clothes, pink lipstick and yellow hair extensions.

'Mi go a shop fi mi mudda,' she told Olga, and tried to get away.

'Tek me to ya yard. Mek we talk wid ya mama.'

Joy *beg* Miss Netta for *a bread*, and took Olga back up the hill. As they climbed the steep and muddy path through jungle dripping with dew, Joy heard Babs screaming at Mr Blidgen, who stood impassively in the yard, a box-like figure wearing heavy *government boot*, watching her struggle to peel back a section of roofing, a faint smile on his blunt features.

'Ya want fi tek de raas claat roof from mi picknee head, man. Ya have no heart?' Babs shouted. 'Gimme a couple blaad claat dollar. Gwaan. Raasclaat. An' mi will pay ya back anudder day.'

'I will give you fifty dallar for one zinc,' said Mister Blidgen in his gruff voice. 'Horry up and lift it now.'

'Babs, w'appen?' Olga greeted her, for they knew each other from the beach. 'Gal, if ya need fifty dallar, mi can giv' i' ya.'

Babs stopped levering at the roof, and stood up, swinging the hammer at her side. 'What ya want fi de money?'

'Jus' let ya darter here com an' work wid mi on a likker tourist bizness.'

Joy looked at her mother imploringly; she didn't want to work on the beach as a prostitute.

'Fifty dallar ya give mi far her?' Babs asked.

Joy looked down, miserably.

'Ya man. Fifty now, and mebbe de gal bring a likker more home later.'

'Raas claat Olga,' she shouted. 'Ya com fram de devil, wuman. Ya tink mi tek one cent fi turn mi own darter prostitute?'

'Mi nuh say she turn prostitute. When mi say dat?'

'If she go a beach wid you, she nuh gonna turn blaad claat Christian. Ya is one beach prostitute, Olga, and so also is mi one beach prostitute, but mi nuh gonna mek mi darter one, not for ten tousan dallar mi will nat do dat.'

The sound of an altercation always drew people towards it in Cousins Cove, where two people losing their tempers, and maybe even coming to blows, was considered top entertainment. Maxwell, searching for goats that had slipped their tether, rushed to the yard gleefully, and from other directions came ten or fifteen adults and *picknee dem* to watch the action, and stir it up a bit if it looked like fizzling out.

'Nuh call mi one prostitute, Babs,' Olga shouted. 'Mi work pon de beach in tourist bizness now. You is one prostitute.

Ya would tek five dallar to fuck one donkey excep the donkey never wan to.'

'Blaad claat!' Babs screamed, and hurled the hammer, which sped, spinning slowly, through the air. It missed Babs and struck Mr Blidgen on the shin.

'Ya blaad claat wuman,' he shouted and stomped off into the bush.

'Ya let one wuman lick ya?' shouted someone after him, but he didn't rise to the provocation, and muttered to himself all the way back to his yard.

Olga left the yard and descended the path to the Main, putting the incident behind her. Being a prostitute had taught her the gift of stopping herself remembering selected events from even the most recent past. Without this gift the job would *mad* her, the way it did so many other girls.

She waited on the Main for the minibus back to Lucea in the shade of a tree shared by two boys, Vinton and Oneil, who were *idling pon de roadside*, watching the white man in his yard on the other side of the road planing timber for furniture. She noticed how he didn't fling his tools into the dirt the moment he'd finished with them, the way Jamaican men did.

'Who dat white man?' she asked the boys.

'Him one teacher de England government send down since tree mont fi teach de ignorant picknee fi read and write and learn carpenter bizness.'

'He cool?'

Oneil laughed. 'Him kinda cool, but him nuh drink liquor or go wid prostitute, so forget 'im.'

'Cho!' chided Olga. 'Ya chat nuff likker boy. Him marry?'

'Nuh man, 'im live pon him own.'

The thud of a bass line, first detectable in her feet, and then ears, followed by the whine of a VW Combi engine gunned at full throttle, heralded a minibus, which Olga stopped and boarded, climbing in beside the driver in the comfy front seat – the prerogative of respected citizens like Policemen, footballers and prostitutes.

Back at the Grant yard in the shadow of the fire station, where seven adults lived in three rooms, there was a flood. She picked her way around and over deep muddy puddles and jumped onto the porch, which shuddered when she landed. The house had smelled of mildew ever since her brother O'ell, and her father Sparrow, *tief* the gutter from the fire station to sell, so that when *rain farl*, water swept off the eaves like Dunn's River Falls onto the Grants' previous roof.

The thought of Steve's soundly built house with its brand new roof was one thing Olga could not erase from her memory, and when a week later she was on the phone to Rudy, and heard the *fire chock* was going to Cousins Cove, she shouted, 'Hol' on!' to the boys. 'Mi soon com back,' and dashed to her yard to dress up for the whitey with the new house. It took a few minutes, naturally, but the guys on the fire truck were happy to wait for Olga. When she arrived she had stripped off her jewellery and wore her mother's print cotton church dress, which buttoned chastely to her throat, had long sleeves, and a full skirt that came down unflatteringly over her knees.

'Mi kiant believe it,' the driver of the fire truck shouted. 'Olga give up whore bizness and turn Christian.' Then without any urgency, he activated the siren and bell, and floored the gas pedal.

At Cove she alighted from the truck and walked to the white man's yard, through all the rushing villagers, drawn in the opposite direction by the siren, bell and smoke from D. Brown's shed. She found the white man working on his furniture beside his lagoon. Crouched next to him, a youth, Nickretta Blidgen, older brother of Michael and Oneil, carefully watched his every move.

Short, with narrow shoulders, a wide bottom and splayed feet, Steve Poole had a long nose on a sad face, and looked as if a great deal of effort had been repaid with only the most limited success, yet undaunted, he persevered. He originated in Bolton, a small northern English city, where he'd lived uneventfully for twenty-seven years before accepting a Voluntary Service Overseas posting to Jamaica.

'Ya mind if mi sit in the shade of ya tree, sah?' Olga asked.

'No, lass. Sit right down. Make yourself comfortable. Hang about, that needs a wipe. You be happier if I fetched you a chair?'

'Tank you.'

When Steve dashed off, Olga said, 'What ya do here?' to the boy.

'Mi learn carpenter trade,' Nickretta answered her. 'Mister Poole one good teacher.'

'Mi nuh want ya here. Go way. Go way. Gwaan, run on ...'

The boy, drilled into obedience by his bullying father, Mr Blidgen, obeyed without a word.

'Where's Nicky gone?' Steve asked sunnily when he got back with the chair.

'Soon as teacher back turn, student run off. It alway de same.'

'He's a good lad, got a good eye and a strong arm.'

Olga said, 'Mi try an' stop him. Ya nah mind if I watch you?'

'Goodness me no,' said Steve.

'Only I never talk to no white man before,' she continued.

Later, she asked if she could swim, which seemed to necessitate unbuttoning every single one of the fifteen buttons down the front of her mother's dress, even though she could have slipped out of it easily after opening only four. She turned modestly away from Steve, but felt his eyes boring into her back, and heard the saw he held stuttering for the first time in its groove.

'Mi can bathe in mi brassiere and panties?' she asked, turning to him in her white lingerie. Steve could not take his eyes off her gorgeous body. 'Only I don't got no swim-suit.'

The closest Steve had got to sex in Jamaica was a few tentative conversations with a certain Miss Markham. Miss Markham stood six feet two inches tall, had greying hair and a matronly, no-nonsense attitude, with which she ran the Post Office counter in Lucea. When she saw Steve through the plate-glass Post Office window, she took his mail out of the pigeon hole to be ready to call, 'Mister Poole! Mister Poole! Your mail,' when he came in. Steve was em-barrassed at jumping the three-quarter hour queue, but that never occurred to Miss Markham, who flashed him her toothy smile, because she was a bit buck-toothed, and chatted a while about this and that. Everybody knew the white man liked Miss Markham, but it seemed like both of them were too scared to make the first move.

Making the first move was not something Olga had a problem with. She swam for about thirty seconds, keeping her feet on the ground, emerged wet, and stood before a deeply blushing Steve asking if he had a towel. Blackie, passing down the road, glimpsed the two of them out of the corner of her eye, and thought, *This mash op Miss Blanche Markham's chance with Steve.*

Olga noticed Steve's outdoor shower, housed in a shoulder-high corrugated zinc booth in the shade of banana trees that nodded in the breeze wafting off the sea. When

Steve came out of the house flapping a towel, and checking it over for dirty marks, Olga shouted, 'Over here, Steve, ya didn't mind me taking a fresh?'

'A shower? Of course not.'

When she took the towel, she allowed the door of the shower to swing open a little more than necessary, and her nude wet body was branded onto his memory. From that moment, Steve Poole was smitten.

Ten days later, Olga moved into Steve's yard. Miss Citarra saw her taking her bags of clothes out of the back of a minibus, and that *eveling* the whole village was sombre.

'It look like Olga control Steve now,' Blackie said to Miss Linnet, with a laugh.

'Ya man,' agreed Miss Linnet. 'She run out fram Steve yard all de *picknee* dat Steve teach carpenter trade. It terrible, man, terrible. Mi kiant believe he kiant see Olga is one whore.'

Love blinded Steve. And Olga never put a foot wrong while she courted the poor man, though when he left the house, she went to a little carved cupboard he had made and mounted on the wall, and took out and handled Steve's dark blue passport, her head a blizzard of stratagems. Pretending to be a virgin, she allowed him to deflower her. Steve had no idea sex could be that good; he emerged shaky and stunned from his bedroom every morning, and taught his lessons at Cove Primary with his head full of what he and Olga had done the night before in the candle-light of their room.

The village lived in mourning for the old Steve, whose yard was open to children, and whose tools were always available to be borrowed – for Olga told him to say no when people came and *beg him for one pick, or buster, or hax, or ammer*. She turned him against the village, and filled his head with lies about Miss Citarra, Miss Linnet, Yvette, and everyone else, so he walked past them without stopping to talk. No-one dared tell him the truth about Olga; you could easily get killed for doing something like that, and anyway Olga would somehow lie her way out of it.

It was only when Vinton hurried off the minibus from Lucea one afternoon, saying he'd seen Rudy, Olga's second husband, looking for Olga in town, that the village saw some good in the whole episode, for this surely meant they were going to be entertained. People grouped up casually at Steve's end of the village waiting for the bearded German youth to turn up, which he did, with a rucksack, on a minibus.

'Excuse me, but I am looking for Olga Grant,' Rudy asked Miss Linnet, who had escaped from Mr Blidgen with some excuse, and come down from her yard as soon as she'd heard the news.

'Ya can find ya wife in dat yard,' Miss Linnet said. And Rudy set off, followed by Rushton, Miss Citarra, Yvette, Miss Linnet, Blackie, Vinton, Oneil, his brother Squeecher, little Maxwell and a half dozen *picknee*.

Olga was in Steve's house looking at photographs of life in Bradford in the photograph album. Steve was at Cove Primary, putting in overtime, due home at any time.

'Olga!' Rudy called.

The Cove crowd smiled.

'Oo dat?' came from inside, in a sharp, angry voice.

'Olga. It iz Rudy.'

Olga came to the porch, scowling. Rudy walked across the yard in filthy jeans, T-shirt and worn trainers, his shoulders sloped depressingly downwards by a week of arguments with his parents, a long, long flight, a difficult search for Olga, and a rucksack with twenty kilos of his most loved possessions. He was not a happy boy; he had just experienced the first three days of his life without a car, a house or his generous allowance, and it had not been enjoyable.

'Rudy, ya carry dung mi air-ticket an' passport?' she snapped.

'Olga. I carry down nussink but my love,' Rudy replied, hitching off his rucksack, and looking around with delight at the pretty yard and inviting creek. 'But remember ze song, All you need is love, Olga.'

'If ya nah have no air ticket, den go way, den, ya rass claat German fool. Gwaan! Hitch up ya bag and leave.'

Rudy flinched at the severity of his wife's words. 'But Olga, vot is vrong? Haff I done somesing I am not knowing?'

Olga looked up the Main in the direction of the primary school. Little Craig ran down the middle of the road, his eyes sparkling and his front teeth clearly visible.

'Steve de com!' he called excitedly. 'Steve de com!'

A few hundred yards behind him, Steve hurried to his yard, the prospect of another early night with his fiancée quickening his paces.

'I haf come to live wiz you, as man unt wife, Olga,' Rudy said.

Olga dashed back into the house and came out with the kitchen knife. This wooden-handled stainless steel knife looked like an innocent cooking implement, but it had form: it had been a murder weapon once, in the hands of Sparrow, the father and moral guide of all the Grant siblings; he had inflicted many gashes, and countless times it had been pressed threateningly against the flesh of both enemies and friends.

The look in Olga's eyes as she advanced holding the knife in the air so terrified Rudy that he was rooted to the spot. His mind raced: it wasn't too late to ring his father and beg forgiveness. His BMW would still be in the garage, his flat still unsold.

'But Olga vot is vrong? We can liff here most happily togezzer – and I will try to get my farter to send some money, I promise.'

'Dis marriage finish,' she said, somewhat unneccesarily, and brought down the knife, gashing his arm.

'Lick her, lick her!' Maxwell shouted from the road.

But Rudy knew Olga better than that.

'Mein Gott, Olga, you could haf kilt me. Haf you gone mad?' he stuttered, backing away from her.

'Ya man, and mi will kill ya if ya nah get out av mi yard. Gwaan, ron now ...'

Rudy grabbed his rucksack, and ran, clutching his forearm, out of the yard and down the Main, disappearing from view just as Steve, whistling merrily, came into view. Rudy ended up in Ione's bar down by the seashore, clutching a T-shirt to the wound, which looked rather worryingly superficial, considering how fast he had run. The heavily dreadlocked Ione brought him a Red Stripe that he'd opened on a pair of rusty nails, which Rudy swigged on, tasting the slightly fishy smell that lingered around the cap of every bottle served in Cove.

'Spliff?' Ione asked.

'Ya, danke, tank ya.'

'No problem.'

Ione reached for his stash under the cane thatch roof and *bil one spliff*, which he lit, the white smoke obscuring his head and locks, before passing it to Rudy. Rudy pulled deeply on it. This was his first spliff since landing in Jamaica. It tasted lemony, and full of blossom.

After a long, easeful silence, Ione, who ot course knew what had happened to Rudy, because everyone in Cove knew everything, said, 'Life go on, eh?'

And Rudy smiled. 'Ya man,' he said, 'life go on.'

When Steve got back to his yard he saw the knife in Olga's hand.

'What are you up to with that knife, Olga?' he asked cheerily.

'Cutting flower dem far de table,' answered Olga sweetly, slicing through the stem of an hibiscus.

He put his arm around her waist and smiled into her eyes. 'Flowers for the table,' he said. 'You know I think I'm the luckiest man in Jamaica, to have someone as wonderful as you.'

Three weeks later they were wed. The day after the wedding, Olga dragged Steve to the Post Office to make sure he posted their passports, marriage certificate and application for her British citizenship to the consulate in Kingston. As usual, Miss Markham served Steve. Naturally, she knew exactly who Olga was and what was in the envelope. Miss Linnet had told her. She had heard it from Miss Citarra, who had heard it from Yvette, who had seen it while she *palish an' shine de flaar* in Olga's house. Miss Markham took the envelope from his hand and hid it at the back of a drawer under some old papers in her desk in her office, where it remained for seven months, until questions from Head Office forced her to put it into the postal system.

There is not a single nation which welcomes applications for citizenship from Jamaicans, with perhaps the exception of Colombia, and it therefore took a long time for the passport to come, the British Immigration Service erecting every legal obstacle they could to Olga's quest, but she was patient, determined, and prepared to wait. And while she waited, she played the part of Steve's wife as well as she could.

Steve taught at Cove Primary and worked without rest on improving the house, the yard, which was almost now a garden, and building more beautiful furniture. After eight months, Olga gave birth to a boy, called Chris. He was laid in a carved cedarwood crib Steve had constructed in the shade of the sea-grape tree on weekends. The boy reached his first birthday, but still the Immigration Department at the Consulate wanted more questions answered and more documents produced.

After a couple of years, Olga's hopes of getting out of Jamaica began to fade. She grew bored with Steve, and became careless. When he went off to the primary school to teach, she wandered over to Roddy Perry's to drink Appleton and idle with him under the almond tree outside his bar, and listen to his stories of life in big cities and travels abroad with people like Bob Marley. She *friend with* Roddy, causing Steve incalculable anxiety and suffering. When Olga gave birth to a second child, a girl, Steve knew the infant was too dark-skinned to be his, but loved the baby all the same. Everyone laughed at a man who had *a jacket*, as another man's child was called, but Steve didn't seem to care; *he pull it round him till it fit*.

Twice a week for three years, Olga went fruitlessly to the Post Office at Lucea, to see if her passport had arrived. As a white man's wife she could go straight to the front of the line, where Miss Markham told her with an ambiguous smile that she had no mail, except from time to time a Jamaica Public Service bill, as electricity had finally been brought to Cousins Cove. Then one hot and rainy morning in June, she was given a package which contained her new deep blue British passport.

By that time her marriage had lasted over three years, and people in Cove wondered if Olga had changed, or if she was still *one bad gal*. Their doubts were cleared up the day she received her deep blue British passport, because she stepped out of the minibus in Cove clutching her package, went into her yard and threw all Steve's clothes out of the house. When he came back from work, whistling a tune as he walked down the road, she met him at the little gate he'd erected to stop Chris wandering onto the Main, and *run him off,* exactly the same way she *run Rudy off.* Everyone in Cove either watched, or knew about the incident.

'Leopard kiant change him spot dem,' opined Miss Citarra.

'Ya man,' said Blackie. 'Olga alway one bad gal.'

Steve came back every day for a month to remonstrate with her, his tearful and increasingly desperate appeals entertaining the crowd drawn from the Back Street, but she *cuss and use bad word* and run him out of the yard time after time, much to everyone's amusement, until he went back no more, and people said he'd gone to live *inna foreign.*

Olga set about selling Steve's house and furniture. She found three interested parties: a Swiss dentist, a blue-blooded Boston ganja smuggler, and an American tourist. She then sold the house, and took the money, from each of them. No-one knew quite how it happened, but most agreed Liar Brown, Olga's lawyer, had a lot to do with the plan. It was certainly by no means the last time a house or piece of land in Cove was sold to more than one whitey at a time.

Olga took the money and emigrated with Chris and May to London, where she soon realised that she didn't have to lie or use people to get what she had always wanted, which was a job, a decent home and the easy life. She was soon settled in a council flat, went back to college, and within four years she was deputy manager of a small building society branch in Balham. She's still working on the easy life, but she's happy with things as they are.

Back in Cove, while the three purchasers argued over

whose house it was, Yvonne, Olga's younger sister, moved into Steve Poole's yard and held the place by force with her elder bothers Donovan and Dougie, shortly before they were both jailed for murder, when the whities dropped their claims.

YVONNE

Yvonne was as pretty as Olga, but because she was shorter, plumper and had an enormous posterior, a *bumpa botty*, covered in cellulite, she was considered much sexier than Olga by those who declared themselves experts on the matter, i.e. every man in Cousins Cove. She had none of Olga's elegance, and in the place of her sister's intelligence was a short-sighted, even stupid, cunning, but she had courage, and few people or things scared her. She was a shining example of someone with no conscience, and keenly followed her siblings into the family trades: petty crime and prostitution, but didn't have their determination or brains to be a success. It wasn't easy to follow the high achievements of Olga – at one point Negril's highest paid whore – and two elder brothers, both of whom were serving impressively long stretches in Spanish Town Jail for robbery and murder. Yvonne managed little more than stealing towels on the beach, and diluting the pure orange juice she sold in Negril with squash and water.

Although essentially a failure in the world of crime, Yvonne felt big and bad in Cousins Cove, which was a peculiarly forgiving and encouraging community for low achievers. You could be the best, or at the very least brilliant, in your chosen field, without achieving a thing. It was enough simply to talk about it. Dreams were as highly regarded as actions; words were as valued as deeds. Everyone had a money-making scheme in the planning stage, and no-one felt any pressure to get it off the ground.

Those who did actually do something, as opposed to talk about it, were assured of success – though it must be pointed out that the threshold for success in Cousins Cove was low and wide. The cricket team, which won only one game the season after the famous match against the Police, was still 'de best inna de island. Serious'. The top athlete, a star of track and field, was Vinton, with his knock knees and immense flat feet which looked like batter poured into a deep frying pan, who each successive year left Cove for the inter-parish trials in Lucea, full of hope, with many slaps on the back, firm shakes of the hand, and injunctions to 'lick dem down', and 'mash dem op', and was knocked out in the first, or very occasionally, second, heat of every event he entered. He was knocked out, in fact, as often as Cove's other great sporting champion, Waller the boxer, who at twenty-five had trouble finding his words after so many blows to his head.

Cove's top tourist operator was Joe, whose newly built bar stood on rocks beside the seashore, not far from the shed he built with Ione, whom he had parted from acrimoniously after an argument about Ione's tendency to long change customers. Joe's new shed was about twelve foot square, with bamboo walls, a pitched zinc roof, and a concrete floor on which was built a mahoe wood bar. Behind the bar was one crate of dusty soft drinks, one of Red Stripe and one of Dragon Stout, a framed black and white photograph of Haile Selassie, the Ethiopian Emperor, and another, unframed, of Bob Marley. In front of the bar were three stools whose height placed your chin at the level of the bar if you sat down. On the bar, in common with every other rum shop in Jamaica, was a ghetto blaster half tuned to a radio station at full volume, and a glass cabinet whose feet stood in bottle tops of water to prevent ants climbing up them and swarming over the *buller, bon, rack cake, or fry fish* which sat in the warm gloom of the showcase for whole weeks before being consumed. The bamboo walls were painted blue, yellow, white and dark green, as each half pot of paint he *beg* from friends ran out.

After everyone in Cove had visited it, looked around, and said 'criss bar, man' to Joe, it fell silent and empty – except for Joe, on a stool behind the bar, his dreadlocked head resting on his folded arms, week after week, listening to the air-conditioned coaches half full of tourists hissing at the bridge, changing down, and then roaring up the hill past his bar, changing back up as they hit the straight out of Cousins Cove. Locals patronised the bar, but they had little money, and had to make one Red Stripe or *saff drink* last three or four hours; yet somehow, like most businesses in Cove, the bar just managed to keep its head above water, being saved from total immersion by the arrival, every six weeks or so, of a car-load of tourists, bored by their hotel and resort town, doing a little exploring. They would fill the bar with their big American bodies and voices, and within an hour triple the monthly takings. Tourists were everything people said they were. If you happened to be passing Joe's at the time, you could easily be asked in, and bought one, or even, in one extraordinary reported incident, three, Red Stripe (and it would have been four, but all Joe's beer *done*), and get to chat with the *whitey dem*, all of whom were incredibly rich, madly generous and extremely friendly.

It was Yvonne who managed to get tourists to stop in Cove for more than an hour or so, and *everybady respect* her for that. She found out that Steve Poole's yard had some magical qualities for the white man. She brought parties out from Negril, and sometimes white men would stay the night, but she was useless at *whore bizness* because she always bugged them for too much money too soon, and they scurried back to Negril. There was one couple Yvonne met on the beach, called Don and Marlene, who came to Jamaica every year around November-time when it was just getting seriously cold in Chicago where they lived, who always stopped by Yvonne's yard on their way to their hotel from the airport.

Don and Marlene had visited two years running when, around November 1990, Yvonne began to think they might reappear. And indeed one dry autumn day, Yvonne, hearing a car pull off the road into the yard, rolled over on her bed, peered through a crack in the woodwork, and shouted, 'It Dun an' Marlene,' to Vinton excitedly.

She had recently taken Vinton off the side of the road where he scratched a living, just, selling stolen or scavenged fruit in tiny quantities to passing motorists. Since escaping Miss Liza's yard, he had no yard to call home, and slept at night wherever he could. *Up 'n' down*, it was called. He was always careful to leave before his welcome wore thin or, before it wore *too* thin, anyway, and never returned to the same yard too soon. In sixteen years alive in Cove he had managed to accumulate only four, treasured, possessions: *one brief, and tree shirt*, two of which he had to lend to his cousin Glenroy, to borrow back *one trousers, so he could walk up and down 'pon de street widout shame*. He wanted most of all a gold chain, so girls would talk to him, no, notice him, and *one shoes*. His attendance at Green Island Secondary School trailed off two summers ago, well before he learnt to read or write – but in a world with no books, paper or pens, it was not a problem. He knew that others were doing better than he, and had more to show for sixteen years than one pair of underpants and three T-shirts, but Vinton felt that his life was by no means irretrievable, and with the right breaks he could come good – find a girl who would talk to him – and even make some bills.

When Yvonne installed him in her yard to babysit, guard against *tief*, wash up, cut and rake the yard, in return for a roof over his head (unless Yvonne had friends staying, when Vinton had to sleep under the house *in the housebottom*), and the occasional look at her snowy portable TV, his real education was about to begin.

After they all said hello, and Don and Marlene said how warm it was and how beautiful the sea looked, Yvonne said, 'Ya need a drink after ya journey. What ya want?'

'Well, what are you offering?' Don asked.

'Anyting. Beer or saff drink.'

'I'll have a Red Stripe.'

'Don! It's only four o'clock!' said Marlene.

'Relax. We're on vacation, and this is Jamaica, honey.'

'Ya man. In Jamaica it no prablem.'

'Well I'll take an orange juice,' said Marlene. 'Do you have fresh orange juice?'

'Ya man,' said Yvonne, going into the gloom of the house. Vinton had come round to the back door.

'Get mi one Red Stripe and one saff drink, orange. Horry. Hol' on.'

'Dun,' she called. 'Ya need one spliff to chill out?'

'Oh wow,' said Don. 'Well, I guess so …' he replied.

'It is a little early, honey,' said Marlene, 'and we still have a way to go on that terrible road.'

'No problem,' said Yvonne. 'Spliff can clear the brain for drive. Den ya can constentrate. Alright, just a small one.' She thrust a few notes at Vinton, and whispered, 'Get mi one spliff. Run. Horry now.'

Down at Joe's he found the bar shut. Quite often Joe was so high when he arrived at work, he went round the back under a fig tree, climbed into his hammock and waited for a customer without noticing the front door was closed until he came to shut up at the end of the day.

Vinton called his uncle's name. 'Dread!' he shouted, but nothing came in reply, so he went on down to Ione's shed on the seashore.

'Dread,' he called to Ione, who was crouching by a pot on a charcoal fire in the little kitchen behind his bar. 'Ya have one Red Stripe and one saff drink?'

Ione moved slowly to the cold store, a hole in the sandy ground behind the bar where half a dozen bottles – his entire stock – sat in warm water that three days before had been chunks of ice, bought off the dripping *ice chock* that supplied all the bars along the Main from Mo-Bay to Negril. He found a bottle of beer and a fizzy orange.

'An' mi need one spliff,' Vinton added when Ione wiped the bottles on a rag that smelled of fish. Ione returned from his stashing place under the cane thatch, and Vinton said, 'Ow much for dat?'

Ione looked long and hard at the two bottles. Then he said, 'Red Stripe six dallar, saff drink tree. Dat ... dat ...' his voice trailed off, and he was left gazing intently at the bottles in silence.

Vinton wished his youngest sister Amoy was there. She was nine years old and the village's champion mathematician, reader, writer and speller.

'Dat nine dallar,' said Vinton quite confidently.

'Ya man,' smiled the dread.

'Ow much far de spliff and wizla?'

'Say ... say ... say ... five dallar. Dat mek ... dat mek ...' he started laughing softly to himself.

'Nine dallar an' five dallar. Dat fourteen.'

'Ya man.'

Vinton gave him an orange twenty-dollar bill with the picture of a bauxite mine on it. Ione drifted off into the dark recesses of the shed and returned with a handful of notes, which he then looked at in a surprised way, as if they had landed in his hands by magic. He shook his head and laughed. 'It com to ... It com to ...'

'Fourteen dallar.'

'Ya man.' He stopped and stared at the money again. 'Ow much ya give mi?'

'Mi give ya one twenty bill.'

'Ya man.' Long pause.

'Ya owe mi six dallar.'

Ione looked at the money in his hand. 'Mi nah have six, man. Me only have four dallar bills an' one ten dallar bill.'

Vinton was aware that there was a solution to the problem, but felt that Don and Marlene were going to be gone before Ione and he got it. White people did everything so fast.

'Tek de twenty. Give me de change later.'

'Ya man. Respec.'

Vinton left the shed and ambled back to Yvonne's yard, running the last few yards.

'Ow much?' Yvonne shot at him as he handed the drinks and ganja in the back door.

'Twenty. Drinks nine. Ganje eleven,' he answered, giving Yvonne back her change. He knew she knew the price of drinks, but had gambled on the ganja, whose price fluctuated with supply and demand.

'Dun!' she called, and gave him the ganja where he sat on the porch.

'Oh wow. How much do I owe for the draw?'

'Fifty J. Call it four US. An maybe a likker tip far de boy who ron and carry it.'

'Sure,' said Don, digging in his pocket again.

Vinton, standing shyly at the corner of the house thought to himself how Yvonne was a hard task mistress, but had a soft side to her.

'Here.' Don gave a single US bill to Vinton. A US dollar! His first! *Wickid.*

'Tank ya, sah,' he said, fingering the bill lovingly.

'What ya carry dung fram a foreign far mi?' Yvonne impatiently asked Don. 'Ya know ya got to give mi someting,' she piped gaily. He made the mistake of not bringing Yvonne a present last year – she was so demanding he had been lucky to get away without her peeling Marlene's watch and jewellery off her body – so he didn't make the mistake twice.

Yvonne unwrapped her gift hungrily until she saw what it was – a kitchen apron with Don's company logo on it – and lost interest so quickly she didn't even say thank you. Vinton looked at it and thought he could wear it on the street and the girls might love it. It was worth a try, anyway.

After a spliff and a drink – Marlene taking only one sip of the bright orange confection in her bottle, but upon seeing Don with his spliff she said, 'All right, maybe I'll have a quick pull on that' – the procedure was as follows: Don went to the car, took out masks, snorkels, fins and swim suits, and they swam for twenty minutes before taking a shower and driving on to Negril. Vinton led them to the water's edge, carrying their state of the art diving equipment just to get a feel of the newness of it, even if only fleetingly, saw them safely in, and said, 'Ya wan ya car clean, sah, while ya swim?'

'Oh right, great. And keep an eye on it, thanks,' Don called, and pulled down his mask.

The reef, through a snorkelling mask, was a teeming, bright and beautiful world. The coral, predominantly red, grew in extraordinary shapes – in huge pillars that seemed about to teeter to the sandy sea floor; great mansions, hollowed out like catacombs with giant bulging brain corals protruding from their sides; and near the surface, in pale fingers of delicate traceries, reaching through the water to the sunlight. Amongst this ruined underwater world darted thousands of bright fish; from tiny electric blue minnows in shoals half a million strong, through striped, spotted, brindled even, fish, to giant rays that swept out from the shadows with the sinister, deliberate slowness of a dangerous and fearless animal. While Don and Marlene were immersed in this world, only stopping to stand on the coral every now and again to clear their masks and exclaim, 'Wow, isn't it just unbelievable. I mean really?' before dipping down back into it, Vinton made his way back to clean the car.

'Gi' mi dat one US dallar,' Yvonne snapped at him, as he gazed with stunned admiration at the Civic.

'Nuh sah! Dun give i' a mi, Yvonne ...' But it was useless, so he pulled it out of his pocket and handed it over. At the pipe under the avocado pear tree, he filled a pan with water, found an old discarded sock of Yvonne's and went back to the car, moving fast so as to have plenty of time touching the beautiful automobile. It was a five year old Honda Civic, and you couldn't get much grander or newer than that in Cousins Cove.

He had never, in his whole life, handled, let alone owned, any new manufactured object, until he worked for Yvonne. Everything that he got hold of was second-hand, no, fifteenth-hand, at least, and had long before lost the lustre, feel and smell of newness. He longed for something with a price label on it, something straight from a shop, with plastic and cardboard packaging to strip off, but only ever got his hands on things picked from the dust of a yard where they had been thrown down by the last owner.

While wiping the back window, Vinton saw, on the back seat of the car, a photographic bag with something metallic, and new-looking, sticking out of it. It was a camera, a *criss* camera, with one *wickid* big lens, and the name PENTAX written across its top. He tried the door; it opened. He sat in the back seat with his legs out the door, and picked up the camera. It was heavy, and felt good. He lifted it to his eye, and after a few difficulties was looking at the steering-wheel and speedometer through the viewfinder. *Ya man.* That would make *one nice phota.* He made the click and whirring wind-on noise with his mouth. He knew the sound from the tourists who always took photographs of the old fishing canoes from Joe's Bar. He couldn't work out why anyone would want a picture of Jagwar and Oncle Dicky's dug-out canoes. If he were them, he would have taken a picture of the Rental car, or Joe's flush toilet, or the street light – something new and *criss* like that.

He saw a pair of sunglasses under the bag, and pulled them out. They had a weight, too, like all the expensive things tourists brought with them. He tried them on and looked in the wing mirror. He brought the camera near his face so he could see it in the reflection, too. *Ya man, dat look kinda cool.* When he slipped the glasses back, the big bag moved and revealed Marlene's handbag beneath. Vinton saw the pale green edge of some bank notes, and after investigating a little, had Marlene's wallet open and was fingering four or five hundred US dollars in cash.

'Put i' back, ya idiot, Vinton,' Yvonne snapped, slapping

the top of his head. 'Dat nat de way fi get de money. Ya want fi we to go a jail? Den nuh touch i'. Gwaan, move out a here. Go dung a sea an' keep watch far Dun an' Marlene.'

'What is you gonna do?'

'I,' said Yvonne, slipping into the driver's seat and touching the key in the ignition, 'am gonna tek de rental far one likker spin.'

'But ya kiant drive, Yvonne,' Vinton blurted out. He knew she had only got a licence because *Afficer* Donovan of Green Island Police Force (Traffic Division) had given it to her for sex.

'It easy fi drive. If Chicken George can do i', any fool can do i'. Go an watch far Dun.'

Vinton stood back and watched Yvonne pilot the Honda unsteadily onto the road. When its front wheels were half way across the tarmac she pulled on the hand break, got out of the car, leaving it in the middle of the road, and dashed back across the yard and into the house. A minibus and car came abreast round the blind corner and swerved with a cry of tyres, narrowly avoiding the Honda, then Yvonne appeared carrying a pair of sunglasses, and climbed back in the car.

She had no destination in mind, nor errand to run, but there was nevertheless a definite purpose to her journey. Her object was to cruise up and down the Main and possibly onto the Back Street, so that as many people as possible could see her driving the *criss rental car* and be reminded of how big her status was, before getting the car back to the yard and parking it.

Yvonne was the most glamorous person in Cousins Cove. The people knew she was bad, but loved her for the new and exciting things she brought into their lives: the long bamboo pole that waved in the breeze above her roof, with the rusting antennae tied by string to its top, was the source

of immense civic pride, even though the pink portable TV
at its other end barely produced an intelligible picture. It
meant, though, to people passing through, that Cousins
Cove had a TV. Yvonne loved the glamour of being the most
modern girl in the village, and felt a certain responsibility
to live up to expectations. Whenever she got her hands on
a new appliance she proudly *brandish* it to the *likker people
dem of Cove*. It was she who gave people their first feel of a
Walkman. The headphones were passed from head to head
producing startled and awed expressions as Kenny Rogers,
slurring on underpowered batteries, growled out his lyrics.
So powerful was the little machine that even Rushton, deaf
to everything else, caught a snatch of music and laughed
joyfully at his first aural contact with the outside world for
decades. Yvonne also introduced the camera to Cove, taking
a lot of pictures of people which were never developed
because they didn't have the money to *clean de film*. No one
minded though – posing for the pictures was enough of a
thrill. She also bought the pressure cooker to Cove. She had
gone into Larmonds Record and Novelty store in One Way
Street, Lucea, to buy a Hi-Fi, but discovering that she didn't
have enough money, went for a pressure cooker instead.
With the remains of her funds she bought some diced beef,
and hurried home to impress everyone in Cove. On the long
journey from the factory in Taiwan, where the pressure
cooker was manufactured, to Lucea in Hanover, where it
had sat in the shop for three and a half years, it had become
parted from the instruction manual, so Yvonne relied on
instinct to discover how it worked. One thing she knew
about beef: it took a lot of cooking. She dropped it into the
pot, added some water, seasoning, scallions and carrot,
screwed the lid down hard, put it on the paraffin flame, and
stood back. Within quarter of an hour a wonderful scent of

beef stew filled the room. It was time to call in the small crowd gathered in the yard. In trooped Miss Citarra, Yvette, Craig, Nakissia, Oneil, Rushton (who since the Walkman, believed Yvonne had access to miraculous inventions) and Miss Linnet, all of whom admired the clean lines of the pressure cooker and commented favourably on the smells emanating in hisses from it.

'Mi go a Negril now, and nyam de beef when me com back tonight when it cook proper,' Yvonne announced, as everyone left the house. 'Vinton,' she commanded. 'Sit here and watch de pressure pot till me com back.' Negril being nineteen miles to the east, and Yvonne's mode of transport being a minibus, Vinton settled in for a minimum two and a half hour wait in front of the sizzling pot. After an hour, though, when he had invited Oneil into the house for company, the smell of well seasoned beef stew became too much for the two hungry boys to resist.

'Let we tek off de top an' eat a couple spoonful of meat before put it back to cook. Yvonne never gonna know,' Vinton suggested.

'Ya man,' agreed Oneil, 'she never gonna give we no beef herself.' Too often Oneil had sat with Vinton in Yvonne's yard, and out of the corner of their eyes watched Yvonne single-handedly consume a meal for three, before shouting at Vinton to wash up the plate and pot.

Vinton had trouble unscrewing the lid, but Oneil, who was good with his hands, saw that a hammer and piece of wood would do the trick. He put the wood in place against the boiling pot, and gave it a sharp crack with the hammer.

There was a mighty explosion. The lid flew off the pot, and a fine layer of beef stew was spread evenly over the walls, ceiling, faces and clothes of Vinton and Oneil.

'Jeeezus, Chris'!' laughed Oneil.

'De pressure pot vex!' said Vinton.

'Mi kiant believe i'. But i' taste good,' Oneil said, picking a strip of meat off a T-shirt that said MY DAD WENT TO JAMAICA AND ALL I GOT WAS THIS LOUSY T-SHIRT, and putting it in his mouth.

'Mmm. It can go on,' agreed Vinton.

'But what Yvonne gonna say?'

'Yvonne never gonna know. Yvonne kiant know or else she gonna kill we.' So the two of them, armed with a wide-headed screw-driver and a general purpose kitchen cloth scraped up the mess, put what they could of it back into the pot and screwed the lid back on. When Yvonne returned she ate her stew and pronounced it an unqualified success.

That had been months before Don and Marlene called by, and she felt it was time to reassert her position as Cove's most exciting resident. She turned the car right, and took it slowly up the Main towards Chicken George's house, where she knew it would out-trump his immense Grundig TV. Vinton watched her leave on her Royal Tour of Cousins Cove, and made his way back to the sea.

It wasn't long before Don and Marlene's snorkel pipes began to move back across the reef towards Vinton, where he sat anxiously on the rocks. Behind him, there was no sign of Yvonne or the car. Soon they were drawing themselves out of the water, ripping off their masks and saying, 'Oh wow, that really is incredible, I mean that's awesome, it really is. Jesus, there are people who'd pay hundreds of bucks to do that ...'

'It sure beats the D train down town on a cold Monday morning,' laughed Marlene.

When Don noticed Vinton sitting on the rock, he said, 'Hi, there. Everything okay?'

'Ya man,' said Vinton, and had recourse to the phrase

Yvonne always used in a crisis with tourists: 'This is Jamaica, man. No problem!'

'Sure!' laughed Don.

Vinton looked up through the seagrape trees for signs of Yvonne. All he could see was Craig, hanging around hoping for a tip from the white man. He thought he could probably get *Don dem* to the shower and then to Yvonne's bedroom, where they had left their clothes, without seeing the *rental* wasn't there, because Steve Poole's hibiscus hedge hid it, but after that Yvonne had better get back, or there was gonna be *one 'ole eap o' trouble*. He wondered where she was, imagining her taking the rental gently down the Back Street on the way back to her yard. In fact, she had her foot hard down on the gas pedal and was five miles out of Cove on the road up to Blenheim. Having cruised past Chicken George and ensured he saw her in the car with Marlene's Pentax round her neck, she decided to go up into the hills to check a *Police* who had been giving her the eye on the beach for a couple of weeks. Maybe he'd want to take a ride with her. She thought about Don and Marlene. Yes, she'd have to hurry a little.

On the way to the shower Marlene said, 'Did you lock the car?' and in a lower tone added, 'Only my bag and money are in it.'

'Will you relax, Marlene,' Don replied. 'I've known Yvonne years. We're amongst friends.'

'So you didn't.'

'I'm not sure. Hey! you ...'

'Ya man,' replied Vinton.

'No-one's been inside the car, have they?'

'No man,' replied Vinton.

'See?' said Don. 'Now just relax. Please.'

They loved the open-air shower, and ran laughing to the

house and Yvonne's bedroom while Vinton sat unhappily on the porch looking out onto the empty road. Suddenly Don came to Yvonne's bedroom door with a towel round his waist.

'Anyone been in here while we were swimming?'

'Nah sah,' answered Vinton.

'There must have been,' Marlene screeched from inside, 'my watch has been stolen.'

'Darling, we don't know for sure yet …'

'Yes I do. I put it here with my clothes. I told you this place was fucking unsafe. I knew we should have gone to Tahiti. The South Sea islanders just aren't into this stealing shit.' She, too, appeared at the door. 'You see anyone sneak in here?'

'No. Nobady com in here.'

'Well where the hell is my watch then? It was a fucking Rolex. I paid over a thousand bucks for that watch. Just what is it with Jamaicans? Did you come in here while we were swimming?'

'No. Mi swear mi didn't. Mi sit pon de rock dem while ya bade.'

'Oh, right, sure, you just acted as lookout for your pals.'

'Let me have one look,' Vinton said, approaching them. He'd seen this before. *White people get high, lose tings and say dem tief.* He entered Yvonne's room, and began a search. In the little cupboard on the wall that Steve Poole had made and Olga had been unable to prise off and sell, Vinton found Yvonne's bible, with a woman's wristwatch pushed under it. He took it out.

'That's where I put it. I forgot I hid it.'

'No prablem,' said Vinton.

'VINTAN!' he heard shouted.

'Please excuse me,' he said to the whities, 'that is Yvonne.'

She was back. But the car wasn't in the yard. 'VINTAN!' he heard Yvonne scream again.

He followed the shout out onto the road, where Yvonne stood twitching by the car thirty yards from the yard, the Pentax resting on her full bosom.

'It burn outa gas,' she said to him. 'Wishart Dun dem?'

'Dem change in fi you room.'

'Quick. Ron now to Ranald and beg some gas fram him.'

Vinton sprinted off up to Ranald's yard and managed to get some gas, though the only receptacle available for its transportation was a washbowl, round which the pint of petrol swilled as Vinton trotted back to Yvonne.

'Give me dat,' she snapped, pushing him out of the way, but when she brought it to the gas tank the fluid dribbled off the bottom of the bowl in an arc onto the tarmac. 'It want one fonnel. Ron and fetch one fonnel.'

But Vinton knew there wasn't a serviceable funnel in Hanover, let alone Cousins Cove. He dashed into the hedge and plucked a wide and waxy leaf from an almond tree.

'What ya doin' wid dat? Mi need one fonnel ya idiot.'

'Dis can work, Yvonne. Pour it now.'

With remarkable smoothness, the gas ran down the groove of the folded leaf and disappeared into the gas tank.

'Now get ou' de way,' Yvonne said, and started the car.

Marlene and Don sat on Yvonne's bed, too consumed by embarrassment at falsely accusing Vinton of theft to notice the sound of their car returning. They emerged sheepishly a few minutes later, when Kadim, Yvonne's high-heeled, six year old daughter, was coming home from school.

'Vinton,' Yvonne whispered out of the back door.

'Yes?' answered the boy.

'Lock off de current.'

He went to the main fuse box and threw the switch to off.

'Go inside an do ya homework,' Yvonne ordered Kadim, 'it late.'

The sun was indeed setting. Kadim went in, and then came back to the door and addressed her mother.

'Moma, mi kiant see to read book cas it too dark.'

'Switch on light, ya idiot.'

'Mi kiant switch on light, cas corrent gone.'

'It bad for child to read in dark?' Yvonne asked Marlene.

'Sure, it can ruin a child's eyes. What's wrong with your lights?'

'Mi kiant pay de bill and dem disconnect we. Only ten US, but mi poor and kiant afford it.'

'Oh Don, did you hear that?' Marlene said. 'The little girl has to do her homework in the dark because Yvonne can't pay the ten dollar electricity bill. Can't we do something?'

Marlene was thankful for this opportunity to efface her earlier meanness – and for such a tiny sum.

'Sure, hon,' Don reached into his pocket. 'But I've only got eight bucks on me.'

'Don't worry,' said Marlene, moving off the porch and going to the car. 'I have some.'

She came back with her handbag. Vinton looked at Yvonne, upon whose deadpan features he searched in vain for a hint of a smile. Marlene took out her wallet and withdrew a ten dollar note.

'Here,' she said, quietly and enjoyably, as she gave it to Yvonne.

'Ten dollar for bill, but twenty-five bucks for reconnection fee,' Yvonne said.

'They do that here, too? That's what they do in the States. They're terrible these big corporations. Here.'

The sun was submerged in the sea, and the short sweet cool Jamaican dusk was upon them. Don said they had to get on. As they kissed Yvonne goodbye, and promised to see her again the following year, she said, 'Nuh forget mi present.'

They drew out of the yard and headed west to Negril.

'That was a great stop,' Marlene said. 'The swim was out of this world, and that boy was sweet, you know? And it was real nice to be able to help out, wasn't it?'

'Sure was,' said Don, smiling as he thought about the week of sun and fun and harmony that lay ahead of them. The visit had completely changed his wife's mood. 'It's right what they say, isn't it? Jamaica – no problem.'

Back at Yvonne's yard, as Yvonne put the 35 dollars into her pocket, she caught Vinton looking at her.

'Mi one teevee?'

'No,' replied Vinton.

'Well why ya look pon mi den?'

'Mi nah look pon ya,' he answered.

'Good,' she said. 'Now switch on de current an' cook up some rice and peas far mi. Mi ongry. Horry.'

And Vinton proudly tied Don's apron with the company logo on it around his waist, and set about his duties.

DROGS BIZNIS

When Driver *get back from a turn inna Kingston at him mumma's yard*, he came down from his yard *inna de ills* to show off the sunglasses he stole from his brother, and inquire amongst friends who was the best fisherman in Cove. His elder brother Buru had some *gangsta* buddies in Allmans Town, Kingston 4, who *do some drogs biznis* with Colombians, and needed a reliable sailor to pick up a consignment of cocaine dropped into the sea at a prearranged spot off the north-west coast of Jamaica. Living *inna de ghettto* they knew no fishermen, but Buru told them that his brother Driver lived near the coast in Hanover, and he could ask him to find someone to do the pick-up.

Driver first *buck up pon* Jimmy U-Roy Fairfax, who *idle* in the deep shade of the big almond tree by the fishermen's canoes.

'Whuppen'?' Jimmy greeted Driver.

'Yes, Jimmy,' said Driver, settling on a fat root that threaded in and out of the sand. 'Tell me one ting, which de wickedest fisherman in all of Cove?' he asked.

'De best fisherman? Con, Wadder, and de udder shooterman dem catch nuff pound of fish. Dem clean lick down all de fish dem in de Cove wid speargon.'

'Mi nuh mean shooter men, mi mean boat fishermen.'

'Boat fishermen? Dat easy. Jagwar de best. Him fish far

tirty odd year and know all de sea up an' down. Dat man can see straight trough water. And de fish love him, dem haffi love him, cas dem alway catch by him. Or Oncle Tom. Even when nobady op and down de coast fram Negril to Ochi kiant catch nuttin, Oncle Tom come back wid a boat full of snapper.'

'Which fisherman de best boatman?'

'De best boatman?'

'Ya man. Which fisherman know de sea and boat and ting better dan de udders?'

'Driver, why ya want fi know dis?'

'Cas Buru need one man wid a boat fi do a likker drogs biznis wid.'

'What kinda biznis?'

'Dat mi nuh know, cas him nuh tell me no detail plan dem. All mi know is dem need de bess boatman in de village.'

'For de purpose ya state, de answer easy: ya look pon man right now.'

'Uuuh?'

'Mi can elp ya brudder no prablem. Ya com to the right guy.'

'Bot Jimmy, ya stop fish since four year, and ya nuh ave no boat, and ya lost easy out at sea when ya have ya boat. Remember dat time one starm come up fast and the sea rough up, and nobady kiant find ya till de coast guard ketch ya baffling for life off Negril Point?'

'Dat cas fi Byron canoe weak.'

'Ya man. Now mi remember, ya tief Byron canoe dat day.'

'Shot op, man. Dis biznis serious. Mi know what ya brudder want – one boat fi pick op drog fram sea. Dat easy, and mi can beg one fibreglass craft fram som fool in Lances Bay wid big engine, so nuttin kiant wrong.'

'No sah,' laughed Driver, 'ya nat gonna do no biznis wid Buru ...'

'Mi know what biznis dis is. Dis cocaine biznis, tross me. And dat coke wort 'ole eap o' money ...'

'Ya man, mi know,' said Driver, 'and the dealer dem know too, and ya kiant mess wid dem or dem kill ya. Serious.'

'Dem kill ya, sure.' Jimmy paused, then grinned, adding, 'If dem catch ya.'

'If ya mess wid dem, dem ketch ya. Tross mi. Dem rut'less. Dem love fi kill, dem love i'.'

'Listen,' said Jimmy, drawing Driver closer, 'ya tell ya brudder dat mi de wickedest fisherman ...'

'Nor!'

'... and you and mi got out fi check de drogs ...'

'Nor, Jimmy ...'

'Out at sea we tief maybe half pound or tree pound ...'

'... No!'

'... and leave it tie up by fish pot, com back fram a sea and tell dem dat when we find de coke one bag brok and coke lost.'

'Jimmy, ya kiant do dat wid dis posse. Dem roff, trost me. Dem kill ya quick as dem smile at ya.'

'Ya know how much dallar half pound coke wort'?'

'No, an' mi nah want fi know.'

'Five tousan' US. Half pound ... Tree pound wort near twenty tousand US.'

'Twenty tousan' US?'

'Ya man.' Jimmy's obeah mathematics worked its magic on Driver's resistance. 'Dat twelve tousand five ondred US for each o' we.'

Jimmy borrowed a boat, which six weeks later, shortly after dark, they pushed off the sand, clambered into, and pointed out to the black sea, scraping the hull horribly, because Jimmy'd forgotten the lanes in the coral reef. They had no charts, no watch and no compass with which to find the rendezvous.

Far out at sea Jimmy shouted, ''Top de engine …'top de engine.' When Driver killed the outboard, Jimmy said, 'Ssh. Mi tought mi 'ear one airplane.' Driver looked terrified. They sat and listened to the lapping of the warm black sea on the hull. The moonlight illuminated the buoy, plastic bag, tape and *scissor* in the bottom of the boat. 'Nottin,' announced Jimmy. The next thing he said, half an hour later, was, 'It soon com. Tross mi.'

When, nine hours later, dawn broke greyly over the slither of land on the horizon, Jimmy got Driver to start the engine, and pointed the prow back to Cousins Cove. As they bounced along, Driver scrabbled around the bottom of the boat for the tape, scissors and other equipment related to their planned deception, and threw it overboard.

'What ya do, ya idiot?' shouted Jimmy.

'Mi dash i' all away.'

'Mi need dat tape! Nat de bouy, no! … Jeeezuss.'

'It all got a go, Jimmy. Dis a problem situation we is in. Mi nuh gonna take no chances.'

'Us don't do nottin wrong. We do everyting right. Relax, tek it easy. Dem nuh gonna vex wid we.'

They roared past the fleet of fishing canoes paddling out to sea at dawn, pulled the boat carelessly onto the sand and were just about to disappear for a few days *inna de bush* when they noticed a group of men sitting under a tree watching them. It was Buru, looking excited, his Kingston friend from Telaviv posse, an out of uniform policeman called Nini Hibbert, and two strangers. One had a bald head and a pair of silver revolvers wagging under his earlobes, the other was a short, fat, moustached Latin man.

'Whuppen'?' Buru asked.

'Alright,' said Jimmy.

'Everyting cool den?' Buru asked, unable to contain his happy excitement.

'Ya get trough?' asked the Kingston *yout*, who was called Fumes.

Jimmy looked about him at the mangrove bushes, and lowered his voice. 'The plane don't come,' he said.

'What do you mean?' asked the man with the moustache.

'We sit an' wait all night, but we nah hear or see nottin. De airplane never com. Mebbe it have problems and kiant leave to com up.'

'Were you on the right grid reference?'

'Ya man, for sure. We was der. We was der, waitin, and nottin don't com.'

'So where is your map and compass?' asked the man.

'We trow it inna de sea when we come in. Don't we destroy all incriminating evidence, Driver?'

'Ya man,' said Driver miserably.

The guy with gun earrings told the others to search the boat. Jimmy said to him: 'No plane com, man, believe mi.'

'Ya man, plane come. Now it sit at Montego Bay airport,' said Fumes.

'And it don't got no coke on it?' Jimmy gulped.

'No. It hasn't. Because the consignment was tipped overboard,' said the boss, the short man with the moustache.

'Where?' asked Jimmy.

'At the correct position at the correct time.'

Jimmy leant towards the little Colombian. 'Dat what de pilot say?'

'Yes. Yes.'

'Him musta drop it someplace else where him bredren wait, so him can tief it fram you.'

'That's not possible.'

'Why nat? Is you one o' de pasingers on de plane?'

'No.'

'Ow many people on board wid de pilot?'

'He was alone.'

'Well den, bas.' Jimmy lowered his voice to a whisper. 'Ya kiant trust nobady. Dat pilot one tief. Believe Jimmy Fairfax. De pilot one traitor.'

'No he's not.'

'Bot 'ow can ya know, bas?' Jimmy whined, in his most paranoia-inducing manner.

'Because I am the pilot,' the man answered, 'and I threw it out.'

Without pausing, Jimmy said, 'Good. Dat rule out dat den. So. Us know the coke drop. Some fisherman most see it come, dem most. Let mi go and talk to mi bredren and aks a couple question up and down. Mi will have ya coke back by tonight. Tross mi. Nuh problem.'

Everybody watched Jimmy closely. Driver cleared his throat. Jimmy smiled weakly.

'Ready?' he asked brightly. 'De quicker mi go, de quicker ya get ya coke.' He made as if to go, but *Afficer* Nini Hibbert stood in his way.

'Ya nuh go nowhere till de bas tell you, annerstan?'

'For sure, no problem afficer.'

The man with the revolver earrings talked in a foreign language to the boss. Then he nodded at the cop. The cop leant towards Jimmy. 'Ya have till tonight to find the consignment.'

'We meet back here at sunset. Understand?' the boss said.

'Mi annerstan,' said Jimmy.

Driver nodded sickly.

'Dem annerstan,' said Buru. 'Dem annerstan that if dem nuh find we coke, dem gonna dead.'

'Get de message?' the cop asked.

'And no funny stuff, all right?' said earrings.

'Dem kiant try no funny stoff, cas dem know mi will find dem, wid ease,' said the cop.

'Sure,' said Jimmy, sunnily. 'Tross we, tross we.'

When the men had left, all crammed in Nini Hibbert's police car, driver turned on Jimmy. 'Ya idiot!' He ran his hands through his locks and stamped his foot. 'Mi told ya not to mess wid Buru. Why mi listen to you? Why?'

'Cas mi clever, and mi alway have a nex idea.'

'Ya alway have a nex bad idea.'

'Not dis time. Not dis time, Driver. Listen. What we want fi happen?'

'Fi find de lass coke.'

'Right. Or fi lose de Colombia man and him friend dem.'

'Dem nuh gonna go nowhere widout dem coke, Jimmy.'

'Bot maybe someting can happen to dem. Someting bad, eh?' A smile curled his sly features.

'Cho,' spat Driver. 'Ya kiant kill dem, Jimmy. Dat kiant work.'

'Nat kill dem, Driver. Get dem remove.'

'Who remove dem?'

'Police.'

'Police?' repeated Driver, trying to work out another of Jimmy's stratagems.

'Mi talk 'bout Crimestop.'

'Crimestop,' said Driver, and then recited the radio advert: 'Don't hide it, tell it. Crimestop.' Crimestop was a confidential Police phone line for informers.

'Com ya,' said Jimmy, 'us gonna mek one phone call.'

The two of them spent most of the afternoon looking for a serviceable telephone box, ending up outside Green Island Police Station, both crammed into the public phone box at its gate. Jimmy punched the number into the phone.

'Dis gonna deal wid de prablem,' he said, sweating profusely. 'Yes sah!' he suddenly said into the receiver.

It had been a quiet morning on the Crimestop desk in Montego Bay, so when the line rang, *Afficer* Nini Hibbert, who had just come on shift, answered it within two rings.

'Crimestap,' he said, without enthusiasm. Since his suspension pending the inquiry into his robbery of the Sav La Mar Post Office, and his subsequent acquittal, the Superintendent put him on the Crimestop desk because his presence on the street in uniform was found to be too inflammatory.

'Ya sah. Dis one citizen callin bout drog dealer dem in de parish av Anover.'

'What ya information?' *Afficer* Hibbert asked, disinterestedly, bored of the succession of interfering nobodies and malicious *liards* who were the only people to call Crimestop.

'Mi know where ya can arrest two Colombia cork dealer, two Kinston dealer and one corrupt Police,' Jimmy said.

'Dat so. Where?' Hibbert said, not bothering to stifle a yawn.

'Ya know Cove?'

Hibbert sat up abruptly. 'Cousins Cove?'

'Ya man. Go dung a Cove 'bout sunset, ya can pick dem up near the sea side. Ya kiant miss dem. Dem have one airplane at de airport dem use for smuggle cork.'

'Interesting information. How you learn bout dis?'

'Inside information. But it true.'

'May I ask your name?'

'Jost call mi a concern citizen.'

'Yes sah. Tell me, sah. You want a reward for this information receive?'

In the phone booth Jimmy smiled at Driver, put his hand over the receiver, and said, 'Dem even gonna give mi money for dis!' Into the receiver he said, 'Afficer, mi do dis far mi country, ya know? Dis country is full of drog dealer and criminal and it drag we down in de eye of de world, ya know? People inna foreign say al dem Jamaicans jost drogs dealers and bad boys and prostitute. It de job of de honest citizen, fi clean out de contagion of dishonesty and criminality, bot, bot if you want fi give mi a couple dollar for outa pocket expense and ting, dem can be mi will give it to mi ole moma, cas mi nah want nottin fi miself, bot fo him mi will trouble ya.'

'Alright. Where ya want to meet mi?'

The good thing about working in Negril was you saw plenty of new things. Candy had one of the best jobs in tourism, standing all morning waist deep in the water off Zoo, raking out the weeds so the whiteys didn't have to step on any plants when they went for a swim. He saw *ole heap o gal dem widout bra*. Bla had a good job too: wiping bar seats at Rick's Cafe in Negril when customers in damp swimming costumes got up to leave. Yvette *have* a job lowering the chain at the gatehouse of the Negril Tree House to let cars in and out. She saw some *wickid* cars in that job. The bad thing about working in Negril was you lost touch with the latest events in Cove. But when the tourism workers got back after their shift that evening, they were all brought up to date with the latest developments as soon as they stepped off the minibus, because the whole village *chat nuff bout* Jimmy and Driver *an de drogs biznis*. Sitting on the rail of porches at dusk, standing semi-naked around standpipes, and in the middle of the backstreet, people *group up fi talk pon de subject.*

Blackie's shed was a bar Vinton and Oneil built out of ironwood posts and bamboo on captured land beside Yvonne's yard. It listed heavily to the left when you stood in its doorway looking into the gloomy interior, where Blackie usually stood behind the bar in front of her stock of six Red Stripe, four Dragon Stout and half a dozen *saff drink.* She once tried to extend her lines to *tin milk, mackrel, and peanut,* but Vinton and his younger sister Amoy *nyam down all de stock* whenever her back was turned so she gave up. The bar had a bench, on which, that evening, she lay peacefully sleeping, her big shiny body rising and falling, and a stool, on which Rushton, Miss Citarra's brother, sat. Rushton was a white-haired, sleepy-faced man, whose amiable features formed easily into a one-toothed smile. Vinton, seeing the old farmer inside, pulled Oneil into the shed to tell Rushton the news. Vinton knew that Rushton was the only person who hadn't heard the story five times, on account of his acute deafness, and wanted to tell it again.

'JIMMY IN SOME DROGS BIZNIS DAT GO WRONG!' Vinton shouted.

A smile spread across Rushton's face. 'HIM DOUBLE CROSS DEM?'

'MI NUH KNOW. CAN BE. SOMETING GO BAD. MAXWELL SEE SOME HEAVY YOUT FROM KINGSTON SHOUT AT JIMMY DIS MARNING AFTER HIM COME BACK FROM INNA DE DEEP.'

'And he didn't take no bait when him and Driver go a sea, but leave it on the seashore, and never com back for it, so dem nuh fish,' interjected Oneil, though Rushton got none of it.

'DEM KILL JIMMY?' Rushton shouted happily.

'NO MAN, DEM LET HIM GO. BUT DEM WANT HIM NOW, CAS JIMMY GO A GREEN ISLAND AND RING CRIMESTOP FI TELL DEM ABOUT DE DRUGS DEALERS AND EVERYTING EXCEPT HIMSELF AND TOLD DEM FI ARREST TWO COLOMBIAN AND SEND HIM BACK DOWN. AND HIM ASK FI ONE TOUSAND DALLAR FOR HIM INFORMATION. ONE AFFICER KNOW JIMMY VOICE AND DE POLICE COM A COVE FI BEAT JIMMY. WHEN JIMMY HEAR HE RUN OFF INNA BUSH.'

Rushton was laughing at the thought of Jimmy spending a few days on the run.

'Mi kiant belive 't. Him call Crimestop and dem com after him,' said Oneil.

'Dem say now dem try fi find de cocaine inna de sea,' said Vinton wistfully, 'so mebbe somewhere out dere,' Vinton looked out to sea through the unglazed window in his mother's shed, 'there's a ole eap o' cocaine float around.'

'De yout from Kingston and de Colombia man rent all motorboat fram Sandy Bay to Green Island fi go out and look for dat coke. Can be dem will find i',' Oneil said.

'Remember dat time Maas Algy find ten fifty gallon drums of gas floating out a sea inna de deep, and bring dem all in tie wid cord behind him canoe?' asked Oneil.

'Dem find all kinda ting out a sea; one time dem find airplane,' said Vinton excitedly. It was a Cessna ditched by a drunken American smuggler on a Christmas morning ganja run that went horribly wrong.

'WHADDAT?' shouted Rushton.

'MI SAY YA CAN FIND ALL SORT O TING AT SEA.'

'YA MAN. YA NEVER KNOW WHAT YA CAN FIND PON DE BEACH,' Rushton shouted back. 'DIS MARNING MI DE DOWN DE SEASIDE EARLY AND MI FIND FOUR BAG O' BREEZE WASHING POWDER WASH UP PON

DE SAND. MI KIANT BELIEVE I'. IT MOSS BE A GIFF FRAM GOD.' Washing powder was sold cheaply at the market in transparent plastic bags.

'WHAT YA DO WID DEM?' Vinton asked.

'WHAT? WHA' YA SAY DER?'

'SO WHA' YA DO WID DEM?'

'MI TEK DEM BACK A YARD AND MI WASH FI MI CLOTHE DEM. WHAT ELSE MI GONNA DO WID DEM?'

'YA TEK UP ALL FOUR BAG?'

'Nuh shout, ya fool,' Oneil advised Vinton. 'Ya wake Blackie,' he added in a whisper.

'Ow mi gonna find out bout it if mi nuh shout, idiot?'

'AV COURSE! YA TINK MI WASTE WASH POWDER?'

'DO IT CLEAN CLOTHES?' asked Vinton, laughing.

'YA MAN, BUT DER SOMETING WRONG WID DAT POWDER. IT CLEAN GOOD, BUT IT NAH SUD, AND I' NUMB UP FI MI ARM DEM WHEN ME WASH DE CLOTHES DEM. DAT WHY SOMEBADY TROW IT INNA DE SEA.'

'YA ARM GO NUMB? OW MUCH YA USE?'

'MAYBE NEAR QUARTER POUND.'

'Jeezus,' said Oneil quietly. 'Mi kiant believe dis.'

'SO DE REST LEAVE?'

'TREE OR FOUR POUND LEAVE. BUT MI NUH WANT IT, SO MI GET RID A I'.'

'WHAT YOU DO WID I'?' Vinton and Oneil held their breaths. Vinton checked to see Blackie was still sound asleep. This wasn't the kind of thing you wanted your mother in on.

'MI DASH IT AWAY.'

'YA DASH I' AWAY? WHERE?'

'WHERE? IN DE TOILET PIT INNA MI YARD.'

Leroy Mckenzie was the biggest drugs dealer Vinton knew.

There was Lance, Cove Bug, and recently Ises in the village, but they weren't really drugs dealers, they just *hustle a couple spliff when tourist stop* and the opportunity arose. Leroy Mckenzie was a real drugs dealer. He had a Benz, and a big wall house on the hill far above Green Island Secondary. He smuggled enormous volumes of ganje, by boat and plane, and built a legitimate business on some of the proceeds, buying an 800 acre estate near Orange Bay, with its own private harbour, well out of sight of curious eyes. He planted and soon harvested rows and rows of mango, banana and coconut trees, and built two long sheds to breed chickens. He was a clever man; everyone said it. Before dealing drugs he was head of English at Green Island Secondary School, where he'd married one of his star pupils, beautiful sixteen year old Sunita, Ran of Rack Top fame's sister. He sometimes threw a *couple dallar* to the *picknee dem* playing at the pipe in Egypt when he drove up to see his in-laws behind Cove.

But Leroy Mckenzie was a ganja dealer; coke dealers were different. There was one in Negril with a sports Benz with a gold grill and mascot, and a blue neon frame around his number plate. Vinton had seen him. *Jeezus. Ya kiant believe i'. Trailer load of gold chain roun him neck, wickid watch, and choperators roun him hand and ole heap o ring, size ya kiant believe, tross mi, roun him finger and thomb dem.* With just a single piece of his jewellery, Vinton could pull every girl in Cove, except Bubbles, who at sixteen had grown so plump and beautiful it'd take two or maybe three.

'Mi gonna do a likker business, den,' Vinton said to Oneil.

Outside, in the snowy moonlight, Oneil said, 'Ya nah gonna go dung a Rushton yard?'

'Ya man. Fi sure,' Vinton said across Oneil's laughter.

'Ya gonna, ya gonna, ya gonna put fi ya hand inna Rushton do-do?'

Vinton looked at Oneil seriously.

'Not Rushton do-do?' Oneil shouted again, laughing as he staggered backwards.

'Ya know how much coke wort'?' Vinton asked.

'It nat wort dat, man. Nuttin wort dat.'

' 'Top ya noise, ya eediot. One bag o' coke, say two pound, wort ...' Vinton, having no idea, thought of the largest sum of money he hoped it was worth, and said it: '... it wort sixty US.'

'Sixty US dallar?'

'Ya man.'

Oneil laughed. 'It wort more dan dat. Come on,' he said, and headed off across the pasture towards Rushton's yard.

Vinton stopped him. 'We want one flashlight,' he said. 'Vices have one but it want one bulp.'

'Con have bulp. Vices have battery dem?'

'No. Yvonne have battery in fi her tee vee. She in Negril tonight. Mi will get de battery and de flashlight. Ya get de bulp.'

They met up on the road outside Blackie's shop, and assembled the torch, which produced a faint yellow pool of light on the tarmac.

'Give it mi,' said Vinton.

'No man,' said Oneil, laughing and running off towards Rushton's yard and *tilet pit*.

There were three sanitary sytems in Cove. Most of the *little people dem feed de crab*, that is, crouched in a thicket, or edging, or bit of bush, and afterwards covered it in leaves or the sandy soil. However, privacy was becoming harder to come by; more and more people were clearing bush and building houses. The second way was the *tilet pit*, one of which Rushton had, amongst maybe ten others; this was a two-metre deep hole covered by concrete with a small opening, on which, when no expense was spared, a wooden thunder box was poised.

The third kind was the *flush tilet*. There were only two of those in Cove: one in Chicken George's yard, which had a padlock on the outside of the door to deter toilet tourists, i.e. those many people who wanted to come and stare and wonder at a flush toilet. The other one was in Seeta's new wall house, which stood in his yard not far up the Main from Miss Citarra's. Seeta grew rich quickly, driving tourists around in his *criss* minibus. For a short while he employed Oneil to clean the minibus and his house while he was working. While Seeta was out, Oneil invited in his friends to look at Seeta's possessions, and Vinton accidentally took a photograph with Seeta's camera of Oneil with his feet on Seeta's sofa – yes, sofa, even Chicken George didn't have a sofa – watching Seeta's pornography on the video. Four weeks later Seeta *clean de film* and saw the picture. He ran Oneil out of the yard and never paid the last six weeks' money, but there was nothing Oneil could do about that. Naturally, Vinton and Oneil had closely inspected Seeta's *flush tilet* ... The flush itself, triggered by the neat little chrome *hangle*, was impressive, and they tested it so often it broke, and Oneil had to take the top off the cistern and fiddle about with it until he got it going, though it was never the same again. Both sat on it for hours but were unable to give it a full test because they couldn't relax enough on the seat to do do-do.

Rushton's *tilet pit smell rank*. It caught the boys' nostrils before they pulled back the rusty zinc door of the hut and stepped inside. The torch panned across the box sending a dozen *teenagers*, two-inch cockroaches with glistening brown backs, slyly to cover.

'Point him down der,' Oneil said, removing the thunder box.

They moved towards the hole, which Vinton grimly estimated to be about the size of his waist. The light went down the hole. Neither said anything, then Oneil hissed, 'Jeeez. Us. Chrise.'

Vinton giggled.

They saw a one and a half metre pyramid of faeces, the whole surface of which was crawling with cockroaches and maggots.

'Over dere. Dere.'

'Ya man.'

Rushton had thrown the bags in at an angle, so they were embedded about halfway down one side of the pyramid. Oneil counted them. 'One, two, tree ...'

'No,' said Vinton. 'I'll count dem. You get dem.'

Oneil laughed, 'Tree.'

'Dere is de brok one.' The torch caught the white powder spilling from a split packet. Three cockroaches investigated it with long twitching antennae.

'Cockroach coke yard,' said Oneil.

'Dem want fi party.'

'De coke can reach?'

'Dat mi nah know,' said Oneil.

'Try,' urged Vinton.

'Bwoy, ya kiant talk to ya bredren like dat!' exploded Oneil, standing back and crossing his arms. 'So why you nuh try fi reach i'?'

'Cas ya hand longerer dan fi mi hand.'

It was true; once he was the tallest gangliest *yout* in Cove, but recently it had become Hanover, and possibly western

Jamaica. That's why one of his names was Longboy. Oneil
sighed, and lay down on the floor with his head over the
hole. A cockroach sped out onto his shoulder, and then his
face, jinking to avoid Oneil's slaps and running down his
neck into his T-shirt, where it was finally flattened with a
mighty blow against his chest.

' 'Top ya noise,' Oneil shouted at Vinton, who started
giggling again.

He put his hand into the hole; more roaches jumped onto
it, but he ignored them as they scurried over his head and
across his mouth. 'Hold de flashlight steady, ya'eediot and
'top laughing. Here. One ... two ... tree ...'

Thus he recovered each bag, including the broken one.
Vinton took two of them down to the standpipe on the road
at Egypt, a minute or two away, rinsed them down and hid
them in the grass before going back for the other two. As
they gasped for breath in the fetid heat of the hut, both tried
to think only of what they would do with the money. Vinton
first imagined huge quantities of food – dumpling, roast
breadfruit, yam, and rice, all cooked by Mama who, though
hard on him, and had many times beaten him with machete
and stick, and thrown *rock stones* at him, could cook up a
plate of fry fish and rice and peas like nobody else. But he
was going to be rich. Rice? Rice was for *de likker people dem,
de sufferers, de poor people.* Rich people ate chips. He conjured up vast tables covered in Whoppers, cheeseburgers,
chicken nuggets and chips – all from Burger King Gloucester
Avenue, Mo-Bay. But then he thought of clothes: jean
trousers and shirt, matching, with pearly buttons, and Bally
shoes, or Nike, or, the very thought sent a thrill through
him as he washed a bag clean with his hand, both! He could
be the only *yout* in Cove with two pairs of shoes. And flies
with a functioning zip. Nobody in Cove had one of those.

And he could get *a socks*. But then came thoughts of girls.
If you were rich you could have a trailer load of girls. Go-go
girls, who knew how to dance; he'd keep one all for himself,
or two; he could afford it.

Oneil's fantasies ran on different lines: first he would buy
Miss Linnet, his mother, a TV and video, and a fridge
freezer if he could afford it, and afterwards some clothes for
his sisters Marvia and Marcia, and a shoes and a visit to
Dr Bury for granny. For himself, he bought a saw, plane,
tape, plumb line, hammer and set of three chisels, so he
could follow his brother Nickretta into the carpentry trade.
If you could work wood well, and quickly, you could really
make money, he thought to himself as he brought up the
last pound bag of cocaine. He then dashed to the pipe,
stripped to his underpants, and gave himself a thorough
bade with little bits of soap you can always find in the long
lush grass around a pipe. Vinton rolled Oneil's trousers and
shirt around the bags of cocaine, and walked, with Oneil
striding alongside in his underpants, back towards Blackie's
shed.

They decided to secrete the drugs in a hollow guango tree
by the pasture, and sleep close by to keep a watch out. They
were soon on the Main, feeling the warm tarmac under their
feet, when they heard an argument in progress down by the
fishing boats, deep in the mangrove trees, out of sight. But
it wasn't like a normal fight, when two people *cuss and use
bad word* with each other at the top of their voices and
everyone in earshot grouped up to listen and laugh.

It was the Colombian with the silver gun earrings. He was
shouting, but no-one was shouting back at him. The boys
crept closer through the bush to see: four uniformed *Police*,
the moustached Colombian and another Jamaican *yout* were
ducking three gasping, choking men in the shallows. Two

Police cars were pulled off the road and hidden in the bush behind them.

They heard a voice splutter, 'Please God believe we. Mi nuh touch ya cork. Mi swear i'. Mi swear i'.' There was another splash, and silence.

'Look like dem ketch Jimmy,' Oneil whispered.

'An' Driver and Driver brudder Buru,' Vinton whispered back.

The four pounds of cocaine he was carrying seemed suddenly a very dangerous load for someone with his keen sense of self-preservation. Oneil crouched down, the moon glinting on his long thigh. Vinton crouched too, and suddenly heard a loud retort, like a length of calico being ripped at speed, explode from his bottom, the inevitable consequence of a double portion of Blackie's *jack domplin, mackrel an' dasheen* hastily consumed for lunch on top of two *saff drink* and eleven ripe mangoes.

'Oo dat?' shouted one of the Police. There was silence but for Buru, Driver and Jimmy's gasping. The *Police* walked towards the boys, a flashlight glinting in his hand. 'What ya do der?' He shouted when he saw them.

'Mi a go a do-do, sah,' Vinton replied.

'Wha dat ya hold?'

'Washing far mama fi do.' Vinton held up the bundle to show the Police; a trickle of cocaine spilled from the open bag onto the ground.

'Ya Persil bag brok,' said the Police. 'Ron on now, find someplace else fi do-do.'

'Can be too late fi dat,' Vinton said under his breath.

'Ya sah,' said Oneil.

✳   ✳   ✳

The idea that night-time was for sleeping and day-time for waking never caught on in Cousins Cove. In other villages, when night fell, they climbed exhaustedly into bed and woke only at dawn. But to many men and women in Cousins Cove, dusk was the signal to get up and sample the unmissable tropical night. When the moon was bright and high in the starry sky, the opportunity for meeting members of the opposite sex to chat with and make friends with in the moonlight was too good to stay at home. People had to get out the yard and walk *up an down*. As the moon waned over the following days, and the nights perceptibly darkened, the friendships formed under the full moon were consolidated in the moonshadows, and finally consummated when the new moon set early near the end of the month, and darkness offered sweet secrecy.

During the days, Vinton and Oneil hovered always within sight of the guango tree, and at night they *chill out* under it – sleeping fitfully, waking with a start, and talking in lowered voices to friends and girls who passed by in the dark.

About every four hours for ten days, Vinton said to Oneil, 'Nah tell nobady, bout dis, annerstan? Nobady. Too much people looking for it fi take no risk.'

Oneil looked at him skeptically, knowing that it was he, Vinton, who was the big mouth.

The next day, at dusk, as the setting sun reddened the cliffs at the mouth of the cove, Trouble crossed the pasture and approached Vinton and Oneil.

'Mi can tek a look at de drog dem?' he asked Vinton.

Oneil looked at Vinton. Vinton said, 'Mi only tell him cas him can help we sell it. Ya have connection, true, Trouble?'

Fifteen year old Trouble said, 'Ya man. Fi sure. Mi have associates, ya know? Seen?'

They led Trouble to the tree. Vinton said, 'It five days since nobady see de Colombian or no Police. Even Jimmy and Driver walk up and down pon de Main now.'

Both had emerged three or four days after the beating, Driver with a limp and Jimmy with a black eye and a new name, Drogs, which everyone called out when they saw him.

'Dem nah a com back,' said Trouble, staring at the bags of coke. 'It time to market de merchandise.' He used terms he'd picked up from videos Miss Citarra watched.

'Where we gonna sell i'? Tek it a Negril?'

'No man,' counselled Trouble. 'Dem will rob you of i' and den kill ya. Sell i' here in Cove.'

'Mi kiant sell i' from Yvonne yard. She have two whities stay.'

'An' Mister Blidgen gonna kill we if mi sell drog from him yard.'

'Ya man,' Trouble and Vinton agreed. 'All o' dat.'

'Let we sell i' from fi mi yard,' said Trouble.

'What 'bout Miss Citarra?' asked Vinton.

'Tip her couple dallar, she cool.'

The following day they took a pound-bag of cocaine to the back room at Miss Citarra's, and with Craig looking on closely, and the toddlers Nakissia and Najia crawling amongst them, the three boys filled a hundred plastic bags each with about two grams of cocaine, and knotted the tops.

'How much we charge for each one?' asked Vinton.

Trouble picked a figure out of the air. 'Six US, or ninety J,' he said.

Vinton smiled and shook his head slowly from side to side as he filled another bag. 'Mi kiant believe dis. Mi gonna rich.'

For a day or two, business was slow. Ran and Babs came round, but had no money, so just stood for hours looking at the bags of coke. A couple of *yout* tried to hustle it to tourists who stopped at Joe's Coffee Shop, but they were the wrong type, and Joe told them to quit it. Then a whitey called Jared, the son of a prosperous New York businessman and poet, who had dropped out in Jamaica on a generous allowance, and who lived in a little house on some land his father had bought, was brought to Miss Citarra's house by Craig. He put a ten-inch line the thickness of a pencil out on the top of the broken television, and made all the children laugh when *him sniff it*. After that he bought three bags for cash, and left with Babs and Ran following him to his house. From then on, business picked up. Lance's elder brother stopped by in his minibus and bought a few bags to take to Negril, and he too was soon back, along with a couple of heavy *yout*, who took ten bags, and paid in US dollars. The next evening, Oneil had to run back to the tree for another *pound*. By the end of that week, people were calling at Miss Citarra's yard all hours of the day and night. She didn't mind. She loved it, and would prod Trouble or Vinton or Oneil if they were sleeping and scream at them to serve the customer.

Vinton was meanwhile also in demand at Yvonne's yard, where he was cooking, cleaning and helping out a couple of whitey tourists called Jane and Chris from London, England who rented the place from Yvonne for a couple of weeks. They looked respectable, *like Christian*, so he tried to give an impression of being reliable and uncorruptible to them, and kept quiet about the coke yard he ran on the other side of the road, that by now was never empty, because not only were people always pulling up to buy coke and drive off, but quite a few customers were living in the yard, smoking on the front porch or lying twitchily asleep by the back step *till dem spend down all dem money*. Things were so hectic that Miss Citarra only managed to keep going by stirring a tablespoon of coke into a big jug of *beveridge* – sugar and water – which she, and the *picknee*, sipped all day.

Vinton's and Oneil's coke yard was a big secret that nobody knew about except the whole of Cove and a few score others, but they were protected from betrayal because the village was proud of the huge find, and overjoyed at last to witness a commercial success within the village limits. Everybody except the Christians wanted to see it flourish, but the Christians knew better than to report them to the Police.

Chris and Jane left Yvonne's yard for the airport at the end of their holiday. They thanked Vinton for looking after them, gave him their address in London and told him to look them up if he was ever over. Having a foreign address on a bit of paper was almost as glamorous as foreign travel in Cousins Cove, so Vinton treasured the scrap, and kept it in a lada bag *inna de bush* with his few other personal possessions.

Yvonne came back wearing new clothes of stone-wash denim she'd bought with the rent money.

'Vintan,' she snapped. 'Clear up de back room and shine de flaar dem. Some guest from Kingston come fi turn in mi yard for a couple day fram tomorrow. An' rake de yard, an' ron an' buy mi one tin mackerel fram Maas Greville, an',' she added, perhaps sensing it was getting a bit harder to push Vinton around, 'tek tree dallar fram de change fi yasel.'

Later, when he was on all fours rubbing at the dyed pine floor with the coconut brush, sweat dripping off his nose, Yvonne stood watching him, greedily eating a bun and cheese. Only the thought that he had sixty US dollars hidden away, and a half share in the remaining few pounds of coke, sustained him.

'Dem say sambady buck up pon de coke dat lost,' Yvonne said as she bit off another knob of bun and cheese.

'Dat so?'

'Dat whad mi hear,' Yvonne said, her pretty mouth chewing cake. 'Ya ever hear of Telaviv posse?'

'Ya man. Everybady hear o' dat.'

'De men dat com fi stay tomorrer fram Tel Aviv. Dem want fi find who have dem coke. Dem bredren o' mine from old days. Dem heavy, man, heavy,' she added with a dreamy smile.

'Dat so?'

'Ya man, so look after dem good while dem stay in mi yard. What dem want ya give dem it. Annerstan?'

'Sure, Yvonne, no problem.'

They arrived late at night, when the village, except for Miss Citarra's yard, was silent, emerging from a blacked-out BMW wearing sunglasses, one of the bredren carrying a sports holdall. Vinton was immediately dispatched by Yvonne to wake Blackie and open up the shed for a dozen hot Dragon Stout.

'Shed close,' she shouted through her wooden wall.

'No Mumma, ya got to open up. Yvonne friend dem want couple drink.'

'Tell dem fi drink water from de pipe.'

'Mumma, dem from Telaviv posse inna Kinstan.'

There was rustling inside, and the wooden louvred shutters opened. Blackie's podgy hand held out the key to the padlock on the shed. 'Nuh touch nuttin yaself, boy.'

'Yes Mumma.'

Vinton entered Yvonne's house to see the holdall lying open on the floor, with the men sitting round oiling two handguns and *one Uzi*. He steadied himself on the lintel, and then handed out the bottles, getting no thanks, or even acknowledgement of his presence. Only Yvonne addressed him.

'Wait outside in the yard,' she snapped. 'And nuh com near de house.'

Vinton crouched beside the road thinking about the guns when a car drew up from the direction of Negril, and a guy shouted, 'Wishart de coke yard, boy?' out of the window.

'Der not no coke yard ere,' he replied, choking on the *fry fish an' buller he tief from Backie shed.* A motorbike then drew up from the other direction with four youth on it, two white and two Jamaicans. They all got off and the bike fell over, but they just laughed before stumbling across the verge to Miss Citarra's yard.

'Dat where i' is,' said the man in the car.

Vinton called out to Craig, who was patrolling the Main, despite it being four in the morning, for customers.

'Ron fetch me Oneil,' Vinton whispered to him over Mister Poole's old hibiscus hedge.

When Oneil came, Vinton told him all he had seen and heard.

'Us moss stop Citarra sell more coke straight way,' Vinton said with terror in his voice.

'Let I ron over and tell Citarra fi stop sell coke, close down de yard and cool out for a couple day till de posse ride outta town.'

'Ya tink dat kian work?'

'No, but mi kiant tink o' nottin else dat might.'

With those hopeful words Oneil slipped away into the darkness, passing the four men on the motorbike who were arguing at the tops of their voices about who could drive the fastest with them all on board.

Oneil came back with Trouble flashing his ratchet knife at his side.

'Wishart de gun men?' he shouted. 'Nobady gonna tief ya coke fram ya, Vinton! Dem try, mi cut dem troat.'

Trouble had clearly been at Miss Citarra's beverage.

'Nuh joke man,' said Vinton desperately, while Oneil tried to hold him back.

Then someone came onto Yvonne's porch.

'Ssh,' said Vinton to his friends.

'Vintan,' Yvonne whispered, sharply.

'Mi de com,' he replied, pushing Trouble behind the hedge. 'Tek dis man inna de bush and show him where fi hide him bag, and den stay wid i' until mi call ya.'

'Ya man.'

Thus Vinton led the gunman, who he heard being addressed as Fumes, into the thicket of sea grape and wist that grew up around Yvonne's yard. In a darkenened clearing he said, 'Dis place good fi hide.'

Fumes passed him the bag effortlessly, said, 'Nuh bodder de bag, and no let nobady elkse touch i', annerstan?' and then moved off silently the way he came. The bag was heavy. Vinton put it down with a muffled clinking noise on the sandy ground and crouched beside it. He could smell the gun oil. A moment later there was a rustling of the bushes and Oneil appeared.

'What Miss Citarra say?' Vinton asked.

'He gonna try fi ease back de cork deal dem.'

Vinton looked down and shook his head. 'Dis ting gonna bad,' he said.

Oneil said, 'What inna de bag?'

'Gon dem,' said Vinton.

'Gon?'

'Ya man. One tirty-eight Taurus revolver, an' a tirty-two semi-automatic, and even one Uzi.' The youth of Jamaica knew the names of all the guns.

'Why dem want one Uzi in Cousins Cove?' Oneil asked.

'Fi kill we,' answered Vinton miserably.

'Jeezus,' said Oneil slowly, as he absorbed the truth. 'So what we gonna do?'

'Dis,' said Vinton seriously. 'Load up de magazines. Mi tek de Uzi, you hangle de two pistol dem. Mi kick down de front door and squeeze off couple hundred round inna de house, and you hide roun' the back and kill anybady who run out the back door.' He looked at his wrist. He had no watch, but said, 'Al right. Synchronise watches.'

Oneil said, 'Ya idiot. How can ya joke at time like dis?'

'Mi nuh joke,' said Vinton. 'Now is time for de Cousins Cove posse fi strike back at Telaviv. Ya man. It gonna easy now us ave de weaponry.'

'Vinton mi know yah too coward fi even open up dat bag.'

'Cho! Nuh talk to de don like dat.'

'So what we gonna do?' Oneil asked again.

After a long pause Vinton said, 'Mi tink mi better try fi talk wid Yvonne. Maybe she can elp we.'

When later he tapped on Yvonne's bedroom wall, there was the sound of rustling and a man's low voice. He should have known Yvonne would *link op wid one o' de bredren*.

'Yvonne, it Vinton. Mi need fi talk wid ya.'

'Wishart de bag?' the man's voice snapped.

'Oneil watch de bag.'

There was some murmuring in the room, then the door opened and Yvonne slipped out.

When they were away from the house, standing by the lapping sea at the edge of the yard, Vinton said, 'Yvonne, ya know ya say dat somebady buck up pon de coke?'

'Ya man. Ya hear who?' she asked excitedly.

'Ya, mi know.'

'Good boy. Tell mi. 'Oo?'

'Mi an' Oneil.'

'You an' Oneil? You an' Granville?'

'Yes.'

Yvonne paused while her mind raced over the possibilities for personal gain that this intelligence presented her. Her first thought was not, it must be admitted, for the welfare of her employee and his friend.

'You an' Oneil?' she repeated.

'Ya,' said Vinton miserably, hanging his head.

'Wishart de coke?'

'Mi hide it inna one tree.'

'Good boy. Ow much ya ave?'

'Two bag and one half.'

'Ow big de bag dem?'

'Like bag o' sugar. One pound. Ya tink mi gonna dead?'

'Mebbe nat if ya do as mi say. Anybady elkse know bout de coke?'

'Ya.'

'Oneil.'

'Anybady elkse?'

'Ya man. Ole heap o' people know.'

'Bumber claat. Ya eediot, why ya tell dem?'

'Cas mi sell some o' de coke fram Miss Citarra yard.'

'Ow much ya sell?'

'Mebbe two or tree hondred US.'

'Jos a couple of gram. Dat no problem.'

'Good,' said Vinton, smiling for the first time in three hours. Then he asked, 'Ow big is one gram? Like half a bag o' sugar? Gram like pound?' But Yvonne wasn't listening.

'If ya nuh wanna dead, den bring mi all de coke and all de money. All av it, an me try fi cool out de Telaviv bredren. Gwaan now, and com back soon.'

Back in the seagrape thicket, Vinton said to Oneil, 'Ow much dallar we gonna give back?'

'Mi ave two ondred and ninety US, an six ondred J.'

'Ow much ya gonna give back?'

'What ya mean, boy? Cho! Jus do what de woman say or de don kill ya.'

'Dem nuh scare mi,' laughed Vinton. 'Mi ave two ondred and mi gonna give one ondred and ten US and couple ondred J.'

Early the next morning Vinton and Oneil were lined up in Yvonne's house in front of Fumes and his two *bredren* from the Telaviv posse. On the table that Mr Gay had made so lovingly for Olga and the kids, stood two pound bags of white cocaine. Vinton had given Yvonne two and a half, but the half bag had mysteriously disappeared. Next to the cocaine were two hundred and ten US dollars in crumpled notes. Beside that was a 9mm pistol, and beside that was Fumes' hand, ready to pick it up and use it.

'Ya want we fi believe dat ya find four bag o' coke pon de beach, and sell tree pound, dat twelve ondred gram, an get tree ondred US far it?'

'De yout one liard,' said one of the gunmen, darkly. He stood up, took the gun off the table and put it against Vinton's temple. Vinton thought to himself that he had two options: one, to bluff it out, and the other to tell the truth and beg for mercy.

'Tell de man de trut' Vinton,' Yvonne said.

Vinton thought: Come on. Be like a bad boy. Big up your status. Bluff it. But he said, 'Mi sorry sah, mi just remember mi have anudder couple dallar dat mi forget complete about. Mebbe mi kian ron an' fetch i'.'

He ran to and from his hiding place in the bush

and was soon back with the money, which he laid on the table.

The sinister small gunman laughed. 'Ya want we fi believe dat all de money ya have?'

'Ya sah. Dat all de money we take.'

'Far twelve ondred gram?' The man brought the gun up to Vinton's head again.

'Mi swear.'

'Ease up, Badeye, de yout tell de trut',' said Yvonne, with a little look at Vinton which said you are going to shine a lot floors and run a lot of errands for this.

With the exception of Badeye, the gunmen inexplicably started to laugh. Vinton was hurt. 'Why ya laugh?' he asked.

'Why we laugh? Cas ya sell out cocaine wort forty tousand dallar.'

'Ya nah have no more coke leave noplace? Nobady have no more?' asked Badeye.

Out of the corner of his eye, Vinton saw Yvonne look at him. He felt the gun jab into his side.

'None leave but dis, sah,' he said, and gave Yvonne a look which said I don't think I'll be shining quite as many floors or running so many errands as you thought.

And ya no give no money to nobady elkse?' asked Badeye.

'We give a couple dollar to Miss Citarra,' Oneil said.

'Oo dat?' they asked Yvonne.

'De lady who yard dem use over de road,' Yvonne explained.

'Ow much ya give her?'

'Mi nah remember.' Out came the gun again, this time to be pressed into Vinton's kidneys from behind. 'Two ondred and tharty US, bout.'

There was a small crowd already assembled at Miss Citarra's yard all looking for coke before Badeye strode out of Yvonne's yard and, pausing for a huge coach of tourists to roar by, trotted across the road. Craig saw the dark, oiled metal of the gun he held nonchalantly at his side, yelped 'Wickid!' and skipped along behind him.

'Wishart Miss Citarra?' Badeye shouted at the house. 'Com ya.'

'Oo want her?' Miss Citarra called from inside.

'One man 'bout a likker business.'

'Mi nah have no coke leave. Go way fram ere. Dat finish.'

'Mi know dat finish. It mi who tek i'. Now come out, mi want fi talk wid ya.'

Miss Citarra came to the door. She sweated and had to support her enormous bulk on the frame.

'Granny,' said the man, 'mi hear ya ave someting dat belong fi mi.'

'Nuh sah. Everyting mi ave, belong fi mi. Now go out mi yard yout, before mi mek ya.'

The assembled and fast-growing crowd of spectators drew in their breath with admiration. There was Craig and his sisters Nakissia and Najia, the girls with buckets of water from the pipe on their heads, there was Linda from the back street, wearing one high heel shoe and one trainer, there was Trouble, looking bleary, and Trevor looking excited, and there was Miss Liza, who stopped on the way to catch a minibus to Lucea, in addition to a few assorted coke heads. All of them saw Miss Citarra insult the gunman, and turn casually into her house, and all of them saw the gunman's face twist in fury at being *dis* by an old woman.

'Yo, Granny. Mi talk wid ya. When mi talk wid ya, nuh move off till mi tell ya. Somebady tell mi ya sell drog here.'

'Dat no concern of you,' Miss Citarra shouted from inside.

'Ya man. It is so. Cas the cork ya sell is fi mi and mi bredren cork.'

'It nuh go so, boy,' Miss Citarra answered, coming to the door again. 'Dat coke lost at sea, and somebady find i'. Mi no tief. You is de tief, come fi get mi money. But you nah gonna ave i', so ron on, ya likker man now.'

'Dat coke belong to me, so give mi mi money.' He lifted his gun for the first time.

'Ya want fi kill mi? Go on, shoot, ya blaad claat fool. Kill mi. Bot ya nah gonna get no money, cas dat belong to mi.'

Badeye started to talk, but Miss Citarra turned into her house, saying, 'Bumber claat,' and pushed the door closed behind her. Badeye lost his temper at this. He ran at the house, leapt onto the porch and burst inside after her, slipping his gun into the back of his belt as he moved. He was inside for only a moment before the crowd heard the horrible crack of fist on flesh and bone, followed by the thud of a foot well practised at brutal violence stabbing into an abdomen again and again, with sickening force. There followed the terrible sound of a body crashing heavily onto splintering furniture, and the moan that came from a spasm of tortuous pain.

Half a minute later the door opened slowly, and the hunched, groaning figure of Badeye, half crawled, and half stumbled out onto the porch. Miss Citarra appeared in the door frame, holding the gun.

'Gwaan back a Kinstan!' she shouted. 'An' nuh com back ya if ya nuh want mi fi beat ya again.'

In Yvonne's house, Fumes and his *brudder* were loading the coke and the guns into the holdall. When they heard Badeye call them, all three got into the BMW and sped out of the yard and out of Cove on the road to Mo-Bay, Ocho Rios, Fern Gully and Kingston.

Miss Citarra sold the gun to some bad boys in Negril for thirty US dollars, Yvonne sold her half pound of cocaine to the Police in Negril for one thousand US, and Vinton and Oneil spent the next few weeks in each other's company, tending to avoid their friends, with their tedious jokes about selling forty thousand US dollars of coke for three hundred dollars. One of their favourite occupations was sitting on the rocks behind Blackie's shed, staring out to sea, looking for anything small and white floating free on the water.

TUFFEE AVE A VISION

Giarbage was no problem in Cove. If you have *giarbage,* you *dash i' away inna de bush or inna de sea. Den it no prablem.* *'Cept the whitey always complain 'bout litter an' giarbage, and that make the government do someting 'bout i'.* A tourist in a *criss Rental* would pull up by Joe's bar, or Ione's shed, step out on the soft pale sand, gaze at the sparkling sea in the pretty bay with miles of wet green jungle all around him, and then notice a candy wrapper maybe the size of a postage stamp that was hidden in the grass and say to his wife, 'Can you believe this, honey? Look. Litter. How can they ruin it like this?'

But in Negril the problem got serious. The hotels were flinging their garbage into the sea, and sometimes it drifted back onto the beach right in front of the sunbathing tourists. The coloured plastic packaging looked good floating on the water, but it *vex* the tourists, and they just called it dirty. Nobody had the courage to tell them that the plastic garbage wasn't nearly as dirty as the raw hotel sewage being flushed into the sea by underwater pipe just beyond the rubbish.

The *big people dem dat own Zoo, Sclandals, Negril Tree 'Ouse* and the other big hotels found a piece of government land by the Main in Orange Bay and *mek it turn domp.* There were a few yards on it, but most of the *likker people dem* who lived in them were happy about the bounty that suddenly came their way, for the dump was a big success: *chocks* loaded with *giarbage com dung* from every hotel, restaurant and bar in Negril in the west and as far as Lucea in the east. Soon the *domp* was six chains wide and nearly a mile long, an immense, stinking, smouldering treasure trove, for the white man binned all kinds of things which were by local standards not rubbish at all. A cursory search yielded pornographic magazines, batteries that weren't flat, lada bags, books, children's toys, and razors. An hour spent in the company of the limping dogs, busy children and slow-moving adults of the tip, could be rewarded by a camera or watch, which although non-functioning, was nevertheless a prize.

The smell was not good, everybody admitted that, and it grew thicker and more noxious when the new slaughter house near Grange Hill began dumping scraps of cattle hide and rendered carcasses which festered spectacularly in the hot sun. In the heavy humidity and soaring forty-degree afternoons of the summer, the stench grew so bad people said you could see it. When the wind blew from the east, you could smell the Orange Bay dump so unmistakably nine miles down the coast in Cove that it became one of the seven wonders of the village.

High on the hill above Orange Bay there was a *criss* new housing estate for the rich people. The homes were all wall houses, with fancy concrete walls around the gardens, carports with a door that went straight into the house, and ornate wrought-iron security bars on the porch, where the big people sat to enjoy the breeze wafting off the Caribbean. Everyone said that if the smell got as far up the hill as the Orange Bay Estate the dump would be closed. It did, and no lesser man than Judge Horace Walpole led the campaign to close it. He wrote a long letter to the Gleaner, he made representations to Andy Chin, the local Member of Parliament, and attended

a special meeting of the Negril Town Council. He even rang
Barbara Gludon on JBC radio to complain about 'the deplor-
able pollution caused as a result of the instigation of an
unauthorised rubbish facility at Aringe Bay', but none of this
worked. The Negril Chamber of Commerce said that the
dump had to stay if the government wanted tourism to increase in western Jamaica. As the tourist industry was the
only thing keeping Jamaica from absolute bankruptcy, nothing was done. The *domp* grew and grew, and smelled worse
than ever, so bad, in fact, people were forced to invent a new
word to describe it. They stopped saying, 'Dat domp smell
bud,' and said instead, 'Dat domp green, man. It green bud.
Serious. It greeeen.'

Right on the top of the hill, some quarter of a mile above
the big people's housing estate at Orange Bay, lived Leroy
Mckenzie, the biggest ganje dealer in western Jamaica. He
built an ornate white concrete house with four balconies
and dozens of yards of concrete balusters. There was a
swimming pool full of his fat children and extensive grounds
patrolled, they said, by armed *bredren* of the Don. When
the stench reached Mckenzie he spoke to the Negril Chamber
of Commerce. They explained once again the impossibility
of moving the dump or closing it down. He spoke to them
again. The next week news came through to the people that
the *domp* was moving.

The question was where would the *domp* go? There were
certain limitations: it had to be on the Main, or near it, and
could be no further than twenty miles from Negril. The
Negril Chamber of Commerce identified various pieces of
land: and each time a place was mentioned, the *people dem
rise op gainst i'*. Little London was suggested and then
dropped, because of local opposition, and then Green Island
was identified. Every other village supported this idea, if only

to prevent the dump coming their way. 'It moss be Green Island.' Vices argued in Cousins Cove. 'Consider de name. The place call green cas it gwine green.' But Dr Bury, who owned the land in Green Island, and who negotiated a lucrative rent for the site, had his yard surrounded by furious villagers and was forced to drop the project for his own safety.

The next place they picked was Cousins Cove, but at dawn, the day after the rumour swept through the village, Blackie and Miss Citarra formed a roadblock on the Main with the eight *picknee* from their yards. The roadblock was considered the basic democratic right in Cove, more basic than voting, which only people who could read and write got to do. But anybody could form a roadblock, and many did, because only if you stopped the traffic did the *big people dem* listen. Although Miss Citarra and Blackie and Trouble tipped over trash cans, and burned tyres on the road, stopping all the traffic, they were only actually after one car, a black Toyota Landcruiser which came through every morning at seven twenty, driven by Mr Dunbar McFarlane, a member of the Negril Chamber of Commerce.

When Craig ran down the line of cars to the barricade shouting, 'Mumma, him a com, him a com,' the two women whose combined weight was thirty-seven stones, or 518 pounds, bore down on the poor man, who quickly pushed down the lock on his car door when he saw them. Half the crowd didn't know what the issue was about, and the other probably wouldn't have minded the *domp* anyway, but after a swift discussion with the two women, Councillor McFarlane agreed to keep it out of Cove all the same.

Cove had no official council, or instrument of local government with any influence whatsoever. Village government was undertaken entirely unofficially only when it was needed, by anybody who could be bothered to do it – like

Blackie and Miss Citarra with the road block. In Lances Bay things were run differently. They had a parish council, with a sub-committee for economic development, and they had an active Rotary Club and Kiwanis Club, all of which had the main aim of developing Lances Bay, because Lances Bay was determined to go places. This is how, against the wishes of *de mijarity av de likker people*, Lances Bay made a formal request to the Negril Chamber of Commerce for the *domp*. The terms were straightforward: in return for a mile of tarmac road up into the hills, the electrification of thirty houses above the Main, and a rent of thirty thousand J a year, they were prepared to fill up a long undisturbed gully half a mile long and three hundred yards deep, thick with mighty cotton trees, and harbouring a clear-water stream, with the hotel rubbish from Negril.

Councillor Harold Hoyte (chairman of Rotary Club, Kiwanis Club and the Lances Bay Masonic Chapter), with the deputy chairman of the Lances Bay Parish Council, The Honourable Mrs Shirley Hoyte, resident magistrate, proudly made the announcement of the successful bid for the *domp*, at a specially convened meeting in the Lances Bay Primary School.

'This development is a major step forward for our community,' said the Councillor, to a round of appreciative applause from the seated, and hatted, burghers of Lances Bay. But at that, from the back of the hall a bare-chested rastaman with long locks and sleepy eyes called out, 'Dis one fool ting. Ya nah fill de land av Jah wid pollution fram de white man, or Jah com down and seek retribution wid one tundebult or eart quake or orricane dat will smite ya dead.'

''Top ya noise, Tuffee,' somebody shouted. 'We want corrent in fi we yard for teevee and fridge. We want our village to get rich. If ya nah like i', den bwai, gwaan fram ere.'

'Ya man!' a few people yelled, laughing. 'Ya want to poor al ya life ya eedit dread?'

'Money is not my richness,' Tuffee declaimed at the voices railing against him. 'My richness is to live and walk pon the earth barefoot.' This brought a gale of derision from the *baldead* standing around him. At that, he picked up the rod he was never without, hoisted his bag onto his shoulder, and with his head held proudly high, he started his walk back to his yard, high in the hills, overlooking the gully which the Parish Council were going to fill to the brim with *giarbage.*

The majority of land in Cove was owned by Mr Webster, who had a family of children whom he loved, but who, it turned out when he died, inexplicably left all his lands to the lawyer who made his will, a man of Asian extraction who resided in Canada. When squatters, led by Miss Citarra, became recalcitrant, he sold it in a job lot to a white man whom Yvonne cleverly brought to Cove from the beach in Negril. He had little idea of the political powder keg he was buying.

Only one section of the coast wasn't owned by Mr Webster, and that was an exquisitely beautiful strip of land on the western side of the cove, across the creek from Blackie's shed and Yvonne's yard. When you walked through the woods to the sea you came upon a lagoon perfect for swimming, flashing with tropical fish that darted into caves hollowed by the crystal sea out of limestone cliffs. This plot fell into the hands of a Chinese–Jamaican business man called Mister Ronny. Everybody in Cove had big plans, and Mister Ronny was no exception. People hoped he was going to build a sky-scraper hotel with *one big car park,* but he went one better than that: he was going to flatten the forest to build a container port, complete with warehousing and cranes, and dynamite the coral reef at the mouth of the cove to form a deep water harbour for freight shipping. For days they bragged about their luck up and down the Main. Even Trouble, who had relocated to Negril, and had lately been scorning Cove whenever he returned on a visit, had to admit the plan was *wickid.*

Cove engendered great plans, schemes big enough to lift the place out of the ranks of other sleepy fishing villages and transform it into a top resort, where tourists milled about in hundreds, carelessly throwing bucks around. Ran's Rock Top Cave was planned to be a Dunn's River Falls, but no-one ever came to the smelly dank cave and the sign went mouldy and fell off the tree. A German called Hojan built and opened a huge and ugly restaurant called The Poseidon, but its massive car park grassed over with disuse and the place closed down. If only half the plans came off, Cove would be like Negril, or Ochi, but unfortunately none did, and the cafes, sheds and bars remained determinedly empty, the *fry fish and bammy and bon and cheese* in the glass showcases consumed only by the people who made them and their friends, while all day and all night hissing coaches full of tourists roared by on their way to and from the airport.

Mister Ronny's surveyor and builder spent two days surrounded by *picknee* on Mister Ronny's land, planning the container port. They discovered the sea had undermined the rock and made it unsuitable to build heavy structures on, so the whole scheme was scrapped. Mister Ronny put the land up for sale and began to look elsewhere to locate his container port. Chicken George was going to offer him fifty acres he owned, until it was pointed out that land without sea frontage wasn't very useful for a port.

Mister Blidgen, who had hoped to be a subcontractor on the wharf, said, 'Seem like nottin never gwine big up Cove now,' and talked of leaving the village where he was born and raised fifty years earlier. Only the two German men who netted little tropical fish from the reef for exports to pet shops in Germany, and who had built a big house on the hill on the proceeds of the business, were happy that the project had fallen through.

Mister Ronny's land was finally sold to a bond dealer from New York called Kevin who wanted to quit the city and start a new life. Kevin was a stocky man of thirty-five who wore a bandana, combat fatigues and had an abiding interest in guerilla warfare and the art of survival in the jungle. He cut a clearing in the forest and erected a palisade of sharply pointed staves, as if at any moment he was going to be attacked. Behind the staves he lived a manly existence amongst his tools, bedding down in a hammock slung across the inside of a camouflaged tent.

One day, while sawing down trees on the edge of his property he came upon a small encampment made by Tuffee, the dreadlock who had fled the *domp* in Lances Bay. There was a rough bed made of old sugar sacks under a cane trash lean-to, and a wooden bench by a fire that burned on a mound of ash two feet high. Tuffee looked up from the fire and saw Kevin crashing through the undergrowth with a machete in his hand and a combat knife strapped to his shin.

'What the hell are you doing here? This is my property. Get off it.'

Tuffee took a long pull on the brown paper spliff he held in his hand, and then passed it to Kevin, bidding him sit down.

'No way man,' Kevin snapped angrily. 'I gotta sort this situation out. You're squatting on my property.'

'Den mi will pick up mi bag and rod and go. Bot first let we smoke a spliff of ganje, far de Lard say "He causeth the grass to grow far de cakkle, an' herb far de service of man, that he may bring forth food pon dis eart'".'

'That's the bible, right?'

'Ya man,' smiled Tuffee, holding out the spliff, 'so let we give tanks and do de Lard's work.'

Kevin took the spliff and settled beside the fire, watching the thin plume of blue smoke rise up into the jungle canopy.

'You got too much ash on that fire. It's gonna clog the flames. You wanna clear it out, or better still construct a concrete incinerator. Then you'll get an efficient fire without any heat wastage. Plus you can throw trash on it.'

'Dis flame never out, day and night dis fire burn for Jah. An' mi never put no trash on i', only logwood and can be ganja ash, not cigarette or no plastic or nottin unrighteous. Dem tings Babylarn. Den de ground and de bush and de air, and maybe de people,' here he gave Kevin a distant, but winning smile, 'take good vibes from de fire. Mi ave one vision from Jah, and Jah tell mi fi com down a sea an' burn logwood trough de day and night, and ya haffi live ya vision.' His head then disappeared from view behind a huge white cloud of exhaled ganja smoke.

'This herb tastes good,' Kevin remarked.

'Yah man, herb is the healing av de nation, ya know? Herb like fruit. Keep you healty, mind clear, a true.'

'Ya man,' agreed Kevin.

'The more people smoke, the more Babylarn fall.'

They sat in silent contented contemplation for an hour and three quarters, which was a short while by Tuffee's standards. Kevin's stoned head spun with a vortex of non-sequential thoughts along with the sight of the shirtless dreadlock beside him, his matted brown hair cascading down his muscled brown back. High above them, a flock of green parrots screeched amongst the shards of sunlight in the dark canopy. Kevin had planned to 'drop' these trees with one of his buzz saws, for 'security reasons'. They impeded 'clarity of vision'. But sitting with Tuffee by the fragrant hardwood fire he felt that perhaps he would put off the job till another day. It was the first time in two weeks he had stopped strutting about with a weapon of some sort in his hand, and contemplated where he was.

Later, Tuffee explained to Kevin that Jah had sent him a second command in another vision: to build a tourist bar on Kevin's plot of land. Incredibly, Kevin listened carefully, and said, 'Well I guess if Jah told you to, we'd better get on and build it.'

Kevin loved construction, but it was obvious from the beginning that he hated tourists – he wasn't that keen on people; the palisade of sharpened stakes was hardly a welcome mat, after all, but he was charmed by Tuffee, whose rastaman ways cast a spell over him. The tourist coaches, which were audible from his property, got on his nerves. Like a lot of foreign white people in Jamaica, Kevin felt he wasn't a tourist, and thought that the presence of other tourists devalued his own experience, which he considered authentic, while theirs of course was phoney and commercialised.

He imported a lot of expensive woodworking machines

from the States, like computerised lathes and turning machines, and Tuffee brought down some dread *bredren* from *inna de hills* to work them. Within a couple of months all the machines were broken, but by then a large circular bar had been built, full of hardwood chairs and tables, at which the dreads lounged comfortably for most of the day.

In addition to the heavy machinery and tools, Kevin imported a stencil set, with which he set to work making a lot of off-putting signs for his customers. There was a fine tradition of signage in Cousins Cove. Every one of Cove's tourist atractions and businesses was signed on the Main; indeed, the sign was the most important part of the enterprise in Cove. For some, a bar or some other flimsy attraction was merely an excuse to design, commission and erect a sign. There were twelve signs on either side of the Main in Cousins Cove Bottom Side. Coming from Mo-Bay, the first was Hojan, the German's sign for The Poseidon Bar Restaurant and Grill. The bar went bust within three months of opening – a real success story for Cove, but the sign lived on for years, its rather deformed porpoise flapping in the breeze for months before finally being recycled as a table top by Roddy Perry. His SUNSET BAR AND VILLAS AND RESTROOM sign, in bright yellow with black writing, was the next sign. From then on, they came thick and fast. RAN'S ROCK TOP CAVE started off quite small, but when the business failed to attract tourists, instead of examining the disgusting state of the cave, which was used by all Ran's staff as a latrine, he did what every struggling business in Cove did: increase the size and claims of his sign. His new one was two metres square, and read STOP AT WORLD FAMOUS RAN'S ROCKTOP CAVE TOURIST SPOT COACHES WELCOME. It drew in no more customers, but was much admired by the village, and *did big up Ran's status.*

The next sign, a few hundred yards on, was opposite Driver's shed. It was a small metal government one on a pole that had read NARROW BRIDGE, but was painted over by Driver to read COOL BEER. It goes without saying that in Driver's shed there was no beer cooler than the tropical climate, but nevertheless the sign did make tourists stop in Cove because it dramatically increased the number of collisions on the river bridge, so it was considered a tremendous success. Joe's Coffee Shop had three signs, advertising fresh orange juice, fried fish and coffee, at various points over the next fifty yards, and then beyond him, as the road rose and began to leave Cousins Cove Bottom Side there was a *criss black and white* sign for Blackie's Shed, that read PLEASE REPLACE ALL DIVOTS, which Byron had found floating in the sea near the big Tryall Hotel golf course in St James, and another, past Yvonne's yard, which Trevor and Oneil put up which said ONE STOP COOL DRINK FISH LUCKY STRIKE TOURIST VIEW POINT. This sign represented a new development in the Cove business community: it was a stand alone sign, with no business of any kind attached to it. Much admired, it gave its owners all the kudos and fun of having a sign without any of the hard work, worry and of course cost, of actually running a commercial enterprise.

To these signs Kevin added many more. Tuffee wanted to open the bar before it was finished, but Kevin said, in an early indication of disinterest in actually serving any customers, that nobody should be allowed in until all the building and landscaping was completed. This dumbfounded Tuffee, who could see how adequate the facilities were and how beautiful the gardens were looking. Often, if the palisade gate was left open accidentally, passing tourists, seeing the delightful location, pulled over and wandered in asking if it were possible to get a drink and have a swim in the lagoon. Kevin always chased them out rudely. There was another problem attached to waiting until the building was completed, as far as Tuffee was concerned: no building project in Cousins Cove had ever been completed, by anybody.

A name for Tuffee and Kevin's bar, Rainbow Circle, came to Tuffee in another vision from Jah. Kevin produced a huge six-colour sign to hang outside the pallisade, as well as many smaller ones for erection within. Four, on the Main, read DO NOT PARK HERE, and one over the doorway read WATCH YOUR STEP. It might have been meant figuratively, but there was actually a small and undangerous step down on the path below it. Inside, were many more: DO NOT PASS THIS POINT. NO LITTER. NO IDLERS. NO FOOD OR DRINK IN THIS AREA. NO CHILDREN. Had Tuffee been able to read them, he would have been dismayed, but as he couldn't, he loved them. Encouraged, Kevin made more signs: when Tuffee built a handsome mahoe and cedar bench overlooking the lagoon, a *flex* spot to sit and watch the sun drop into the sea at sunset, Kevin added the final touch: a painted sign saying DO NOT SIT.

Tuffee managed eventually to persuade Kevin to open the gates to customers, if only for limited periods. Kevin tried to close the place between the months of November and May, i.e. the tourist season, 'for maintenance', but Tuffee played his trump card, and said Jah had sent him a vision in which Rainbow Circle was open all year round. Kevin then tried to restrict the hours of opening, 'for security reasons', but could only enforce them while he was present. When tourists did turn up, he couldn't deny they were open and resorted to other off-putting techniques. He'd hand out menus saying things like, 'Oh, by the way, everything's off,' or 'I don't advise the fish, the chef got food poisoning from it last night. Well, we think it was the fish, it could have been the chicken or the vegetarian dish. From the vomit all over the kitchen sideboard it looked and smelled like fish.'

Outside the palisade, where the *likker people dem of Cove group up inna de shade of de guango fi watch proceeding*, a debate about Tuffee was well advanced. People had seen him arrive with his rod and shoulder bag from Lances Bay and set up camp beside the sea, and presumed he was a *rental dread* trying to *capture land* from Mr Ronny. Except there was something special about him: he had cursed Lances Bay, a whole village. Even if the curse was empty, it was impressive enough, for words really meant something in Cove.

Maxwell, who had spent time staring at the logwood fire with Tuffee before Kevin turned up, was the only inhabitant of Cove to admit to liking Tuffee. Idling with Driver in the shade of the long-armed guango tree, he said, 'Nuh mock de dread,' when Driver *dis* Tuffee.

'Ya man,' said Driver. 'Mi like all colours. We all de same. Black, white, whatever. Cept rastafarians, wid dem lang hair and beard. Me don't like dem, man. Dem wortless. For sure.'

'No man, rental dread wortless, who take coke and tief white wooman monny,' argued Trevor. 'But Tuffee not rental. Him bongo dread. Him nyam only ital food and burn logwood fire all trough de night. Ya haffi respec Tuffee. Serious man. Him ave one vision from Jah dat tell him fi build one tourist bar in Cove.'

Driver laughed at that.

'Nuh laugh, man,' warned Trevor. 'Nuh mock de dread. Him cast spell pon Lances Bay.'

'And what happen to Lances Bay after him cast him spell?' Driver spat. 'Eh? Mi tell ya what. Nottin. Jah don't send no rental dread no vision. Him just tell Kevin dat fi get one job.'

'No man. Him say monny is nat him richness.'

That made Driver laugh, long and loud, and all the other people who were listening, Michael, Squeecher his brother, Sophia and Oneil, laughed too.

Kevin had to make a trip back to the States for a hair transplant to cure his baldness, about which, you could tell from the bandana, scarves and large assortment of hats he sported, he was tortuously self-conscious. Of all his problems, it was the one he need not have worried about: in Jamaica there was no distinction made between short hair and pattern baldness. Both are called *bald ead*. Kevin could not have picked a country where baldness had less of a stigma attached to it. To many Jamaicans baldness had a cachet; it meant you could afford *fi trim at de barber*. One entertainer even boasted about it, calling himself Shinehead. So many people shaved their heads nobody even noticed who couldn't grow hair, and certainly nobody cared. There was not even a word for baldness, it was so inconsequential. Still, Kevin went to the States for his hair transplant, dreaming perhaps of returning two weeks later with locks like Tuffee's.

While he was away, the gates of Rainbow Circle were thrown open, and the place filled with curious, slightly nervous tourists, who swam, drank, and just *chill out* with Tuffee. He loved working as a waiter. He had difficulty understanding the whities' English but that didn't matter. Dreads did not need to know English; it only diminished their mystery and exposed them to difficult and searching questions about their religion and lifestyle. Tuffee just *laugh an' chill an say ya man, ya man*, until it was obvious he'd said the wrong thing, and then he *say nor man, nor man*. Seduction of tourists by rastas more often than not turned on some kind of misunderstanding, and had both sides been able to understand each other fully, would never have occurred so frequently. The fact is, and this was what *vex bald ead bud, de white gal dem love de rastafarian.*

Rasta is a religion for the twenty-first century. It has all the ingredients for huge growth in post-Christian times. With no written rules or formal church structure anybody could define what it involved without fear of being wrong. From the start, it was the perfect religion for people who no longer wanted to be in a flock. All of its adherents were archbishops in the matters of liturgy and theology. Yet in addition to this, Rastafarianism had all the conventional components of a world religion, starting with a magnetic and charismatic messiah, Emperor Haile Selassie, the coolest black man in sixteen centuries, who stared out of his portraits with a lot of attitude, wrapped in a leopard-skin stole. The religion's St Paul was Marcus Mosiah Garvey, the man who roared, 'Rise up you mighty people!' and inspired black people all over the world, before the white man jailed him, and as hymnographer there was Bob Marley, the man whose blood was made of equal parts of *riddim an' love.* He was the only musician, black or white, who had not made one bad record. On top of this, Rastafarianism had a few additional features suited to the modern era – it was a religion that had its own haircut: dreadlocks, the first black hairstyle white people were really jealous of, and incapable of having themselves. And of course, uniquely, it had its own drug: ganja. And it was a good drug, the best drug; probably the only drug in the world, pharmaceutical or recreational, whose reputation was improving with time.

When the tourists came into Rainbow Circle, Tuffee moved amongst them bare-chested, his sun-drenched locks cascading down his slender back. Sometimes he would get high and *kick back* with a nice white girl beside the lagoon. There was one beauty who kept returning to Rainbow Circle called Julia, for whom it was particularly wicked to play hookey and lie beside a semi-naked rasta while the rest of her class were back at her private school in Connecticut. Tuffee once spent an hour and a half with her watching the green parrots in the forest canopy, and would have spent longer except he suddenly remembered he had taken a food order from a table of eight tourists and had forgotten to go by the kitchen to inform the chef.

When Kevin came back after the operation, Tuffee showed him the tin of bank notes he had collected in his absence, but Kevin was *vex*. He took particular exception to Julia, whom Tuffee had installed in his rastaman hut on the cliff edge above the lagoon.

'She godda go. Today,' he told Tuffee. 'I mean, you never said anything about having strangers hanging round the property day and night. I'd never have agreed to that. Never.'

'She nuh stranger, Kevin. She cool. She cook and wash and help wid every likkle ting. Come and meet her. You like her.'

'I don't even want to say hello. I know her type. Just get her ouda here, okay? And close the gates. We don't open for another six minutes.'

Kevin brooded alone in his bunkhouse with his mirror, appalled by the unnatural furrows of hair planted on his scalp. On the third day he emerged from the toolshed with the largest of his three buzz saws and, strapped ten feet up the big guango tree, began to sever the upper branches of the beautiful, noble tree. It was a tree old enough to have given shade to resting slaves; its generous crown spread not only over the customers at the bar and restaurant, but also out over the palisade to the Main where they gave cool shade to anyone idling on the Main between eleven and three-thirty. Tuffee woke when he heard the sound of the

chain biting into the wood and came out to ask what was
going on.

'Kevin. Com dung man from up der. Nuh chop down
dat tree. It give shade for we fi live in. It Jah tree. Ya kiant
kill dat, man.'

'Don't you listen to the radio? There's a hurricane forecast.
Hurricane Frederick. When a hurricane comes it's standard
procedure to pollard the biggest trees so they don't get
uprooted, that way they grow back after the storm has
passed. It's standard US Army procedure. It's in the US
Army field survival manual.'

'Dat one fool ting, Kevin. Mi never hear nobody do dat.'

'Sure. The US Army's wrong, of course it is, Tuffee. I
mean what do they know compared to you? I mean they
only have the most advanced data and technology, not to
say experience, in the whole world. But they are wrong. Of
course. That must be it,' he said, yanking the cord on the
saw.

'Bot Kevin. Everytime dey say horrican come on de radio
it alway turn back. Alway, an' it never com to Jamaica.'

'This wasn't a local news item. This was a report from
the Caribbean hurricane tracking centre,' he shouted over
the idling buzz saw.

'Ya kiant believe dat man pon de radio. Nobady know
where a horrican go. Only Jah know dat, man.'

Kevin laughed sarcastically. 'The hurricane tracking centre
is in Miami. That's the US. They use a satellite. I don't mean
to mean to be rude about Jah, but when it comes to the
prediction of hurricane movements, he don't know shit
compared to a twenty million buck satellite.'

'Dat Babylarn, dat satellite, dat spy biznis. Nobody can
know de wedder bot Jah.'

'Yeh, sure, well don't believe it if you don't want to. You're the one who's gonna get killed by a falling tree in a hurricane, not me, thanks. Haven't you ever heard of your own Minister for Disaster Preparedness?' It was a portfolio in the Jamaican Cabinet that Kevin approved of. 'I just heard him on the radio, man. He was on JBC half an hour ago warning the whole island about Frederick.'

'It never gonna com, man. It alway turn back ...'

But Kevin pulled the ear protectors round his head and proceeded to slide the screaming chain into the trunk of the mighty tree. After half an hour's cutting, and another twenty minutes of hammering wedges into the incision, the top of the old tree gave a horrible groan, and then a cry, before crashing down into the undergrowth behind the bar. Kevin ran over to the felled timber, climbed up on it, like a hunter on a rhino, his buzz saw in his right hand, wiping sweat from his big brow with the back of his left hand before resting it on the machete in his belt. To some frightened tourists who came up from the lagoon to see what the commotion was, he explained about dropping trees: 'You drop something big like this, you don't feel like doing it again in a hurry, you know? It's like every time I kill a fish scuba-diving. I don't feel like killing for a few days after. I mean like you do all the butchering, tearing out the guts and vital organs, and so forth, and you're, you're ... I'll tell you one thing, you really get to know a fish when you kill it, and you really get to know a tree when you drop it ...'

The tourists were soon driven back to the lagoon, and Kevin walked bow-leggedly to the bar looking for some shade to drink a beer in, as the place where he normally sat was now blasted by the brightness of the mid-morning sunlight. While gulping his Heineken, the radio on the counter broadcasted an update on hurricane Frederick: the alert was downgraded as Frederick was blowing itself out west of the Caymans, and was now no longer a threat to Jamaica.

Tuffee refused to burn any of the felled wood on the sacred fire because it was against his religion.

'Where does it say that in the bible?'

Tuffee took a long toke on his spliff, and blew out the bluey-grey smoke in twin horns from his nostrils. 'It written, Nuh cast unrighteousness pon de eart or pon de flame, for de lard Jah will cast ya inna de bottomless pit,' he said, proving himself to be, by the standards of his religion, a Biblical scholar.

'Look Tuffee,' Kevin said, 'I think it would be better for both of us if you thought about moving on from here. Okay?'

But the very next day, Kevin told Tuffee he could stay.

Some tourists came in that afternoon and asked Tuffee what had happened to the decapitated guango tree.

'Dat orrican damage,' Tuffee answered.

'Really?' they answered. 'Wow! We never heard you had a hurricane.'

'Orrican Frederick,' Tuffee said. He could see Kevin listening while changing a tyre on his jeep.

'Did it do a lot of damage on the island?'

'None at all, man,' said Tuffee shaking his head. 'Dis only damage it do.'

Kevin threw down a spanner and stomped off into the bunkhouse.

Later, coming up behind Tuffee as he meditated *pon de sunset* Kevin said, 'I changed my mind. You better go. You better leave. I mean if you like to make jokes about me to customers on my own property, you know. It's not cool any more. You can stay tonight, okay, but put that fire out and be gone by tomorrow night.'

Tuffee replied to Kevin, 'Ya kiant order mi fram dis land.

Dis land a fi mi now. Mi work pon it and live pon it and sweat pon it and dat mek it mine. Ya kiant mek mi go. Only Jah can mek mi go.'

When word of this exchange got to the street, Driver said to Maxwell, 'Tuffee try fi get monny fram Kevin. Just like mi say. Didn't mi say dat?' He turned and appealed to Rushton, who heard nothing but said, 'Ya man.'

Trevor said, 'Tuffee tell mi dat monny nat him richness. Him one bongo dreadlocks man, believe mi.'

Tuffee refused to leave Rainbow Circle. A few weeks later, to break the deadlock, Kevin offered Tuffee money. He said he could have 50 US if he went, but Tuffee said, 'Mi nuh one prostitute, Kevin. Dis ting wort more dan money.'

'Well whadya want?' asked Kevin, touching the top of his head to check the implants, some of which were septic.

'Mi nah want monny. Mi want fi stay where Jah tell mi fi stay.'

But nobody except Maxwell believed Tuffee, because people wanted rastamen to be hypocrites, and people said, when they talked about it, which was often because everyone was interested, 'Tuffee believe him can get more dan fifty US fram Kevin.' And whether or not they were right, Kevin raised his offer, in units of 40 US, to 170 US. Everytime Tuffee *walk pon de street* the people would hail him up and say, 'Yo, dread. Dat ole eap o monny Kevin a give ya. Tek it while ya can, ya know?'

'Mi know it plenty dollar. Bot what need mi av US? All mi need is air fi breathe and food and water fi live. Jah a tell mi a build Rainbow Circle. Ongle Jah can mek mi go.'

On the day he raised his offer to 200 US, there was another hurricane warning on the radio. Kevin heard that there were some whities over at Yvonne's taking elaborate precautions, as per the Minister for Disaster Preparedness's instructions on JBC. At the edge of Yvonne's yard a crowd grouped up to laugh at the whities taping windows, packing their clothes and filling all the water receptacles. Kevin pushed his way through the crowd to set the whities right, but by the time he got back to Rainbow Circle he had to admit the weather looked unusual. There was the warmest, most humid wind he'd ever known, and the sea looked unusually predatory.

Kevin tuned in to the Minister for Disaster Preparedness, but the one disaster the Minister hadn't prepared for, a direct hit on the Ministry by a hurricane, had occurred. The antennae, telephone and power lines were swept off the Ministry's roof, and nothing more was heard of the Minister for Disaster Preparedness for three days, by which time Hurricane Gilbert had struck the island and long since left.

Hurricane Gilbert stalked along the spine of the island, taking only six hours to decimate the entire country. After it passed, Vices estimated that it left only nine unbroken panes of glass in the whole of Jamaica. It arrived in Cove at about sunset, though the winds had been ferocious for a few hours before then, bending trees back and forth and making the fronds of coconut palms resemble hair underwater. Kevin left the corner of the creaking, moaning bunkhouse to see if it looked like any trees were going to crash down onto the roof. He saw bits of corrugated zinc, torn from the roof of Ione's shed, fly at sixty-five miles an hour in the gloom down the road towards some children who were still out having fun in the gusts. He looked at his enormous guango tree stump, and made a mental note to point out to Tuffee how well it fared in the storm.

A few hours after dark, the wind doubled and then trebled again in ferocity. The bunkhouse squealed and groaned, the walls puffing out and squeezing in. Up on the hill, Mr Blidgen, seeing his roof coming loose, tied one end of a thick rope to a rafter, the other round his waist, and braced himself in a doorway to hold it down. With an almighty scraping and ripping sound the roof came away and lifted Mr Blidgen, his legs kicking madly, up into the air. He landed thirty yards away from the house and was dragged seventy yards more through mud and brush before the rope finally snapped. He scrabbled away to safety, and his roof flew up into the sky twisting and turning like burnt paper over a bonfire.

Miss Citarra was old enough to have seen and remembered Hurricane Charlie in 1955, so she knew the correct form. You had to do three things: first, she prayed to *the Lard Gad almighty far deliverance*; second, without delay, she escorted her six dependant *picknee* to Cove Primary School, and third, she immediately set off on foot with Trouble to Green Island to loot a fridge freezer from Barry Lee Shung's hardware store.

Kevin left the bunkhouse at four a.m. for an inspection. He stood in his doorway, terrified. The wind by now was absolutely non-negotiable; outside if it didn't kill you it was only because you were lucky. The guango stump he had so carefully pollarded was flattened. Beside it, the circular bar and restaurant was blasted into a thousand splinters, most of which were travelling at speeds over one hundred and ten miles an hour to Negril. The wind was so implacable it even bent the government road sign (the one that said COOL BEER) that was made of steel and offered almost no wind resistance.

The pounding eased back at dawn, and as the light grew, stunned and dishevelled people came out to see the damage. Many wept to see their houses vanished and their yards flattened.

Mr Blidgen and Miss Linnet stood, stunned, in front of the pile of splintered timber strewn across their yard.

'De lard send dis fi ponish we far our sin dem,' Mr Blidgen declared.

Miss Linnet, looking at the devastation, thought, 'Mi never sin dis moch. Why de Lard ponish mi? And why de Lard let Jimmy house stand but blow our house to West-morland? Jimmy sin plenty. Plenty.'

All over Jamaica, millions and millions of tears were shed, but in Cove at least, there was also some laughter.

Miss Citarra failed to loot a fridge freezer from Lee Shung, but got a microwave instead. She staggered back to her yard, where Yvette was picking up splinters of house.

'Momma, de house mash op.'

'No worry bout dat, gal. Look what mi get wid Trouble. One teevee.'

An animated group of Seventh Day Adventists *group up* in front of the Jehovah's Witnesses' Kingdom Hall, which, before Gilbert, was a huge proud structure forty feet tall, and after, an L-shaped fence three foot high.

'De Kingdam all mash op, man,' they said to each other, all laughing. 'De lard com and dash i' away.' More laughter. 'Dem nah gonna build back dat for monts. Look a' i', it al brok dung, every board and every zinc is gone. Mi kiant believe i'.'

'Ya haffi laugh!' screeched a big fat lady, a pillar of Seventh Day Adventism. 'Ya haffi laugh.'

Some places were inexplicably spared, and left completely untouched, as though the storm had a sick sense of humour. Blackie's bamboo shed stood exactly as it had before the hurricane, with even the half consumed *saff drink* that Amoy put down to pick up her most valued possessions, her school books, before her flight to Cove Primary, still standing on a windowsill no wider then two inches.

The worst hit village was Lances Bay. So there was something to cheer up the *likker people dem of Cousins Cove*. The hills above and around Lances Bay were stripped of every square inch of vegetation. Every single wooden house was shredded or flipped over and left in the mud, and those which were concrete were flooded by the overflowing river and filled with mud and pulped vegetation. Of the newly installed electricity poles nothing remained except odd lengths of high voltage cable tangled around the legs of broken goats and cattle.

In Cove it looked bad enough, as though a war had blown through, not a storm; and in the days that followed, displaced refugees, feeding stations, and queues for food and water became commonplace. Kevin loved it. He strutted around topless with his chainsaw in one hand, a dagger strapped to his shin and a machete in his belt. For a brief few days he forgot about the mess on his scalp.

Low-flying aircraft dropped food by parachute which was distributed to the villages. Cousins Cove Bottom Side got a pallet of 144 tins of French snails well past their sell-by date. Vinton hungrily opened them up and *nyam* one.

'Can go on,' he told Oneil and Trevor, nodding.

'No sah,' Oneil said. 'Mi nah eat slug. Me rather hungry den dat.'

Trevor went to look for Tuffee. He felt the bushman would know what to do. At Kevin's a group of people were talking.

'It just lucky nobady dead, dat what mi say,' said Miss Linnet, sent out by Mr Blidgen on a search and rescue mission for bits of missing roof. All over Cove fights were breaking out as people disputed the ownership of twisted pieces of zinc and splintered siding boards. She had in her arms one three-foot length of snapped 4 by 2, clearly identifiable as Blidgen's house by its brown paint.

'No man, two people dead in Lances Bay,' said Michael. Trevor looked at Tuffee.

'One landslide of giarbage mash op Councillor Hoyte house and yard, and kill him an' him wife. Dem say de goverment should not have put de domp uppa Lances Bay, and now it gonna move again.'

'Dem dead like de Dread say dem will dead,' Trevor said.

'Ya man,' said Michael. 'De Dread set one curse pon Lances Bay. De Dread kill two people in Lances Bay.'

Tuffee said, 'Mi nah do nottin. Mi ongly prophet. Jah kill dem cas dem sin gainst de air and de water and de eart wid pollution and giarbage.'

'Rispec, Dread,' laughed Trevor, vindicated. 'Rispec to the max.'

Tuffee went silently to collect his few belongings. At his fire he closed his eyes and looked up at the sky. 'Mi give tanks to Jah, far deliverance,' he intoned. 'Irie vibes.' Then he wrapped a burning ember in some silver foil, tied it with wire to his rod, picked up his shoulder bag and walked towards the gate.

'Where you going, Tuffee?' asked Kevin.

'Mi go a home, Jah a tell mi de time is ready fi start anudder logwood fire inna mi old yard a' Lances Bay. Jah have clear de way far mi.' He squared his shoulders and prepared to leave.

'Hey wait,' Kevin said, coming up close to him and lowering his voice. The group of onlookers bent forward to listen. 'Look, about the money, what with all the rebuilding costs, loss of business etcetera, I don't think I can give you the full two hundred bucks. How about eighty?'

'Mi nah want no monny.'

'Hold on, Tuffee, take some at least. Look, I got five bucks in the bunkhouse. Take it or I'll feel bad, seriously.'

The assembled group watched in awe as Tuffee shook his head and hoisted his bag onto his shoulder.

'Goodbye Kevin,' he said and walked back to restart his old logwood fire in his old yard above the valley behind Lances Bay. And all the people, when they heard about it, *dem haffi respec de dread.*

SAYING GOODBYE

Yvonne *run out of her yard* all her boyfriends because she *decide* to marry Chisholm. *He lazy* and *one idiot* and he beat her and *burst her head couple time but he have Canada passport so she moss marry him.* But when, after they wed, Yvonne applied for her visa to go and live in Toronto they *aks her if she have one Police record. Yvonne have one and she know dem nah want nobady fi go up inna foreign wid no record.* To get a Police record *clean* cost five hundred US so Yvonne decided to sell Mr Gay's house to pay for wiping her Police record. She meant to sell the house in the traditional Grant family manner; that is, take the money and then refuse to move out, and threaten the vendor until he gave up trying to get the house, but the *whitey* who bought it was careful, and took her to his *liar* and made her sign *a paper* which he said he'd show to the Police if she tried to stop him moving in, or attempted to move back in herself. Since she *stop friend wid ole heap o police, dem vex wid Yvonne and nah help her gainst de white man.* But she didn't care, she got two thousand US for the house – easily enough to clean her police record and catch a flight *inna foreign.*

The day Yvonne left the house to the whities, Vinton, who had lived in, and under, her house, on round-the-clock call as dogsbody, cook, gardener, child minder and cleaner for five years, had nowhere to go.

'Tek up mi bag,' Yvonne snapped at Vinton, who lugged them to the taxi, into which Chisholm and Yvonne were squeezed to bursting point, bickering over a tube of candy. With the last overflowing lada bag pushed inside, Vinton said, 'Bye, Yvonne,' drawing their five years together to a close.

'Driva! C'mon,' she shouted.

'Next time,' said Vinton, walking slowly backwards.

'Move!' Yvonne shouted at the driver, who had been flirting in the shade with Bubbles, a comely sixteen year old who'd joined the last crowd ever to assemble at Yvonne's yard to see what she was up to. As the car drew off Vinton turned away.

'Hol' on!'

He heard Yvonne shout and the car stop.

'Tan tan!' she called.

'Ya man?' answered Vinton.

'Tanks. Ya hear?'

'Ya man. Rispec, Yvonne. Every time. Ya have a good time up a Canada.'

'For sure,' she replied, giving him the smile he had longed for. He waved her goodbye and picked up his possessions: a rusty machete, *one shorts, one ganzi, couple cassette, broken scissor*, and a *National Geographic* with some photographs of Canada which he had pored over whenever he could to imagine where Yvonne was going without him.

His immediate problem was where to stay. No girl would take him in; they weren't interested unless you had your own place, and he couldn't go back to Miss Liza because he'd *dis* her since living at Yvonne's. Blackie, his momma, was out of the question – she already had seven sleeping in two rooms, and anyway he had *dis* her too. If only he had a father, or knew who his father was, but Blackie would not tell him. If he knew, he'd ask him for shelter or a *couple bucks* at least. He couldn't stay with Oneil because of his father, Mr Blidgen, and he couldn't stay with Trevor because his father beat boys *terrible* for nothing.

While waiting at the edge of Yvonne's yard to make his next move, a taxi drew up with the wife of the white man who bought the house, who had been shopping in Lucea. Cleaning equipment spilled from her arms as she walked across the yard, and Vinton instinctively got up to help her. As soon as she got in the house she let out an appalling scream. Vinton rushed in to see what the matter was, but it was only one of Yvonne's rats running up and down the lounge because its nest in Yvonne's suite had been removed. The white lady stood on a table screaming, while the white man held a shoe in his hand and shouted, 'Don't worry darling, I'll get it, I'll get it.' But Vinton could see he was too slow for Yvonne's rat, so he grabbed his machete and dashed after the rat to kill it. When he skewered it on the point, he held its wriggling body up to the white lady, but that made her scream more.

'Thanks,' the white man said. Then he added to his wife, 'I doubt very much there'll be any more. Will there?'

'No man,' Vinton corrected him. 'Just maybe him wife and four or six picknee.'

'What?'

'Mi deal wid dat. No problem.'

'It's quite all right, thank you very much,' the white man said.

But the lady said, 'Would you? We'll pay you if you get them all.'

So that day and the next Vinton killed five rats, twelve *teenager* cockroaches, and numerous assorted bugs. The whities wanted to kill moths, because they had no idea they were the spirits of dead people come back to visit the living, but when Vinton explained how bad it was to kill them, they learnt to leave them alone.

The whities were scared of a *whole heap o ting: not just bog and roach and rat, but dog, people dem not know, specially if dem carry machette, power cut, and so many other things dem aks Vinton fi sleep inna de back room, like Yvonne did.*

With his sleeping quarters fixed, for a few nights at least, and a few J in his fist (as both pockets had holes), Vinton could *constentrate* on the thing that he really cared about: *girl dem.*

After a month, the whities went back to their own yard *inna foreign.* They asked Vinton to stay as caretaker in the yard, but locked every room in the house except for Vinton's, left clear instructions that nobody was to enter them in their absence, and took the key away with them.

'It is really important to me that no-one enters our rooms while we're away, do you understand?' the white man said.

'Come on, darling, I'm sure Vinton understands,' the white lady said.

'No, I want to make it clear. Vinton, don't let anybody into our rooms, on any account, while we're away. I'll be more than very angry if I find you've disobeyed me. If you let us down on this, you will lose your job. Understand?'

They gave him an immense sum for bills, and departed with tears in their eyes for the airport, leaving him to his own devices.

There were three people in Cove who looked after whitey tourist yards. Michael kept an eye on Ken and Judy's place called Sea Breeze, though he soon lost his job because every time Ken and Judy went back to Boston, Michael forced an entry into their locked cupboards and sold their possessions. Across the cove from Vinton, Volley, a *bredren of Vinton,* was caretaker of a house a couple of white men bought with *drog biznis money*. It was a good job, caretaking, but it could go wrong: when one day Volley's whities were nailed with eight kilos of Cousins Cove ganja in the Bahamas and given twelve years in jail, Volley was left to handle things *back a yard* for a decade on 43 US dollars.

There were ways to keep the bills down: Vinton got Oneil to dig up the road at night to by-pass the water meter, and got Vices to by-pass the *corrent* meter, though he got hurled across the yard when, saying, 'Mi know how it run, no prablem,' he put the screwdriver on the wrong wire. With this done, Vinton then *spend down all de bills money* in couple days on Red Stripe for de boys, domino, clothes, a trim, and *gal dem*.

Vinton *friend* with five girls, or as he called them, *likker beans*: Sophia, Dawn, Jacqueline, Angie and Opal. He invited them one by one to the yard, helped them in through the window and showed them the whities' magazines and books, and let them try on the white lady's clothes and make up, while listening to cassettes on their stereo and running down the batteries in their flashlight. When they were bored of that he showed them his back room, with its chair, broken mirror and bed, which he swiftly fucked them on before bundling them out the back door and trotting off down the Main to look for the next *likker bean*.

These were glory days for Vinton Williams. Pay landed magically in his savings account at the bank, wafted invisibly across the sea from *foreign* to the National Commercial Bank in the new shopping mall in Lucea. The 20 US a month made him by far the highest paid *yout* in Cousins Cove, or at least in Cousins Cove Bottom Side. When Vinton got a large sum of money, which meant anything over 3 US, a marathon gambling session ensued, either poker or dominoes, because that was the most entertaining way of distributing his pay around his best friends, Oneil, Trevor and Vices, who had none themselves. At the beginning of each month the soft nights were rent with laughter, derision, accusations, and screeches of triumph, and little children lying in bed in Cousins Cove Bottom Side went to sleep listening to the smack and crack of dominoes hurled onto the polished surface of the white lady's dressing table, which Vinton, Oneil, Trevor and Vices heaved out through the whities' window to gamble on beside the Main.

One night, two or three years after the whities started employing Vinton, a tourist coach, instead of roaring by at fifty miles an hour, ten inches behind Vices' chair, drew up with groaning breaks and a door that hissed open. Ran, the driver, called out, 'Tan tan, mi just see ya whities at de airport.'

'Jeezus,' exclaimed Vinton, who was wearing an amber necklace he'd found under the whities' bed. 'Tank ya, Ran. Respec. Vices, Oneil, get de table back in a house fass.'

'No sah!' shouted Vices, who was winning the game of dominoes.

'Ya man. Dis a serious ting.'

'Cho!' complained Vices, sulkily. But he stood up, ruefully studying the dominoes in his big hand, and allowed Oneil and Vinton to pick up the dressing table, which was now polished from years of dominoes, and battered from countless entries and exits through the bedroom window.

Trevor ran across the road to repossess the white lady's sunbed from Miss Citarra's yard where Craig, Nakissia and Najia were slumbering on it in their bedroom, and Vices, as soon as he'd finished *racing up* Vinton and Oneil for scratching the table on the window frame, when a little help from him could have prevented it, dashed to his yard on the back street for the white man's flashlight and cassette player, both of which Vinton had lent to him in return for a rhinestone buttoned shirt. Vinton set about cutting the lawn with his machete in the darkness.

Everything was more or less in place when the airport taxi pulled up and the whities emerged blinking and confused after their long journey from *foreign*.

'Everything all right, Vinton?' the white man always asked, after saying hello.

'Ya man. Everyting criss,' Vinton replied.

'Thought I'd surprise you just for once to see what's really going on when my back is turned,' the white man said.

'Vinton! My necklace! You found it! Where was it?' exclaimed the white lady.

Vinton's hand clutched at his throat. 'Mi find it 'bout de place,' he laughed.

'D'you see that, darling? Vinton's found my amber necklace. You are briliant Vinton.'

The white man, who was searching for a key on a big bunch, muttered something to himself. Inside his rooms he turned on the light and looked around. The floor was speckled with the dried leaves of the dogwood tree that had wafted under the corrugated iron eaves on the sea breeze during his absence. He noticed that Vinton had been using the dressing table, cassette machine and a few other things, again. The crisp new pack of cards were now fat and furry from abuse. But in the three years the white man had been coming to Cove he had learnt that nobody could have possessions in Cousins Cove Bottom Side without sharing them, so said nothing, and went outside to sit on the porch, smoke a spliff with the guys and catch up on some gossip.

✳   ✳   ✳

So life go on, an' life sweet far Vinton. He have gal dem, monny, and a yard fi live in. And to top it all, for his eighteenth birthday present the whities wrote Vinton a letter inviting him on holiday *inna foreign*, with them. Amoy, Vinton's fourteen year old sister, the best reader in the village, read out the letter under the single gloomy bulb of Blackie's shed crammed with fifteen people sheltering from a rainstorm. There was Oneil, Maxwell, Vices, Vera, Miss Citarra, Yvette, Craig, Nakissia, Najia, Trouble, Opal, Bubbles, Michael and Jimmy U-Roy who was *wet up from the downpour*.

'Dear Vintan,' she said, *constentrating* hard. 'Since mentioning to you that we were thinking of having you over here for a week or two in return for the three years of wonderful holidays you've given us in Cousins Cove, I have now made the arrrangements ...'

One breezy warm spring morning the white man, swinging in his hammock, had offered the trip to Vinton, but Vinton thought he was just saying it to make the two of them feel good for half an hour. But he really meant it.

'... Here is the ticket I promised to send you.'

'Talk loud,' someone shouted, because the white man's CD player was on volume 9 on the counter.

'Ya man, loud,' Craig shouted. Nobody suggested turning down the CD.

'Don't lose it,' Amoy continued, raising her voice. The additional noise of the rain on the corrugated zinc roof, only inches above her head, made it harder to be heard. It sounded like the ecstatic applause at the end of a show, designed to bring the DJ back on for more. Drips of water began to form under the light bulb and fall onto Craig's upturned face. 'Your flight leaves Montego Bay on Saturday, September de third, at twenty thirty.' Here, Amoy paused. 'That's half past eight post meridian, in the night,' she explained.

'Mi know dat,' snapped Michael, twitching with jealousy. He had worked as caretaker for Ken and Judy, before they *run him outa de yard cas him tief Ken Walkman an' brief*, but they never asked him to go to Boston. Why did Vinton's whities ask Vinton? Michael was glad he *tief Ken and Judy tings*.

'You ony have two months to get a passport, so apply straight away. I enclose a letter of invitation and financial reference for you to give to the Immigration officer at Gatwick airport, so they'll let you into Britain.' Amoy had to pause here while the rain redoubled its efforts and the applauding crowd rose to their feet and punished their palms to salute the return to the stage of the star for a final encore. When it began to fade, Amoy continued: 'We will meet you at the airport. Ring transfer charge if you have any problems.'

Amoy handed the letter back to Vinton proudly, for he was the first member of the noble house of Williams to leave the island. He was to be a tourist. Nobody from Cousins Cove was ever a tourist. It thrilled Amoy. Everybody talked, and then shouted, at once, congratulating Vinton, who was more surprised than most to see the ticket, and had been quite happy with the promise of travel, even if it was subsequently broken, for in Cousins Cove Bottom Side even a broken promise of something fine was a thing to be treasured.

Michael grabbed the ticket from Vinton. 'Dis nat real ticket,' he jeered.

'Ya man. Dat real,' said Vices in his deep voice. He was always the expert on everything, and so big and so argumentative that nobody doubted his authority. But at that moment Ran's huge Blue Danube bus drew up inches from the bamboo shed, and with a hiss of breaks and a clatter of doors,

Ran emerged, shouting, 'Blackie! Fetch mi one hot Red Stripe. Mi kiant drive no more widout a drink fi clear mi brain.'

'Ran,' said Jimmy U-Roy, 'you see ole eap o airplane ticket wid tourists. Dis one fraud?' It was passed to Ran while Blackie levered the top off the bottle on the two rusty nails that Oneil had hammered into the bar the day she tore out two teeth opening a Dragon Stout for a customer. Ran looked at the ticket, his skin glistening with the sweat of the hot and humid night, and drained the liquid from the bottle in one pull. 'Dat look real,' he announced. 'Dat ticket can fly. For sure.' He handed it back. 'Blackie give mi nudder Red Stripe. Dis plane kiant lift aff pon one engine.' He grabbed the second bottle, and wiping the rusty sediment from around its mouth with his shirt, ducked back outside, where forty-three tourists waited patiently in his coach to be driven to their flight home from Donald Sangster International Airport in Mo-Bay.

'Carry mi dung one Walkman fram a foreign,' Amoy begged her brother.

'An' one shorts and jeans shirt,' barked Vices.

'An' one Bally shoes far mi,' added Trevor.

'Bring mi one mattress, ya hear?' shouted Miss Citarra.

'An' Vinton, carry dung one .38 semi-automatic pistol,' piped Trouble, 'cas dat mi need inna Negril. Bud.'

Vinton laughed in their faces and forced his way through the crush to the door. Outside, the rain clouds had moved off towards Lances Bay, and late afternoon sun was shafting in under them. Gullies and culverts burbled as the flood water subsided, and ponderous waves of steam rolled off the tarmac road.

'Yo. Tan-tan,' Vinton heard Jimmy U-Roy call behind him. 'One ting. Com ere.'

Vinton halted. 'What ya want mi fi carry dung? One BMW?'

'No man,' laughed Jimmy, as his thin legs conveyed him up the slope.

'Look like everybady want someting.'

'Ya nah haffi worry bout dat Vinton,' Jimmy said.

'Yes sah. Mi com back dung wid nottin, dem race mi up. Believe mi.'

'Com back? Ya nah gonna com back a Cove, Vinton.'

'Mi nah gonna what?'

'Ya kiant go a foreign and com back a Cousins Cove. Dis one big chance ya have. It never gonna repeat. Tek it and get outa here while ya can.'

Vinton's face lit up at the idea. But then he said, 'An' never com back?'

'Sure ya com back dung. In couple year when ya one big man wid Benz and house and plenty o' gift for we sufferers.'

Vinton stood still and looked over the pasture. Craig waded through the long grass carrying a bucket of water to a tethered cow in the dusk.

'Dem have job and monny and plenty car up a foreign. And can be white gal dem. White gal love up de yardy inna foreign. Everytime.'

But Vinton had heard the white man and lady talking, and it didn't sound easy to make your way *inna foreign* if you were a yardy. 'It nat easy fi get job inna London,' he said.

'Job? Ya nah need job, man!' Jimmy laughed, putting his stringy arm around Vinton's shoulders and guiding him into Vinton's yard. 'Government pay ya fi live der. And if ya have haccident, like get bounce by car, dem pay ya million a dallar.'

'Dat so?'

'Ya man. It call surance.'

'Bot mi nah have no paper fi stay.'

'Nuh worry bout dat. Waller have no paper but him live inna Peckham since tree year.' Waller was a bad boy from Cousins Cove Top Side. *He did drugs biznis and even kill one man inna Police shootout.* It was someone from his own gang, accidentally, but it still earned him the respect of a proper murderer. He'd fled *inna foreign* on a false passport.

'De whities say Police inna Englund always ketch ya,' Vinton said.

'Police inna Englund? Ya nah need worry bout whitey Police.'

'Why?'

'Whitey Police inna Englund nuh carry gon. Waller tell mi.' Jimmy chuckled to himself at the very thought of a cop without a gun. 'So if dem trouble ya, ya just lick dem down. It easy.'

'Dem nuh carry gon?'

'Nuh sah,' said Jimmy, almost crying with happiness. 'No gon! Waller tell mi. Everybady know.'

'If dem nuh ave no gon, why everybady nuh turn tief and robber and bad boy?'

'Cas dem idle. Bot dat tief biznis easy inna Englund. If de Police ketch ya tief, ya just lick dem down and ron way inna de bush fi hide.'

'Bot der is nuh bush inna London. De white lady and man tell mi. Dat why dem like i' here.'

'Well dem liards, cas Chicken George live ole eap o year in Shepherd Bush.' Vinton had to admit that this was true. 'Ya whities nuh tell you de trut' bout Englund cas dem want fi you a stay here, in Cove, fi cut dem yard an' pick up dem giarbage.'

'If mi run off inna London mi gonna need monny.'

'Dat mi already tink bout. Cas ya mi friend, and mi want fi help ya get start inna foreign. Let we go inna ya room fi talk biznis.'

Indoors, Vinton put on the radio to give them privacy. Jimmy smiled his lupine smile and sweated profusely, occasionally wiping his face and head with a hand towel he always carried with him. 'Ow much monny ya ave?'

'Twenty-one US.'

'Twenty-one dallar. Dat can work. Show mi de white man letter.'

Vinton pulled it out of his pocket. Jimmy read the letter and closely inspected the communication with the immigrations officer. 'Dis good,' he said. It was typewritten on crisp pale yellow paper with an embossed letterhead. 'Wid dis ya gonna walk right inna Englund. No problem. Dem nah gonna trouble ya wid dis. No sah. Mi can give ya twenty-one US of ganja for ya bag which can sell for two tousand dallar inna London.'

'Ya man. Dat would be cool.'

'For sure,' said Jimmy, 'it mi idea. Dem alway cool. Every time. Tek de ganje to Waller, and him help ya sell i'. Waller can show ya how ting run inna London. Ya can move wid him posse if ya want.'

'Dat sound cool. Mi link op wid Waller,' said Vinton, glowing with anticipation.

'Gi' mi de monny, den,' said Jimmy.

Vinton laughed. 'Mi nuh need fi buy ganje from you, Jimmy. Byron ave ole eap him will gi' mi.'

'Bot do him know how fi smuggle i' in suitcase? How fi hide i' so dog dem nah sniff i' out? Mi know cas mi bredren inna Kinston tell mi. Ya nuh want fi go a jail, do you?'

'No man.'

Jimmy put out his hand. 'Den dis de best way,' and

Vinton opened his billfold and handed over all his meagre savings.

When Jimmy went, Vinton *kick back pon him bed, wid him hand behind him head*, his thoughts fixed on the *gangsta* life in London. On the radio Bob Marley sang 'When you bend a new corner, feel like sweepstake winner', and Vinton thought, *mi know what ya say*, Bob.

When news broke of Vinton's plan to turn into a drugs dealer, stay in London illegally and join a gangsta mob, opinions were divided. Most people said they were right behind Vinton. His *bredren*, Oneil, Trevor, Vices and Trouble, were sad to see him go, but never showed it. 'When mi get set up nice,' he told them, 'mi call for ya and carry you up. Tross mi.'

'How long will that tek?' asked Trevor adoringly.

'Mi nah know, bot soon. Tree or seven monts or maybe two year. Soon as mi can. Believe mi. Ya tink mi want fi be inna foreign widout mi bredren?'

Only Amoy was dead against the plan. 'Ya one idiot Vinton Williams. Ya know what happens to drogs dealers? Look at Perry and Minto. Dem inna jail far ole heap o years. And what if you get to London? Ya kiant read or write, you have no trade and no relations to help you. All your family is here. Dis de place you born and raise. Ya kiant stay up dere.' Then she added, quietly, 'ya family need ya, ya know?'

'Ya jealous, gal. Mi fed up wid dis likker place. It too smallish for a big man like mi.'

But there were still some pleasures to be extracted from his last weeks in Cove. His elevation in life to drugs dealer and London bad boy deeply impressed his friends, and drew girls *like magnet draw nail*. Just the sight of an air-ticket made the Cove girls weak at the knees, and he missed no opportunity to push them back on his bed the moment they looked unsteady.

The passport application defeated Vinton, so he asked Amoy to help him, she being the only person he knew up to the task and the owner of the only functioning biro in Cove that week. She filled it in on the counter of Blackie's shed, tears in her eyes. Meanwhile Vinton borrowed a shirt from Vices and went to Lucea to get a passport photograph. The trip did not go well. Before mounting the wooden stairs to the studio he had *one flex trim* with the words BAD BOY razored above his right temple, but the picture *nuh look too nice*. For a start you couldn't see the words at all, but more importantly he looked too black.

'Dat one black bwoy!' Vices shouted with laughter when Vinton nervously showed it outside Blackie's shed. 'Photographer moss have plug out de light cas ya is pure black.' Oneil, Trevor and everybody else who was *high colour* laughed loud, while Vinton, Amoy and Blackie kept quiet, feeling small.

'Give dat back,' Vinton shouted over the hoots and screams of laughter. 'Mi can be black, bot it a mi a go a foreign, nat you – country boys,' he laughed back. But Amoy offered him some money she'd saved for a geography text book, and he went to Mo-Bay the next day to a better photographer who always gave you high colour. When he passed the photo around, Vices said, 'Dat cool. Nice phota.'

'Alright, brown boy,' said Trevor, though Kadian, one of Vinton's *likker beans*, looked at the photo and said, 'Who dat? Dat nuh look like nobady mi know.'

But Kadian had *ole eap o lyrics*.

It was an historic day when the passport came, for Vinton was the first little person in Cousins Cove Bottom Side to possess one. In the privacy of his room he held the slim royal blue book in his big gnarled hands, and felt a lump in his throat. *When mi was one picknee mi nah have nuttin. No shoe no yard no monny no farder, and mi mudder run mi outa de yard. Bot now mi have de first passport inna de community and mi one big man.* His birth certificate, which he had never seen before, slipped out and slid with a faint hiss across the floorboards. He picked it up and looked at it. Out of the indecipherable jumble of letters sprang a recognisable word: FATHER. In the box beside it was written: Walter Carvel Gardener.

There was a man of that very name in the Back Street. Maas Aubrey, they called him. Maas Aubrey? His father? Vinton always pictured his father miles and miles away from Cove, but he had walked past Maas Aubrey's yard, where he lived with his wife Miss Norma Linton and two picknee, thousands of times. Maas Aubrey was cool. Everybody said it. He lent the cricket club his lawnmower and didn't get *vex* when Vices ran it over a rake buried in the long grass and it *mash op.*

Vinton decided to take a walk. He left his yard, crossed the Main after letting a tourist coach thunder by, and took the track up past the *symmetry* to the Back Street. Two nude *picknee* soaped themselves at the standpipe on the corner. He passed on either side of him the wooden houses set back in their yards, until he came to one with a much admired burgundy and cream concrete extension, and a lawn with a clipped hibiscus hedge. For many years Vinton had thought about meeting his father. He planned to step up to him, introduce himself, and maybe buy the man *couple cold Red Stripe and chat bout tings.* He had actually daydreamed about telling him he was going *up a Englund.* Make him proud to have him as a son.

A large, jolly man was playing cricket with two little boys, using a mango tree as a wicket. Maas Aubrey stood behind the bowler and held his arm as he made the delivery. The ball struck the tree and the bowler swivelled round to Maas Aubrey, who shouted, 'Owzat! Well bowl!'

The other boy *fling down him bat*, narrowly missing his brother. Maas Aubrey looked towards the street and noticed Vinton, standing there watching over the hedge, and laughed, saying, 'Picknee nah like him likker brudder to out him.' Miss Norma emerged onto the porch wiping her hands on her apron. Behind her he glimpsed a television. 'Food ready!' she called, and the two boys and their father trooped in, chatting to each other happily. Vinton was left staring at the empty yard. *Ya kiant bitter bout de past*, he told himself. *Dat man nat mi farder. It too late for any man to be mi farder. Dat man Maas Aubrey. Him cool. De past finish. It de future now. Mi bend a new corner now.*

The night before Vinton left, his *friend dem com an' check him, and make gift dem for his journey and new life inna foreign.* They came from all over Cove: Vices with a T-shirt that said JAMAICA NO PROBLEM, and 60 J. Oneil gave him his baseball cap and the 200 J he had saved for a wood plane. His brother Trevor gave him 63 J in coins and some barely used Walkman batteries, and his sister Amoy gave him the 200 J she'd spent five months saving for a geography text book. Chicken George came to shake his hand and give him a London Underground Map. Miss Citarra gave him some *fry fish* in foil, and Blackie brought *round two lada bag of mango, bammy, fry fish, poff, buller and bon an cheese.*

Jimmy crept round with the ganja hidden in two dry coconuts, which had been resealed so well you could hardly see the join.

'Dat com to a likker more dan what us agree.'

'Why dat?'

'Cas dem big, man. Mi get maybe couple pound of ganje in dem.'

'Ya?'

'Ya man. Dat gonna cost anudder four ondred dallar.'

'Far ondred J?'

'Ya man,' laughed Jimmy. 'Bot tink. Dat one investment. Dat four ondred gonna grow to can be couple tousand J inna Englund. And Waller and de crew gonna love ya.'

Vinton sighed. He only had 520 J.

'Dis kiant wrong, Vinton, serious.'

Vinton pulled out all the money he'd been given and handed over 400 J to Jimmy.

'For real,' said Jimmy, beads of sweat covering his forehead. 'Mi gotta go now. Later. Bes of luck, man.'

He was too excited to sleep. The night was sweet: the big moon rose over the hill and burned like a slender flame on the water of the cove. The comforting slap and hiss of the sea on the sandy shore mingled with the chirruping cicadas and tree frogs, and the night jasmine poured its scent over Vinton where he lay restlessly under the open window, thinking of fast cars, shopping malls, underground trains and McDonalds cheeseburgers.

'Tan-tan,' he heard whispered in a girl's voice.

'Ooodat?' he answered, sitting up.

'Kadian.' Kadian, the cutest and most beloved of all his *likker beans*. For that week, at least. Vinton opened his door, and saw the fifteen year old bathed in dappled moonlight. Small, with flashing almond eyes, a beautiful, defiant face, and breasts which were talked about from Grange Hill to Mo-Bay.

'Gal. How ya get here?'

'Mi climb outa mi window and walk trough de bush. Vinton, mi got someting fi tell ya.'

He came down the wooden step and took her arm. 'Talk can wait. C'min side.'

'No.' She shook his hand off. 'Listen. Mi pregnant. Mi gonna have ya baby.'

'Na.'

'Ya man. Serious.'

'Jezus,' Vinton sighed, scratching his head. 'Ya try fi dash i' away?'

'Ya man. Tree time. Mi try fi wash i' out wi Pepsi and baking powda, mi try fi hook i out, mi try everyting, but it stick, an i' too late now.'

'Why ya nah tell mi?'

'Cas mi nah want fi bodder ya.'

'It is mine?'

'Ya man. Mi swear. Mi swear.'

Vinton sighed again. 'Jesus. Dis mi nuh need now. Ya know mi ketch one airplane inna foreign in de marning?'

'Ya man. Dat why mi com. Can ya give mi couple dallar far baby bottle and baby clothes?'

Vinton went into his room and reappeared. 'Mi only hav dis,' he said, 'bot tek i'.'

She held the notes up to the moonlight and counted them. 'One ondred and twenty J? Ya kiant buy nottin wid dat. Give mi more.'

'Mi nuh have no more. Mi haffi give i' all to one guy. Mi swear.'

'Ya liard, Vinton. Ya go pon airplane tomorrer, sure ya have monny.' She turned away and stuck out her bottom lip.

'Mi swear, Kadian. Tross mi.' He touched her smooth brown forearm. She jerked it away.

'Give mi mo' monny.'

'Mi nuh have none.'

'Den mi go back a yard. Mi farder vex wid mi far get pregnant and him beat mi bud if mi nah get back a yard before him wake up.'

'Com inna mi room for one minute.'

'No Vinton.'

'Mi nah gonna forget ya, Kadian. Ya now mi baby mudder. An' mi nah gonna forget mi baby. Tross mi. Mi go a Englund, but mi send down monny and tings for de baby and one day can be bring ya op wid de picknee. Mi want fi be a good farder.'

'Liard. Ya chatt noff Vinton. Good farder. Ya go pon plane tomorrer an' mi and de baby never gonna hear from ya again.'

'Yes ya will, believe mi.'

'Sure. Ya can say it easy, Vinton, bot mi know mi never will. No yout never com back fram a-foreign. Everybady know dat. Good bye.'

He called her back, but she kept walking through the gleaming leaves of the moonlit trees. Vinton said, 'Raas claat,' and lay back down on his bed to wait for dawn.

For centuries, the people of Cousins Cove Bottom Side had been forced into bidding goodbye to their friends and relatives. Torn from their mothers, brothers, sisters and children in Africa, and then sold and dispersed around the Caribbean as slaves, they knew that all relationships could end at any time without warning through forced separation or sudden death.

Vinton's friends *group up* at his yard, all dressed in their finest travelling clothes, even though they were going nowhere, to say goodbye. All of them knew that they would

probably never meet again, for people who went up young
inna foreign, turn English or American, and never made it
back to a place like Cousins Cove Bottom Side. To make
the pain of separation bearable, everybody pretended Vinton
was coming back.

'Likker more,' said Oneil, handing his holdall through the
minibus window. He tried to lock hands with his friend, but
the angle of the seat to the window made it impossible, so
he just held his fist up and smiled.

'Later,' said Trevor, looking miserable.

Amoy was in the shed hiding her tears from everyone.

'Bye Vinton!' she called to her brother. Some of his *likker
bean dem* lined the side of the road looking forlorn, though
not, he noticed, Kadian.

'Ya man, seen,' said Vinton. And the minibus drew out
of Cove with everyone watching it.

When Vinton disembarked at London Gatwick airport, he
had difficulty establishing when exactly he was off the airplane and on English soil. When finally he saw through a
window what he thought was dawn breaking over London,
but was in fact midday on a cloudy November day near
Crawley, he told himself: 'Dis fi mi new country. Now mi
turn Englishman.'

There were so many signs, and whenever he stopped and
put down his bag to read them, people bumped into him.
At a high desk, a *cooly wuman* looked at his passport, his
return ticket, the whitey's letter, asked a few questions, and
then stamped his passport and waved him on. There were
now so many more signs, he gave up trying to read them
and just followed the passengers from his flight. When he

picked his bag off the carousel he followed a man to an exit, and was just reaching the automatic doors at the far end of the customs hall when a white man in a uniform *hail im up.*

'Have you got something to declare, sir?'

'Uh?'

'You are in the red channel. You wish to declare something? Are you carrying more than two litres of spirits or four of wine? Cigarettes? Gifts of any kind?'

'No sah. Nuttin.'

'So why are you in the red channel?'

'Dat mi kiant answer, cas mi nah know what is de red channel,' Vinton smiled.

'Can't you read?' asked the Customs officer, rhetorically.

'Well, mi can read, but mainly certain word. Nat every one, ya see ...'

'Where have you come from?'

'De airplane.'

'No, where did your journey start?'

'Cousins Cove.'

'Which country?'

'Jamaica.'

'How much money do you have on you?'

'Nuttin,' said Vinton openly.

'Please put your bag on the bench, sir.'

Vinton placed it on the steel surface. The customs officer unzipped it, and began to empty it. Up until that moment Vinton had forgotten all about the coconuts. But even when he suddenly remembered them, his external demeanor didn't betray the fact. Many times he'd seen Police miss ganja or knives at roadblocks near Cousins Cove.

'Do you have any firearms? Ammunition? Drugs of any kind?'

'No sah,' answered Vinton with innocent surprise. The

man's hands delved in the bag and withdrew one, and then the other, coconut. Vinton thought about Trouble's eldest brother, Boom Stepper, who was doing a seven-year stretch in a Cayman Island lock-up for swallowing condoms full of coke for Oncle Dick Edmonds, a notorious thief, liar and coke dealer. The white man inspected the coconuts. Vinton remained cool. He, Oneil, Trevor, Vices, Yvette, Trouble and Blackie had looked closely at them in his room, and couldn't see the join.

The white man looked across the hall to a man with his feet crossed on a table in a side office.

'Les,' he called. 'You busy? Bring me the hammer and chisel, will you?'

'Ang about.' Les appeared holding the tools. Vinton swallowed and smiled weakly. The chisel was placed on the hairy coconut and struck with the hammer. At the first blow it sheered off, but for the second attempt Les held it while the hammer fell again. With a sharp crack the nut fell in half revealing two equal cups of white coconut, and nothing else. A miracle. Tank ya, Jah, Vinton mouthed. Respec. The chisel was placed on the second coconut and the same thing happened: it too was empty. *Jimmy U-Roy Fairfax, ya jinall, ya crook*, mouthed Vinton this time, smiling from ear to ear as the white man, most surprisingly, repacked his bag and zipped it up for him.

He planned to get in touch with Waller and the crew and *link op* as soon as possible, but it took a little longer than he thought to get his bearings, and the white man and lady had laid on a programme of sightseeing and events which he couldn't get out of.

They took him down to the bottom of their street to buy a coat and jeans and shirt and brief and sweater in a shop called Emporio Armani, which was *criss* but not as good as some shops he'd seen on the drive in from the airport in a more central part of the city called, he was told by the white man, Lewisham High Street. He was then walked around the corner to buy *one shoes and belt* at a shop called Gucci. Many of his friends in Jamaica bought Gucci T-shirts in the market in Lucea, so that was cool.

He rang the telephone number Jimmy gave him for Waller, but he never got an answer. On the third day he asked the white lady to try it.

'That's out of order,' she told Vinton. 'Either there's something wrong with the phone or the number's wrong. How long have you been trying?'

'Tree day.'

'It must be a wrong number. It looks a bit odd. Do you have an address?'

Vinton passed the piece of paper to the white lady.

'It says care of the Duke of Percy, Peckham,' she said to her husband.

'The pub, I assume, rather than the person,' he said.

'Ha ha. Let's see if it's in the book.'

Vinton rang the pub when she got the number, but couldn't understand the lady who answered, so he passed the receiver to the white lady.

'I'm trying to trace someone called Waller. I have a friend of his from Jamaica staying, who wants to meet up ... Does he have another name, Vinton?'

'Ya man. Him name Sherlock Allen. Waller one alias.'

'He might be called Sherlock Allen. Yes. You know him? Right. Can you give him a message to ring Vinton Williams?' She gave the number and rang off. 'He's the cleaner there. Comes in at six a.m. each day for three hours.'

The whitey's yard was well set up. Ole eap o room on four floor, wid step all the way to de top. Even de picknee have one room fi sleep, one fi play call nursery, and one bartroom, which she share only wid de nanny. Vinton room have tree big window wid fancy curtain and him own bartroom trough one door wid one bard and two tilet, one big an' one small. Downstairs dem ave big kitchen and two lounge full of TV, hi-fi, video, CD, everyting. It nice the way people live inna Englund.

He tried to make himself useful around the house before he turn gangsta. He played with the *picknee*, called Ella. She was coming up to her second birthday and had blonde hair, blue eyes and looked like an angel in the Bible. Often the white man and lady went to meetings. Vinton didn't know what they did at them, but knew they must be in shops because they always returned with big bags full of new things. One time, when the nanny was at the gym, Vinton baby-sat Ella.

The two of them sat on the sofa in the nursery watching *Thomas the Tank Engine* when Ella *start fi bawl*. He took her on his knee and made faces till she *begin fi laugh*.

'You look so sweet!' the white lady said, surprising Vinton. She threw off her coat and put down her handbag. 'Thank you,' she said, 'you're so good with her.'

'Mi like picknee, cept if dem bad and craven like Craig, den mi haffi beat him bud.'

'Look at her, she's so happy.'

Vinton blushed with pride. Then he said, 'Mi gonna have one baby.' He didn't mean to say it, and as soon as he said it, he wished he hadn't.

'You are? Really. Who with?'

'Kadian.'

'Darling,' the white lady called to the man, 'Vinton's going to have a baby.'

'Just one?' the white man answered. 'Which of the harem have you selected for the honour?'

'Kadian.'

'Congratulations, Vinton. At least the mother is beautiful,' he laughed.

'Cho,' said Vinton.

'I can see why you'd roger her, but why on earth she wants to do it with you beats me completely.'

'Cas she love mi up. All de gal dem love mi,' laughed Vinton. 'Mi mash down every gal mi meet!'

'You can take all of Ella's baby stuff when you go.'

'Darling,' said the white man, 'some of it's really expensive.'

'... There's the basinette, bottles, bath, nappies, nighties, the travel cot ...' The white man shot her a look. '... Stop being so mean. If we ever need more we can easily get that stuff here. It's impossible in Jamaica.'

'Ya can carry it dung when ya go nex a Cove?' Vinton blurted.

'No way,' said the white man. 'I'm not taking that lot on the plane. You take it when you go. It's your baby.'

'Ya man,' said Vinton, 'for sure. Sorry.'

At night, Vinton merged into the London scene. His hosts took him to gallery openings in the West End, drinks parties in Chelsea, dinner at Quaglinos, Mezzo, the Soho House and other fashionable restaurants, and late-night dancing at nightclubs or parties in Notting Hill Gate. Vinton drank plenty, but ate little until he got home to Moma's *fry fish, bammy and poff*. Afterwards he lay down under the goose-down duvet on pure linen sheets, gazed about the softly carpeted bedroom with its silk curtains and thought *This the life far mi.*

Waller didn't ring, but Vinton wasn't worried. He rang the Duke of Percy *couple times bot de lady vex and cuss and use bad word*. He didn't need Waller to run away; after a week in the city Vinton knew *how dem ron tings*. He needed a job. No problem. There was *one shop call Affice Angels where dem give out job*. The white lady had told him when he'd asked what it was, and alone he'd located a shop where they *rent and sell house, apartment and yard. Life inna London was criss and easy, smooth an' cool*. You could pick any yard you liked from photographs in the big window.

Most days the white man and lady took him out. They went to the cinema – though always to films with too much chat and not enough *gon and naked wuman*. They went to *ole eap o'* art gallery and museum. One time they took him to an exhibition about *Slavery Days*. There were *ole eap o' old picture dem of slaves and slavery days, and ball and chain and manacle and torture tool*. The exhibits made the whities sad and solemn, and at one moment standing in the gloom in front of a set of handcuffs designed for a child, Vinton thought he saw the white lady wipe a tear from her eye, but it was dark and he wasn't sure. *He nuh fancy that museum too much*. The whities loved the past: they had old furniture, old pictures, and even drank old wine, when the shop sold new wine cheaper! Vinton wanted the future. Not the past. He found it at the Trocadero Centre, a huge building in Piccadilly Circus devoted to electronic games and an exhibition about rock 'n' roll.

After only two and a half hours playing on the machines the white man said, 'C'mon Vinton, let's get out of this hell hole.'

'No man. It criss. Dem would love i' inna Cousins Cove. Love i'.'

That night they went to a party at the White Cube Gallery

for Damien Hirst, then to the Groucho Club where Vinton
sat on the sofa drinking vintage champagne squeezed
between Jarvis Cocker and Damien Hirst. Later, *him vamit
into Damien Hirst's mother's handbag.* When he got home
he lay in bed thinking about the girls he had seen that night.
Then he thought of Kadian, then Sophie, Claudette, Dawn,
Marjorie and the others. In the Groucho there was a man
dressed as woman. *She, he, looked good, and give Vinton a
wink and hold his hand.* Oneil and the guys would laugh
about that. He thought about them. Wondered what they
were doing. He was happy *inna foreign* but missed certain
things: *bon an cheese, fry fish, Red Stripe brewed in Mo-Bay,
doing do-do inna de bush, the big hot sun, which was shrivel
and perish inna London, the warm day, for him stuff up wid
cold, and the moon, which never come out inna London. Bot
most of all him miss Oneil, Maxwell, Vices and the other likker
people dem. And he miss Kadian, too, just a likker bit, and
him tink bout her.*

Sometimes, Vinton ventured out on his own. The white
lady always checked how many layers he had on before he
left the house, and the white man pressed bank notes into
his hand, saying, 'Take this. Have a good time. Remember
to leave enough for a taxi home. Have you got the address
and phone number? Good. Let me give you a little bit more.
Here. Take it. You look after us in Cove, so we'll look after
you in London.' This way Vinton accumulated some money
for when he ran away.

One afternoon Waller got in touch.

'It a Vinton,' Vinton explained into the phone.

'Who?' Waller's low voice asked.

'Vinton Williams. Blackie Son. Joe nephew, and Byron
nephew. Fram Cousin Cove, Bottom side. Jimmy Fairfax mi
bredren.'

'U-Roy?'

'Ya man, U-Roy!' laughed Vinton with relief.

'How U-Roy?'

'Im cool. Im send him best wishes and regards.'

'So. Ya inna London?' Waller asked.

'Ya man.' Vinton looked around to check no-one was listening, but the white lady had left the room and closed the door. 'Mi com a London fi live.'

'Wishart ya stay?'

'Mi stay right now wid som whitey friends inna Knightsbridge.'

'Dem have room or bed for me?' Waller asked quickly.

'No, man, mi gotta leave ere. Mi hope fi link up wid ya.'

'Sure, man. Com an' see me. Let we have couple beers an' talk. Com dung a Duke o' Percy at nine o'clock inna morning.'

In the taxi to Peckham, he counted his money. He had forty-two pounds. It seemed a lot until he got to Peckham and the driver asked for seven pounds. That was 250 J. You could go to Kingston and back on that.

There was trash on the broken pavement and plywood over many of the windows in Peckham. Three black pedestrians bowed their heads into the gusty wind to cross the road. Vinton got out of the taxi and shivered before going into the pub. At the bar there was a big white man on the telephone, with some papers on the bar beside him. He put his hand over the phone the moment he saw Vinton.

'Whadder you want?'

'Mi am looking for somebady call Sherlock Allen.'

'C'min. Oi. Eddie Murphy. There's a mate here for you.'

Waller came out of the ladies' toilet holding a mop. He wore a thick polo neck jumper with a tight T-shirt pulled down over it, a filthy pair of grey slacks and wellington boots. He peeled off a rubber glove and met Vinton's knuckles with his. Both men looked very happy, as if the other one was the answer to their prayers.

'Let me finish up ere and then we'll take a walk up the street.'

Waller took Vinton to a house quite unlike the whities'. It was dark, damp and fiercely cold. The front and back gardens were filled with garbage, and many windows were broken. Waller kicked at the door and called out a name. A big dog started to bark somewhere. A man downstairs grunted, and they went into the basement where he let them into a cold wet room and locked the door behind them. Vinton shivered and sniffed. Under a naked bulb the white man put a little plastic bag of crack on a formica table. Waller felt in his pocket for his pay.

'Ya wan' some?' he asked Vinton.

Vinton shook his head. 'Mi nah lick shit,' he said sheepishly.

'C'mon!' Waller laughed. 'This is ow you keep the cold out, innit? Smoke a pipe and I'll take you up to meet the crew. C'mon. Ow much bread you got?'

Vinton put his hand in his pocket and pulled out his money.

'The boy got some money!' Waller beamed. 'Gimme nother. Eel pay.'

Vinton took a pull on the pipe while Waller held the flame to the crack. He felt great, not at all cold or nervous.

'Alright!' he exclaimed. 'Let we meet de posse now!'

'Ya man,' said Waller, now sweating, 'let we meet de boss.'

They headed up the street, their heads bowed into the cruel

wind. 'You come on the right day, man,' Waller explained. 'Tonight there's gonna be some action. We taken all we gonna take, you know? So tonight we gonna start the street war.'

'Ya man,' shouted Vinton. 'De street war!' This was the kind of talk he'd been waiting for.

'We been taking a lo' o' punishment, you know, but now we gonna sekkle the score.'

'Ya man. Now the yardy here, it time fi sekkle the scar.'

'Ya man!' exclaimed Waller.

In a large council estate Waller knocked on a door. A good-looking black girl opened it. Vinton smiled as sweetly as he knew, but the woman, when she saw Waller, shouted, 'What the bleedin ell you doing ere again? Ow many times I told you to get lost. I don't want you or your friends round ere, right?

Waller laughed, saying, 'Alright girl, take i' easy man.' To Vinton he said, 'C'mon.'

At another house on the other side of the project they gained entry. They went down a thin corridor into a room with four *yout* sitting around smoking cigarettes and looking bored. The teevee was on but nobody watched it, except Vinton.

'Waller,' one of them called. 'Where's me ten pounds?'

'Old on, give me a minute. Hey, Vinton, me beg you ten pounds.'

'Lend it to him,' the first youth ordered Vinton.

'Respec,' said Waller, as he took it. That left Vinton with seventeen pounds. 'This is Vinton. He's just come in from Jamaica.'

'Where d'you come from?' asked the first youth. He was lean, with a trimmed beard and glasses.

'Cousins Cove,' Vinton said proudly, adding, 'Hanover,' when there didn't seem to be any recognition.

'Never eard of it,' the first youth said, and the others laughed. A pretty girl of about seventeen came in the room. She was tall with a cornrow hairstyle. Vinton gave her an openly admiring look, and a big welcoming smile.

'What the fuck are you looking at?' she asked.

'The pretty gal who just walk inna de room,' Vinton answered.

'Nigger, fuck yuself,' she spat. Everybody laughed at that. Especially Waller.

An older man of about twenty-two, good and fat, with a bald head and a big gold chain around his greasy neck came in. 'All right,' he said, commanding everybody's attention. 'We gonna move on them tonight. Everybody ready? Rahim? Kiddy? Sizla? Mucky? Who're you?'

'Mi name Vinton.'

'He just got in from Jamaica.'

'You wanna do some work tonight?'

'Ya man.'

'Cos we gonna need back-up tonight.'

'Yeh.'

'Yeh.'

'You godda gun?'

'Gun?' Vinton swallowed. 'No sah. Mi nah ave no gun.' Then after a moment he added, 'Mi leave dat back a yard.'

'You'll need one tonight,' laughed Sizla.

'We all gonna need one tonight,' said Mucky.

'Ya man.'

'For sure,' they all added.

Vinton was beginning to relax. Talking about guns with his new London crew was his idea of living. Then something terrifying happened: first Mucky and then Sizla reached under their T-shirts and took out pistols, real guns. Sizla slapped his from palm to palm as he bragged about what he was going to do that night, and Mucky kept aiming his at things around the room, pretending to fire.

'They think they got power,' Mucky said. 'But we got power. Right? Fuck them. We got power too.'

'And we gonna sekkle the score tonight,' said Waller.

'Yeh,' said the others menacingly.

Vinton joined in, but wanted to say, 'Can't we settle the score widout gun? Ongly wid chat and curses and bad words?' Because the guns made Vinton tremble.

The big man said, 'I'll be back bout eight with Gambino. So be ready, okay? I'll see what I can do about a heater for you. Later.'

He left. Vinton was hoping he wouldn't get a gun when Waller said to him, 'Gambino's the don. He'll get you a heater, no problem.'

Vinton started feeling not too good.

'Boy. You. Country boy.'

'Ya man,' answered Vinton.

'You got money?'

'Ya man,' Vinton answered.

'Go out and buy some cigarettes and gum. We need some.'

Vinton stood up. But when he got to the door, the one called Sizla said, 'Someone go with him.'

'I'm not going,' said Mucky. 'Freeze my ass off. No fuckin' way man.'

'He don't know nuttin. Relax,' said Waller.

So Vinton went out on his own.

At eight o'clock on the dot two big cars drew up and double-parked outside the house. Vinton, Waller and the other four *soldier dem* tucked their guns into their belts and trooped out into the cars. Vinton was shown into the back of a BMW with blacked-out windows and gold hub caps and radiator grill. Gambino was in the driver's seat. All Vinton could see of him was a big head with close-cropped bleached white hair, a massive jaw and a heavy gold and diamond earing that dangled down to a thick and violent neck. Beside him sat a light-coloured, wiry MC of some repute. Gambino turned to Vinton.

'You the rookie?'

'Ya man.'

'Take this.' He slapped a semi-automatic pistol into his hands. It felt heavy and dangerous. 'Load it up.' He passed back a clip of .32 shells. Vinton fed the bullets one by one into the hungry gun. 'Acquaint yourself with the safety,' Gambino ordered. Vinton clicked the little silver switch back and forth. 'Good.'

Without any sound from the engine, the car leapt forward, pressing Vinton into the black leather upholstery. They sped through wet streets gleaming with reflected neon and street lights. Gambino paid no particular attention to traffic signals.

'What about his initiation ceremony?' the MC asked, indicating Vinton. 'If he's gonna ride with the crew he gotta do the initiation ceremony.'

'Yeh,' agreed Rahim and Kiddy on either side of Vinton, cruel enjoyment in their voices. Vinton swallowed.

'This is his initiation ceremony,' laughed Gambino. The speakers thumped out Coolio rapping "Gangsta's Paradise": THOUGH I WALK THROUGH THE SHADOW OF THE VALLEY OF DEATH ...

Gambino suddenly slowed down. They crawled through a quiet street. Rahim looked behind them.

'Where's Mustapha?'

'Gone to deal with shit-face's wife and kids,' smiled Gambino. 'Right. We're nearly there. Rahim, Boom Stepper, Kiddy. In the building. Rookie, you stay with me to deal with any witnesses and anybody they flush out.' The car drew to a halt outside a minicab office in a three-storey building. 'Right. Move! Go! Now!'

Vinton was just thinking that he had had all the fun he wanted, cruising streets in a BMW with a posse, and was ready to pack it in for the evening and go for a beer with the guys or try to pick up some girls. But he was swept along.

The car doors flew open and the youths rushed the building. There were cries of surprise and then gunshots, some rapid, followed by screams and moans of the wounded and dying. Vinton stood with Gambino, their backs to the car, scanning the building and the street. A top-floor window flew open; shouts could be heard from within, followed by at least a dozen gun shots. A man with blood all over him climbed out of the window onto the sill and tried to reach for a handhold to get himself onto the roof, but a hand from inside caught hold of his ankle and tugged until he fell, his limbs flailing, his mouth twisted and screaming, down towards where Vinton stood. He hit the pavement with a horrible thud. But it didn't kill him, because he started moaning, and tried to crawl forward.

Vinton wanted to say, 'Right. Mi gotta go now, guys. Mi forget mi haffi check one person. See ya. Cool. Bye.'

Kiddy, at the window above, shouted, 'Gambino! They're at the door here. Get them from behind, man.'

Gambino ran into the building giving Vinton the order: 'Finish him off.'

Vinton thought he'd wait to see if the man died of his own accord before doing anything he might regret later. So far, he reminded himself, he hadn't done anything too bad. But the night was beginning to make him panic.

More shots, in quick succession, indicated that Gambino had come up behind his enemy on the stairs. A minute later Vinton heard Gambino roar and then stagger from the building holding his left thigh, which was soaking in blood. Vinton looked at him and thought: *dat too bad. Dem trousers was cool.* At that moment a young girl, no older than Nakissia, six or seven, darted out of an alley to see what the commotion was. She stood on the pavement, her hands held up to her face as she absorbed the horror of Gambino and the dying man on the pavement. Gambino levelled his gun at her and pulled the trigger, but it just went click.

'Kill her, kill her, before she gets away!' Gambino yelled at Vinton.

Vinton wanted to say, 'Bot she just one likker *picknee*,' but decided that it wasn't quite in keeping with the ethos of the Gambino posse. He felt in deep. Very deep. Too deep. The girl turned to run, Vinton raised his gun, closed his eyes as the sight on the barrel came up between her slender shoulders, and pulled the trigger. Nothing happened. The safety catch was on. By the time he fumbled with it and got it off she had disappeared.

The wail of a Police siren got louder and louder.

'The Beast,' Gambino cried. 'Get in the car and drive, arsehole,' he shouted at Vinton, staggering to the passenger seat.

'Mi kiant drive,' Vinton stuttered.

'You want me to drive with three bullets in my leg? Get in. It's automatic. Anyone can drive it.'

Vinton found himself behind the wheel with Gambino breathing stertorously beside him.

'Where's de udders?' he asked.

'Dead. It was a set-up. Someone talked. They knew we were coming. When I find out who it is ... aargh,' he moaned as he tried to reposition his leg. Vinton tried to recall the single driving lesson he'd had in Bessie, Devon's ancient Hillman, in the Back Street. The Back Street suddenly felt a long, long way away. 'Step on it.'

They lurched off, but Vinton soon got the hang of it. Gambino reloaded his gun beside him. 'Give me your gun,' he croaked.

'Dat cool, tanks. Mi ave plenty o' bullet,' Vinton replied.

'Don't be stupid, punk ass. You never know how many you have to kill.'

A Police car got onto their tail.

'Shall I slow down?' Vinton asked, thinking, maybe he could get off with just a speeding ticket.

'No. Faster.' Gambino ran down his window and started shooting back at the Police car. A minute later there was a squeal of brakes and the shattering crunch of a bad collision right behind them as the Police car hit another vehicle.

'Alright!' Gambino laughed. 'That's one problem solved.' He leant back and raised the window.

The chopping sound of helicopter blades in the night air became steadily more audible, and a spotlight hit the car from above.

'Blue thunder,' said Gambino. 'Take a right at the top, then next left. Fast.'

They drew into some disused warehousing near the river. Gambino directed Vinton through a maze of turns with the helicopter hanging overhead. Finally they came to a cul de sac blocked by a tall wire fence with more warehouses and the river beyond.

'Get out. Come on. Fast. If we can get over that fence we're in the clear. There's a tunnel on the other side.'

Vinton looked at the twenty-two foot link fence. He doubted he could climb it, and Gambino would have trouble getting over a bench.

'Open the boot of the car.'

Vinton went round to the back of the car, pressed the button and when the boot sprung open saw a dead man curled up around a holdall.

'Get the bag,' Gambino barked at him.

The bag was open enough to reveal its contents: four sub machine guns and eight bags of white powder. Sixteen kilos of coke.

'Put that on your shoulder and help me up.'

With the heavy bag on his left shoulder, and his right arm around Gambino's wide back, his hand under his wet, warm armpit, Vinton began to scale the fence one handed. The chopper alerted more patrol cars, because the sound of sirens once again rang in the cold damp night air, and soon head-lights panned across the graffitied warehouse walls.

'Faster,' urged Gambino.

A Police car skidded into sight and squealed to a halt. Two cops got out and ran towards the fence, which Vinton, despite holding a 215 pound wounded man and 48 pounds or armaments and drugs, was near the top of.

'Freeze! Police!' one of them called.

Vinton began to think of an excuse to explain away his predicament. It was not easy, even for a Cove man.

'Shoot them, for Christ sake,' Gambino gurgled.

'They're cops. You get life for that,' Vinton said.

'What's wrong with you, punk? Shoot them, arsehole.'

So Vinton, steadying himself by holding onto the fence with his teeth, reached for his gun. He turned, clicked off the safety, aimed and pulled the trigger, again and again and again. Boom Boom Boom Boom. They must have shot back because he felt a warm wet patch spreading all over his thighs. Sweet Jezus, he thought to himself, so much blood, I must be hit bad.

At that moment he woke up. He was bumping along in a minibus from the Donald Sangster International Airport at Mo-Bay on the winding coast road to Cousins Cove. On his lap a mother had placed a sleeping toddler who had *pee pee* all over Vinton's lap. Outside, in the early evening gloaming, the familiar and comforting landscape of Lances Bay passed by.

It was on the way to buy the *gangstas'* cigarettes in Peckham that Vinton decided things looked and sounded a bit too serious for his liking. He was all for violence and *gangstas* – so long as no-one got hurt. When he saw a taxi with FOR HIRE lit on it, he put out his arm and took it back to the warmth, safety, and yes, boredom, of the whities' house, where he stayed for two days before flying back to Jamaica.

Dusk at Blackie's shed. Oneil, Trevor, Vices and Trouble were playing dominoes on the roadside. Opposite, on a hammock, Jimmy swung to and fro drinking *one hot Dragon Stout*. Inside the bamboo shed, Amoy was carefully pinning up the bad passport photograph of Vinton. Behind the shed Blackie was cooking *puddin* on a charcoal cooker, the smoke and sweet scent of which was wafting across the yard where some *picknee* played in the dust before bed. Kadian crouched on her haunches close to Blackie, helping her out in return for being allowed to stay in the yard, for she'd been *run outa her yard* by her father. Across the cove, the setting sun was reddening the cliffs at Kevin's, and the water was quickly darkening. Above, the deep blue sky was merging with the shadowy hills that encircled the village.

For a few minutes everybody but the *picknee* were quiet while they listened to a Bob Marley song on Irie FM, all their thoughts trained momentarily in the same general direction.

'Well I remember when we used to sit,' sang Bob,

'In the government yard in Trenchtown.

Hubba hubba servin the hypocrites

Mingle with the good people we meet.

Good friends we ave, and good friends we last ... (at that, Oneil looked away and took a long swig of his *saff drink*).

Along the way.

In this bright future you can forget your past

So dry your tears I say (here, Kadian looked out to sea)

No woman no cry.

No woman no cry.'

A minibus, Pomp Action, pulled up across the road from the shed, and the door on the far side slid back. It remained there for some time while the passenger, whom nobody could see, disembarked. The crash of the shutting door, and the gunning of the engine heralded the departure of the bus, on its way to Davis Cove, Green Island, Orange Bay and Negril, revealing, after it left, Vinton Williams standing with his voluminous luggage on the roadside.

The guys noticed him straight away, but carried on slapping dominoes on the table. Vinton, passing by them on the way to the shed said, simply, 'Yes.'

And they answered, 'Yes, Vinton.'

Inside the shed Amoy shouted, 'Tan-Tan!' joyously, bringing Blackie in the back door, her face almost breaking with happiness. Behind the shed, Kadian stopped grating coconut for a moment, and smiled, hearing his voice, before starting again. Jimmy, on the other side of the road, slipped off the hammock and disappeared into the hills.

That night far up and down the line, people said to each other, where they gathered by the water pipe or on a porch or under a street light or in a shed, 'Vinton a back – ya hear? Ya man. Him a com back dung a yard. Ya man. Him com back dung.'

ACKNOWLEDGEMENTS

While writing *One People* I drew heavily on the following books: *Acts of Identity: Creole Based Approaches to Language and Ethnicity* by R. B. Lepage and A. Tabouret Keller (Cambridge University Press, 1985), *Jamaica Talk* by F. G. Cassidy (Macmillan, 1961), *West Indians and their Language* by P. A. Roberts (Cambridge University Press, 1988), and all of the incomparable works of Louise Bennet. Anyone interested in the Jamaican language will really enjoy these books. I would like to express my gratitude to Hawthornden Castle for giving me space and time when I needed both. I am grateful to Vangie Clare and Rosie Taylor for many conversations full of insights. I must also thank Sian Austin and Julia Murray Scott for their early encouragement, and Emily Dewhurst for her help later on. In addition I would like to thank all of the inhabitants of Cousins Cove, whose love, friendship and naughtiness remain a constant inspiration. Finally, my greatest thanks must go to my wife Portia, without whose generosity and brilliance I would never have been able to write *One People*.

Payback Press is an independent imprint within Canongate Books focusing on black culture and black writing. The list features some of the most neglected but important voices to come out of urban America this century. Below is the full list of Payback titles currently in print.

Non-Fiction

FIGHT THE POWER
Chuck D — isbn 0 86241 720 1 — £12.99 hbk

THE NEW BEATS
S. H. Fernando Jnr. — isbn 0 86241 524 4 — £9.99 pbk

BORN FI' DEAD
Laurie Gunst — isbn 0 86241 547 0 — £9.99 pbk

BLUES PEOPLE
LeRoi Jones — isbn 0 86241 529 2 — £7.99 pbk

BENEATH THE UNDERDOG
Charles Mingus — isbn 0 86241 545 4 — £8.99 pbk

BLACK FIRE
Nelson Peery — isbn 0 86241 546 2 — £9.99 pbk

BLACK TALK
Ben Sidran — isbn 0 86241 537 3 — £8.99 pbk

PIMP
Iceberg Slim — isbn 0 86241 593 4 — £5.99 pbk

THE NAKED SOUL OF ICEBERG SLIM
Iceberg Slim — isbn 0 86241 633 7 — £5.99 pbk

SPACE IS THE PLACE
John F. Szwed — isbn 0 86241 722 8 — £12.99 pbk

SWEET SWEETBACK'S BAADASSSSS SONG
Melvin Van Peebles — isbn 0 86241 653 1 — £14.99 hbk (includes CD)

Call us for a free **Payback Sampler** which gives you more information on all the above titles. The sampler also contains extracts from our most recent publications together with information about the authors. It is a great little booklet that fits in your pocket and gives you a broader taste of what we publish. Check it out!

Alternatively, if you are hooked up to the internet, look for the Payback Press website where you will find all the latest publication details, extracts from the books and author biographies.

Our books are available from all good stores or can be ordered directly from us:

PAYBACK PRESS, 14 HIGH STREET, EDINBURGH, EH1 1TE
tel # 0131 557 5111, fax # 0131 557 5211
EMAIL info@canongate.co.uk
WEBSITE http://www.canongate.co.uk

All forms of payment are accepted and p&p is free to any address in the UK.

Fiction

UNDER AFRICAN SKIES
Edited by Charles Larson — isbn 0 86241 715 5 — £14.99 hbk

BLACK
Clarence Cooper Jnr. — isbn 0 86241 689 2 — £6.99 pbk

THE FARM
Clarence Cooper Jnr. — isbn 0 86241 600 0 — £5.99 pbk

THE SCENE
Clarence Cooper Jnr. — isbn 0 86241 634 5 — £6.99 pbk

WEED & THE SYNDICATE
Clarence Cooper Jnr. — isbn 0 86241 718 X — £6.99 pbk

THE HARLEM CYCLE VOLUME 1
Chester Himes — isbn 0 86241 596 9 — £7.99 pbk

THE HARLEM CYCLE VOLUME 2
Chester Himes — isbn 0 86241 631 0 — £7.99 pbk

THE HARLEM CYCLE VOLUME 3
Chester Himes — isbn 0 86241 692 2 — £7.99 pbk

THE LONELY CRUSADE
Chester Himes — isbn 0 86241 745 7 — £7.99 pbk

ONE PEOPLE
Guy Kennaway — isbn 0 86241 719 8 — £8.99 pbk

PORTRAIT OF A YOUNG MAN DROWNING
Charles Perry — isbn 0 86241 602 7 — £6.99 pbk

GIVEADAMN BROWN
Robert Deane Pharr — isbn 0 86241 691 4 — £6.99 pbk

THE NIGGER FACTORY
Gil Scott–Heron — isbn 0 86241 527 6 — £5.99 pbk

THE VULTURE
Gil Scott–Heron — isbn 0 86241 528 4 — £5.99 pbk

CORNER BOY
Herbert Simmons — isbn 0 86241 601 9 — £5.99 pbk

MAN WALKING ON EGGSHELLS
Herbert Simmons — isbn 0 86241 635 3 — £6.99 pbk

DEATH WISH
Iceberg Slim — isbn 0 86241 710 4 — £5.99 pbk

AIRTIGHT WILLIE AND ME
Iceberg Slim — isbn 0 86241 696 5 — £5.99 pbk

LONG WHITE CON
Iceberg Slim — isbn 0 86241 694 9 — £5.99 pbk

MAMA BLACK WIDOW
Iceberg Slim — isbn 0 86241 632 9 — £5.99 pbk

TRICK BABY
Iceberg Slim — isbn 0 86241 594 2 — £5.99 pbk

THE JONES MEN
Vern Smith — isbn 0 86241 711 2 — £5.99 pbk

PANTHER
Melvin Van Peebles — isbn 0 86241 574 8 — £7.99 pbk

ONE FOR NEW YORK
John A. Williams — isbn 0 86241 648 5 — £6.99 pbk

SPOOKS, SPIES AND PRIVATE EYES
Paula L. Woods (editor) — isbn 0 86241 608 6 — £7.99 pbk

THE FIRE PEOPLE *(Collected Poetry)*
Edited by Lemn Sissay — isbn 0 86241 739 2 — £8.99 pbk

Blood and Fire
A Jamaican musical heritage defined

Blood and Fire Ducie House 37 Ducie Street Manchester M1 2JW England www.bloodandfire.co.uk